'In...
together three such disparate voices, but Park's classy prose
makes it all worthwhile, building towards poignant reflec-
tions on art, intimacy and meaning' *Daily Mail*

'David Park's eighth novel is his most beautiful yet . . . This
stunning novel conveys the poetry of its subjects through
the prose p...   ...Boyle,
Culture Ni...

A NOTE ON THE AUTHOR

DAVID PARK has written eight previous books including *The Big Snow*, *Swallowing the Sun*, *The Truth Commissioner* and, most recently, *The Light of Amsterdam*. He has won the Authors' Club First Novel Award, the Bass Ireland Arts Award for Literature, the Ewart-Biggs Memorial Prize, the American Ireland Fund Literary Award and the University of Ulster's McCrea Literary Award, three times. He has received a Major Individual Artist Award from the Arts Council of Northern Ireland and been shortlisted for the Irish Novel of the Year Award three times. He lives in County Down, Northern Ireland.

BY THE SAME AUTHOR

Oranges from Spain

The Healing

The Rye Man

Stone Kingdoms

The Big Snow

Swallowing the Sun

The Truth Commissioner

The Light of Amsterdam

The Poets' Wives

DAVID PARK

BLOOMSBURY

LONDON · NEW DELHI · NEW YORK · SYDNEY

Bloomsbury Paperbacks
An imprint of Bloomsbury Publishing Plc

50 Bedford Square　　　　　　　1385 Broadway
London　　　　　　　　　　　　New York
WC1B 3DP　　　　　　　　　　NY 10018
UK　　　　　　　　　　　　　　USA

www.bloomsbury.com

BLOOMSBURY and the Diana logo are trademarks of Bloomsbury Publishing Plc

First published in Great Britain 2014
This paperback edition first published in 2015

British Library Cataloguing-in-Publication Data
A catalogue record for this book is available from the British Library.

ISBN:　　HB:　978-1-4088-4646-9
　　　　TPB:　978-1-4088-4647-6
　　　　PB:　978-1-4088-4636-0
　　　ePub:　978-1-4088-4645-2

2 4 6 8 10 9 7 5 3 1

Typeset by Hewer Text UK Ltd, Edinburgh
Printed and bound in Great Britain by CPI Group (UK) Ltd, Croydon CR0 4YY

To find out more about our authors and books visit www.bloomsbury.com. Here you will find extracts,
author interviews, details of forthcoming events and the option to sign up for our newsletters.

Alberta, above rubies

Catherine

My beloved is gone down into his garden, to the beds of spices, to feed in the gardens, and to gather lilies.

I am my beloved's, and my beloved is mine: he feedeth among the lilies.

Song of Solomon

M R BLAKE COMES SO quietly I don't hear him entering
the room but when I look up he is sitting in his familiar place and his face is full of light. Even his black coat that
in truth has seen better days seems burnished and sheened,
no longer with wear but instead by something to which I
can't give a name. He calls me his sweet rose and his good
angel and when he lifts his hands in customary animation I
see for the first time in all the long years of our life together
that his fingers have no stain or smudge of ink.

'Do you no longer work?' I ask, barely able to believe it
might be so.

'All my work is finished, Kate, and I am free and finally
known. So everything I've put my hand to and everything
done with your help now sits in blessed triumph.'

'It's more than could be hoped for,' I tell him as I savour
the sweetness of his words.

'All the difficulties of the old life are fallen away. The man
who was once a slave, bound in a mill amongst beasts and
devils, has been set free from his fetters,' he says as he wipes
what could be a tear from his eye but which might only be a
tremble of the light.

I want him to come to me, for the first time touch me with hands that have no trace of ink, but he stays in his seat and he's looking at me as if he's trying to remember something, his mind momentarily fogged, until with a shake of his head it's free again.

'But you, Kate, how is it with you?' he asks and, although he doesn't come to me, I see once more the love written bright on his face that he has always borne me and I tell him I am a little solitary but that I try to keep busy and fight despondency as best I can. From the street below there pipes up the voices of children playing and he goes to the window and holding his hand on the glass above his head, just the way he always does, surveys the scene below and says, 'This too is Heaven.'

The light from the window seems to shine through him as he turns again to look at me, so at first I have to blink my eyes until he resumes his seat. When he moves away the sudden stream of sunlight is full of dust's dance, the motes rising and falling like the notes of a silent song. His fingers have left no print on the glass.

'It's good your labours have ended, Will,' I tell him, 'because I don't think these hands would allow me to be your helpmate, or colour as fine as they once did,' and I hold up my hands stiffened with their rheumatism and which in my eyes at least have started to look like claws.

'Kate, my Kate,' he says as he comes to me at last and the coldness of his hands eases away some of the heated pain, 'so many years you've laboured with me. Your faithfulness deserves its own rest.'

'When will I come to you?' I ask.

'Soon, soon. Everything is almost ready.'

I nod but am impatient to see his words come true and whatever the reason for the delay its purpose eludes my understanding. He turns his head briefly again to the window as a street hawker's cry rings out.

'And how goes it with money?' he asks, as he resumes his seat.

'Making ends meet as best I can.'

I feel the sudden urge to tell him about the secret guinea I kept hidden all our marriage against the day it might be called upon but stop myself. Mr Blake is not always wise in the ways of the world or its money, so even now if he were to ask me for it I would have to deny him because the day when it's needed may still yet come.

'Listen, Kate, to what you must do. Take what's left of my collection of old prints to Colnaghi and Co. and try to get the best price you can. Ask good money for the Dürer, the one above the engraving table. Demand to see the father not the son because the younger is a rogue who'll cheat you and tell you the prints are of little value. As a man is, so he sees, and when he views these he'll let profit blind him to their worth. And all that's left – the paper, the tools, the press, every remnant of our toil – offer them to the local engravers, see what can be got for them. Try Richards first – of all of those assassins he is the most honest. Sell too whatever of the paintings you choose and try to find buyers for the store of books.'

'I'd like to keep some brushes and a little of the paint,' I tell him, 'in the hope that my hands might allow me to fill some of my time profitably.'

'Keep anything you wish. And I shall be close by, as close as you always were to me when I worked.'

I am pleased by this and ask him if he would like to drink or eat but he shakes his head and smiles and says he has no need of anything. There are so many questions I want to ask him but already I sense that time is short so one thing presses more than others for an answer.

'Have you seen the child? Have you seen Eve?' and my voice trembles as I ask.

'I've seen her and she's cared for and watched over.'

'Praise God. And how much longer before I can see her?'

'Only a short while. I promise that I shall come for you soon.'

'I believe it,' I tell him, 'and it will be the happiest of all my days.'

Swallows dive and loop across the window. Swallows and children's voices. Light suddenly stretching across the wooden floor polishes the nails. I close my eyes for a moment and when I open them he has gone, gone to walk once more with angels in the groves and to gather lilies in the sunlit gardens of Paradise.

I COLOUR THE PRINTS keeping as close as I can to the original design and at the start I wonder how my hands that are smaller and finer than his struggle to be as delicate in their touch, but in time I take a silent pride in telling myself that our work is indistinguishable. I never fail to be struck by the beauty of the colours – the blues and greens, the violets, the pale oranges and pinks – and sometimes I think these are the shades of Heaven itself. And before long I am able to master the strangeness of such names as indigo, vermilion, cobalt and Frankfort black and be responsible for replenishing them and then there is no place where I'm happier than working at his side amidst the smell of nut oil and varnish, amidst the racks of needles and gravers, the sheets of paper and pumice stones used to polish the plates.

I colour such things as spring alive from the holiness of Mr Blake's imagination that no other man could even think but to dream and sometimes I know his good angel watches over us when he tells me, 'I am under the direction of messengers from Heaven, daily and nightly.' And there are such times when I feel that I have left the earthly world behind and I mount on Jacob's ladder to the very gates of Heaven and I see the angels ascending and descending and my eyes burn with the brightness of what his hand has made. And in his picture he has drawn the angels taking the hands of children and the sky below the burning sphere is deepest blue and star-spotted and as I look at him labour at the wooden press with the woollen cloths and ink-stained rags I say with Jacob, 'Surely God is in this place.'

Now as my days wind surely to their welcome end it feels like I must somehow colour all these pages my memory contin-ues to press and this is the work that is left to me although who commissions it or what will happen to it I do not know. I try to do it clear and clean, keep each stroke true to its edge, but the colours blur and run into each other so it is difficult to under-stand what was lived and what worked at his side, what memory is really mine and which shaped by his imagination. And coming from Battersea to lodge in Green Street, regardless that some would call the distance a trifle, for the young woman I was it seemed a journey into a different world, a slumbering country parish replaced by the noise and fury of the city where the streets were thronged with every class of person in God's creation and not a minute that wasn't filled with the rattle of carriages and post chaises, the scurry of hackney chairs or dust-carts. Smoke from thousands of chimneys, the ceaseless bark of dogs, the street-sellers' cries and sometimes at night the curses of the mob or gangs of apprentices up to mischief. A Tower of Babel where it felt reigned only confusion and chaos. So strange it was that in those first few days I was too timid to venture far beyond the boundary of the street.

And what was more strange than this and which insists on being coloured in darkest hues? A scene that first looked like a representation of Hell itself where spirits and spectres clothed in vestments of black flowed out through its gates into the streets and filled them with their cries. The first day of May and Will tells me it's a holiday given each year to the city's chimney sweeps. A ragged army of young children, the oldest who look no older than seven or eight, the youngest nothing more than little smuts flown from some chimney, processing down the road like black sprites momentarily escaped the enslavement of their work, and they wave and clatter their brushes and tools in accompaniment to their shouts that break free from their skinny, soot-soiled necks to startle birds into flight. Stick-like limbs shiver under torn black rags. Feet are bare. Some are stooped or curved already in their spines. But the faces and hair of these they call 'climbing boys' and 'lily-whites' are whitened by splashes of meal and from their rags flutter little coloured ribbons or shreds of paper so some look like wind-blown scarecrows or tattered ghosts of themselves.

I stand and stare and know I have never seen anything that looks so pitiful despite the laughter of the crowd and when I shudder William rests his hand on my shoulder and leads me away. In the days that follow he's unnaturally quiet and then as sometimes he is wont to do I hear him leave our bed in the middle of the night, his footsteps leading into the work room, and I get up and follow, then sit beside him. He smiles his thanks but says nothing and I sit and watch him work, the night's silence broken only by some drunken shout from far off and the fissle and whisper of the camel-hair brush painting the words and images upon the plate. As he leans over it lit by the lamp and with his magnifying glass in hand I am able to read the words he has written even though they are done backwards and see the child finally emerge before dawn, 'a little black thing among the snow', shouldering a bag of soot and making his way barefoot through winter streets. And as I read the words again he tells me they were given. I understand and when I look in his eyes by the break of day it is as if all the light has gone out of them and his face has a pallor that frightens me.

'I am spent,' he says as he slumps at the table and I stroke his hair but when I try to lead him back to bed he tells me it is light and air he needs so we dress and leave our lodgings, step into the city's dawn. We see the river beginning to snake free from slumber, its slimed mud banks shiny with dew so they look frosted, and he takes me to stare at his sleeping childhood home in Broad Street and then we walk with the morning air cool against our faces. We pass the old almshouses, the brew houses and timber yards, see the homeless huddled in doorways and then a young girl shivering under a dirty shawl, who even at this hour is seeking to ply her unholy trade, calls out and William gives her some little money and tells her she must go home, if there is somewhere that bears this name. She looks at him with defiance as if he is a madman escaped from Bedlam and curses us but beneath the covering of rouge I see the face of a frightened child and I think of the engraving of Jacob's ladder and wonder if some good angel might descend on wings of pity, take the wretched child by the hand and lead her to where her sins will be washed clean and she will be dressed in purer raiment.

The city is slowly beginning to waken and we pass carts already heading to market heavy laden with goods and the drivers sit slumped over their reins as if barely awake, only jerking upright when a wheel hits a stone or the horse tries to stop and drink in one of the muddy puddles that strew the road. We return by the river where there are more of the poor sleeping, packed tight against each other in an attempt to defend themselves from the coldness of the night. Some have tried to find fortification with strong drink and empty bottles are scattered around, the glass flecked by the day's strengthening light.

In the days afterwards he begins his poem 'London' and everything that he has seen and felt makes itself known and I think he has never written anything so righteous or holy but the final lines are a lingering confusion to me:

> But most thro' midnight streets I hear
> How the youthful Harlots curse
> Blasts the newborn Infants tear
> And blights with plagues the Marriage hearse.

And it makes me fearful that somehow he thinks that because such a young woman exists in this world that all love is disfigured and defiled and I don't want to think this but hesitate to ask him in case the answer is not what I hope to hear. So for days I carry her curses in my head, blasphemies made worse because they come from the mouth of little more than a child. Sometimes when they're loudest they make my hand slip and because he has to tell me to be careful my heart is chastened and I make an excuse and leave off the work in pretence there is something pressing I must do about our home.

This morning he promised that he would soon come back for me. When we were but newly in love and he had declared his intention to marry me it took him a whole year to make his words real. I hope he is not so tardy in this his final promise or as sometimes he is in the delivery of work that has been commissioned. The children's voices have faded now with the day's light. I think I must somehow be in Lambeth again so when I look out of the side window I catch a glimpse of the black mud-banked Thames through the gap in the houses, the water the colour of tin. I press my fingers to the glass where I think his have touched but mine leave puddled swirls that are slow to fade.

A whole year in which to wonder if his declaration of love and vow to marry me were nothing more than the empty talk of this visitor to Battersea. Those months were a seemingly endless journey through a wilderness of loneliness and doubt.

'He'll not be back,' my mother said. 'You've let him slip through your hands. And his father has a hosier's shop – you've thrown away a lifetime of nightcaps and stockings, not to speak of gloves and the suchlike.'

At twenty years of age I had already become familiar with the promptings of a mother with too many mouths to feed who was always pushing me towards any suitor who only had to be able to stand upright to be considered a possibility.

And it's true that in hard times love's requirements don't ring so loud but with Will it was never about nightcaps and gloves but only love's purest claim on my heart. Right from that first time I saw him – it can still make me blush like a girl to think of what I felt in those early days when I could hardly bear to be in the same room as him in case everything in my heart was visible on my face.

A handsome man to me, if not to all the world, with what he may have lacked in stature made up for by the breadth of his shoulders, a strength of body and above all the possession of eyes that were full of the deepest life I had ever seen or have seen since. A man of dreams and visions who as a boy saw a tree full of angels and when he described it to me, the very words he used made it so real in my mind's eye so I believed I could see and hear the bright rustle of their wings. I'd never seen or heard the like and sometimes just listening to the unbroken torrent of his words made me feel dizzy as if I'd played that childhood game where partners spin each other round.

He had arrived with what he thought was a broken heart having been rejected by the unworthy object of his desires and, as he unburdened himself that night when a storm rattled the windows and threatened to lift the cottage roof clean off, I simply spoke what I felt when I said, 'I pity you from my heart.'

'Do you pity me?' was his question.

'Yes I do, most sincerely.'

'Then I love you for that.'

So he loved me, without the need for a drawn-out courtship, and he swore that in a year he'd have gathered the funds to marry me properly and take me to be part of his life in the city. And in these present days it pleases me to remember that once I was his teacher, walking out in the country lanes and telling him the names of wild flowers – what pretty colours they cry out for now, each delicate to the eye – and the tools that the men used in the fields and he'd draw them right there and then, making as true a representation as I could ever have thought possible. When he told me he'd never been to school I was foolish enough for a little while to think him like me but I soon understood it could never be so because no man ever knew so many things as Mr Blake. And there were his letters. Every few weeks another one with little drawings in the margins and what was in every letter broke my heart so that sometimes I slipped away to the fields beyond the house and found amongst the grove a secret place where my tears went unseen and unheard.

I keep them still and in the last few days have read each again and am sad that I was denied their comfort all those years ago. And what did he think when he never received a single one in reply? Perhaps his faithfulness after that silent year proved his love more than anything else could. I go to the table drawer and take out the yellowed ribbon-tied bundle and search one even though I know its words by heart and when I find it I read it aloud to the empty room that has been deserted by the day's light and so have to take it close to the fire to let what last flames flicker there help my eyes:

> But that sweet village where my black-eyed maid
> Closes her eyes to sleep beneath Night's shade,
> Whene'er I enter, more than mortal fire
> Burns in my soul, and does my song inspire.

I think it was always my eyes he liked the best. I don't know what colour to use for them and won't look in the mirror in fear of seeing them dull and clouded with age. Some nights by candlelight or the fire's final burn he'd lie and look into them as if he could see into another world. He'd say they were black as jet, as deep as far-off seas, or say some great fire burned there. And sometimes he'd take his fingertips and gently close them saying that if he didn't they would consume him, set his very soul ablaze.

We got married in St Mary's church by the river and I wore wild flowers in my hair and carried a posy of bluebells. But such dread I felt that it replaced all the things I was supposed and wanted to feel and then the moment came, not when I made my vows or received his, but when we stood before the parish certificate and unable to meet his gaze I signed my name with an X. So it was finally made known to him what I had hidden but no words were said and when I looked at him in shame nothing marked his face but love and he took my hand and as if with a fullness of pride led me through the church.

After all my fears and confusions it proved not such a great mystery after all. I took to it quick enough, as quickly as I took to so many things that were unknown to me in my previous life. We'd sit in Green Street where we first lodged and each evening after his work was done he'd teach me to read and write – Catherine was the first word I learned – and it pleased him that I mastered it so well. While he worked during the day I practised my letters when time was spare and read passages in the Bible he'd marked for me. It pleased him too when I'd read them aloud to him as he sat and rested after his toil. And best of all is when I read from the Song of Solomon, 'Let my beloved come into his garden and eat his pleasant fruits.'

Those are the first and best days of love when everything is new and nothing runs empty or needs replenishing. I am his all and everything is rich in its bounty and my skin wears the inky marks of his fingers again and again, whether by fire-light or in the early morning's first rays. And sometimes I fear he will grow tired of me or leave nothing for his work but he also gives me words that are wondrous and full of Heaven's light and he tells me it is a holiness, sanctified and blessed. Once I tease him by asking if he has any strength left to do his work and he laughs and tells me, 'Enjoyment and not abstinence is the food of intellect.'

'Then, Mr Blake, I understand why you possess such an incomparable cleverness,' I say and it pleases him so much he laughs again and it is a sound that is sweeter to me than any other. And then he tells me about a vision that he has had and the great work of poetry that he must write which will confound his enemies and make him known and, although I don't fully grasp all that he intends, his passion blazes like an angry fire until it frightens me a little and I still him into a different passion by kissing his lips and when he says my name in his need his breath rushes warm against my cheek.

There is no shame in love – he makes me understand that – but there are drawings that never get shown and which in truth must be hidden from me. I find them by chance when looking for something else when he is out. And in these there are all manner of creatures engaged in everything that flesh can offer and things that I have never countenanced and in their monstrous strangeness they frighten me so that the hand which holds them trembles under the weight of their excess. Then I hear his footsteps on the stairs and I bundle them away but when he enters we both look as if we are surprised to see each other.

'What's wrong, Kate?' he asks and I try to mask my confusion with a smile but he looks at me as if he knows what I have seen. 'Are you well?'

'I'm well enough, just resting my weary eyes.'

He seems satisfied and takes off his coat to begin his labour and I sit and watch him. He has told me often that he writes when commanded by angels but I think of the drawings and wonder what angel told him to draw these things. And then, but not for the first time, it frightens me that I grasp so little of what exists in him even though I have striven to know him and understand the visions that bring his work into the world.

'What are you thinking?' I ask him almost before I know I'm going to.

'Thinking?' he repeats, 'I suppose just what always plagues me from time to time, not knowing whether to curse or bless engraving because it takes so long and is so intractable, yet it's capable of such beauty and perfection.'

'And anything else?'

'Anything else?'

'Yes, what else do you think in this very moment?' I persist.

'Will there be a sun in the sky tomorrow?'

'Answer seriously, Will.'

'Why do you ask this, Kate?'

'Because I want to know such things as are in your head. To be fully your wife. As you start work on this new design tell me everything that you're thinking.'

'I can't describe everything in words and if I could it would destroy the spirit of my invention and turn the imagination into nothing more than an empty husk. And sometimes I don't know everything but have to wait for it to be spoken through me.'

He stops working and takes my hand and tells me that I have been the truest wife from the day when we married and if he was to tell the world everything that was in his head they would say for sure that he was a madman.

'Who thinks you mad?' I ask. 'I've not heard it.'

'Only because your ears have been stopped by love. "Poor Blake" is how they refer to me when I've passed by.'

'Then they are fools, they are the madmen.'

'And I must prove them so, show them that their minds are manacled and silence every doubter. Nothing I do is the fashion of the age but some day I shall be known. Do you believe that, Catherine?'

I tell him I believe it with all my heart and he kisses me on the cheek and then he holds me until it feels as if he has fallen into a trance and I have to remind him of the work that he has to do. Then as I am about to leave him I hear him say, 'There is one thing I think of, Kate.'

I stop in the doorway and try not to think of the pictures in the drawer that he's never shown to me.

'It's that girl we saw when we walked at dawn.'

'The one who cursed us even when you gave her money?'

'Yes. There's something about her that's stayed with me – the fear in her eyes, the pretence of hatred in her voice that made her sound as if she was fending off the world itself. I've never been so close to someone so utterly lost.'

'She's the girl in the poem, isn't she?'

'I think so. Perhaps.'

He goes to say something more but stops himself and as he returns to his work I leave him and turn to my own but as I make my way through the crowded street think only how the youthful harlot's curse blights with plague the marriage hearse. And already her presence in the world seems to throw a shadow over us, a shadow that will soon lengthen and grow stronger.

A new and a better house and there is work but not always the work that he wants to do and I see when his heart is not in it, his natural passion diverted into narrow tributaries unworthy of the man. And sometimes there is no laughter and he sinks into a black despair. Then for days he is beyond even the reach of love and all the light fades from his eyes and it's as if he sees nothing but a trembling darkness. And at first I try to pull him free from this slough of despond but come to understand that there is nothing that can be done so I say little but stay by him and sometimes he asks me to read and then he appears a little cheered at first until his good spirits slowly melt away again like snow. It's then I ask myself why our love is not sufficient and am hurt and fearful when it doesn't prove strong enough to restore him to himself.

There are times he sits at the table where he engraves but touches nothing, as if to lift the tools would be a burden too great to bear. And seeing him like this makes me pray that some good angel will carry him up on bright wings of hope to where his spirit will soar once more. And sometimes when he falls under what he calls his evil star I make him come with me, ignoring his excuses and pulling on his coat and hat, and then we walk without purpose or direction following whatever impulse takes me or stepping where the sunlight finds a way to slant its path through the houses. We talk little and I think he does not want my chatter and sometimes we journey along the river or into the country until his eyes begin to leave their inner world and see anew what lies at hand. Sometimes on these walks his lips move as if he is deep in conversation with an unseen presence and then I touch him only with the light lean of my shoulder and try to find us good paths in which to venture.

The sound of the engraving tool is always what signals his restoration and then he goes anew to his work with a hunger like that of a man who has been starved and it can come at any time, so often I wake from a troubled sleep to hear its scratch and score in the adjoining room and I give thanks and in my shift I hurry to prove to myself that the sound has not been conjured from my imagination. And at such times he'll look up and smile with all the morning light in his eyes once more and he'll call me to him and kiss my hand and press his head against me and when he speaks of me as 'the blessed hand that lifts him out of despondency' I feel like I am truly his good angel.

Soon after he makes a decision that he will exhibit his work and his excitement overflows and knows no restraint. His heartening sense of the success that must come quivers through his being and I too believe that this will be the enterprise that will change our fortunes because in truth there are times when we need more money – sometimes I think he does not understand how much I have to scrimp and save to make ends meet. He works night and day to get it ready and I think he will be consumed by his own blaze of industry and the works in watercolour and tempera are full of wondrous sights that speak both of Heaven and Albion's history. And there is a painting of the Canterbury pilgrims that is very fine, and as large a painting as he has ever done is called *The Ancient Britons* which is already commissioned.

Such work should be hung in the mighty halls of this city but there is no choice other than to exhibit in 28 Broad Street where his brother James still has the hosier shop and it is decided that one shilling will be charged for entry. Will composes a pamphlet signalling this event that will surely bring him into the light and when he writes it he titles it 'Exhibition of Paintings in Fresco, Poetical and Historical Inventions by Wm Blake' and then all his anger at being kept down by cunning knaves who conspire to bring him ill-fortune makes him issue a challenge, so to those who have called his work an unscientific and irregular eccentricity, a madman's scrawls, he demands they do him the justice of examining it in person before they fall into judgement. And his overflowing energy leads him to have a catalogue printed which my hand helps and we bind it in blue-grey wrappers so it looks most handsome.

All the passion of the enterprise is in his face and his dark star is clouded and far away. Sometimes I try to calm him in fear that his unceasing industry will do him harm but nothing can put out the flame of his work or the excited voice of his conviction that rings out again and again like church bells. And everything is ready and the day and hour arrive but no one comes. I tell him that there is time, that they will surely appear and those who do will spread the word to others, but almost no one does and not a painting is sold except the one already agreed. And in the corner sits the pile of catalogues that consumed so much of our recent efforts and which seems only to mock them now. I want to cry but have to make myself strong and he says nothing, not a word, then goes back to creating illustrations for someone else's work and his head and hand are weighted with despair that I try to dispel with foolish words that have no semblance of truth. He says noth-ing and I want to go into the street and rail against those whose self-serving meanness of spirit has blinded their eyes to his greatness. And I want to shout above their indifference what he has often told me, that he who does not know truth at sight is unworthy of her notice, and how the man who never in his mind and thoughts travelled to Heaven is no artist.

But this world is evil in its cruelty and its mind cannot free itself from the manacles that bind it. So there is a night when I come into the house and find no sign of him but a copy of the *Examiner* open on his table. Nothing I have ever read causes so much pain as the words I find there that speak of 'an unfortunate lunatic whose personal inoffensiveness secures him from confinement' and his work is 'the wild ebullitions of a distempered brain'. Then when I lift the paper away I see the words he has scored in black ink on his desk. It says, 'I am hid.' Quickly I take the paper and feed it to the fire and curse the spirits of envy and malignity that write such abominations. I feel a sickness rising but know I have to find him and that he has gone out into the night without coat or hat.

There is no certainty where he might have headed and I am frightened and wonder if it's the very darkest star of all that shines brightest now in his firmament. Close to our house I ask if anyone has seen him and an old woman laughs and asks if he's run off with the angels but further on a child points the direction he saw him taking. I follow the road that leads me closer to the river; pass the coal wharves and timber yards, the stench-filled dye-works and silent lime kilns, the gin shops blazing with noise and degradations. Somewhere in the distance I hear the sound of a barrel-organ and raucous laughter. The night air has grown cold and a mist clouds the river so the lights along the other shore look smoky and almost dimmed. I pass groups of men already searching and squabbling over where they shall lay their heads for the night and one of them calls after me but I do not turn from my search. Then just when I think I have taken the wrong road and am about to go back I see him, his shirt white in the gloom like a flag beckoning me on even though he stands still as some stone carving. I stop at a little distance and watch him stare into the waters below. He is close to the edge and I am frightened of startling him so I stand silent and pray for the knowledge of what I must do.

'I am like a sea without a shore, Kate,' he says and I am the one who is startled – by his voice and because I had not thought he was aware of my presence.

'Come home, William, it's chilly and you've no coat,' I urge him.

'I have no need of a coat, Kate – I am wrapped in mortality, this flesh is a prison and my bones the bars of death.'

'The world is wrong, Will, the world is a fool. And in my heart I know that some day it will realise what it did and you will be known, known and revered by all,' I say as I go to him and put my arm across his shoulders. But his body is cold and yields nothing to my touch.

'Perhaps what they say is true,' he answers, turning to look at me for the first time. 'Things are sometimes confused in my head. Perhaps I am deceived by the voices.'

'And that would mean I am in love with a madman when I know there is no saner, better man walks God's earth. Come home, William.'

And I try to lead him by the arm but he resists, returning his gaze again to the water, so I have no choice. It is too soon and I have no certainty but I have no choice and so I say, 'I think I am with child.'

Children are everywhere with Mr Blake, in the songs and poems, in the drawings, and in truth I think they play and gambol inside his head. So from that moment when I say those words he is filled with a great happiness that threatens to overflow and in his imagination the child is already born and he writes 'Infant Joy' and the drawing of the poem is very beautiful. He wants me to colour and find delight in it and I try my best. The mother and the newborn child are shown inside an open flower that is the deepest red and signals the opening of the womb. My hand trembles a little and I have to steady it before I give the first copy its colour and see how the mother and child are visited by an angel who brings a holy blessing. And the womb formed by the petals is shaped like a heart and I feel his love and excitement in every line that he has made. I have told him I am with child because I think it might be so for my body feels strange and I tell myself it is because a life grows inside me but I revealed it to him so soon when I am not certain because I could think of no other way of pulling him back to himself.

He is all tenderness and often he lays his hand lightly on me as if he expects to feel the child that grows there and he calls me his sweet infant joy. All the previous disappointment is put behind him and he continues with his work in good spirits, making his plans as always. But I am filled with uncertainty and have had no angel's visit to tell me I am with child so there is only the strangeness, the feeling that somehow in ways I cannot describe things are changing inside me.

He asks me if it will be a boy or a girl and I tell him it is only God's will can decide that. And he says he hopes for a boy but then changes his mind and says best it will be a girl. When I ask him why he tells me that she will be a companion to me in all my days. And he says that if it's a girl he wants to call her Catherine and I laugh and tell him that we cannot have the name that is his mother's, his sister's and his wife's. So he thinks again and decides he favours the name Ruth but suddenly insists she be called Eve because she shall live eternally in the garden of our love and when I consent he skips about as if he himself has become a child.

And there is nothing that drives him to greater fire and fury than to see a child misused. So once in Lambeth I watch him stand at the window and see him stiffen into anger and when I ask him what the matter is, he calls me to watch with him and down in the courtyard below is a boy who has been hobbled with a log as if he is some wayward animal that needs chained to prevent it running free.

'I cannot allow it,' he says and his whole body shakes with fury and he talks of those who would bring slavery to our shores and I try to caution him not to act in reckless temper as on occasions he is wont to do when provoked. But he repeats again, 'I cannot allow it,' and for a second as his hand presses against the glass it feels as if all his fury will smash it into pieces. I lay my hand on his shoulder but it brings no calm and I feel the throb and thresh of his over-flowing anger as if it is a living thing inside him that must find release. And then without his coat he is taking the stairs, his feet rattling them the loudest I have ever heard, and I try to follow but he tells me to stay where I am and in my own fear I have to watch what unfolds from the window.

In the blink of an eye he is in the courtyard below and he is calling the boy to him, beckoning him gently with his arm, but the boy is startled by the agitated appearance of Mr Blake and he cowers a little, his walk, so laboured by trailing the weight, preventing his undoubted instinct to flee and although I cannot hear what words pass between them I can see that Will is tell-ing him not to be afraid and once more signalling the boy to come to him as might be done with a frightened animal. The boy has stopped moving but even at a distance I can see the fear in his eyes and he keeps glancing to the open sheds that stand to the side of the yard. Then there is the muffled shout from someone who is not visible and both Will's head and the boy's turn to look in the same direction. And I am filled with sudden fear and want to run to the yard but know that what-ever is going to happen will have done so before I reach it and so I stand unable to do anything but be a silent watcher.

It's a man, burly and red-faced like a drinker, who steps into the yard from the sheds and he is shouting and his hand waves a piece of wood. I try to bang on the glass to make him know there is a witness to whatever monstrous intentions he harbours but he is striding unaware towards Will who faces up to him and whose own fist is raised in unabated fury and moving furiously up and down as if beating a drum to the rhythm of the words I can't hear. And the man with the cudgel has stopped short but Will continues to advance on him and he is pointing at the boy. Then almost as quickly as he appeared the man turns on his heels and is walking back to the sheds, his arm thrown out in a dismissive gesture and the cudgel held lifelessly by his side, and I watch as William rests his hand on the frightened boy's shoulder before he frees him from his burden then throws it to the ground with all the power his body can muster. As he walks away he looks up at me and I feel all the love I hold for him spring forth and I raise my hand and am rewarded by his smile.

Such a man as Mr Blake deserves and needs a child and I count myself blessed to be able to bring what he so desires into the world. Because now there are no doubts that the child grows inside me and my whole being feels gently nudged and quickened into a newness of life. And William talks of us as Adam and Eve, father and mother to a world that will be conceived without taint or stain because old things will have passed away and all things made new. In the little summer-house at the end of the garden in Lambeth there is a vine that grows which although rich in leaf never bears fruit and we like to sit in the summer warmth this place holds. Although I am uncertain at the start, Mr Blake tells me that art can never exist without naked beauty displayed and sometimes when we sit in it in our natural state and read *Paradise Lost* I feel truly as if I am in the Garden of Eden. One such day, freed from what he calls our 'troublesome disguises', I am startled by the approach of a caller but he tells me there is no need for embarrassment or apology because 'naked we come into this world, clothed only in the Divine mercy' and he welcomes the visitor to our heavenly garden as if nothing is amiss or strange. I tried not to blush but with no more success than I do now at the memory.

The seed inside me has hardly started to grow no matter how often I look impatiently or brush it lightly with the encouraging palm of my hand and I am often sick and it makes me frightened that I shall expel the child from where it lodges in my womb. And I have started to talk and sing to her and tell her her name will be Eve. That summer is hot and it is difficult to stem the stench of the city. The heat coats everything with a sullen lethargy and even the river seems to idle, caulked in the stench of tar and oils and everything else that is inflicted upon it, and I keep as much to the house and the garden as is possible but there are times when the very smell of the paints makes me feel ill and so I cannot help him as much as I like to do. And now this moment must be coloured even though it prints itself sharp and more painful than almost any other page so I am in the summer-house and I let my fingers trace the softness of the vine's leaves. And the colours in my head are pale and delicate – mostly yellows and lilacs with the future sky painted palest blue. I wonder too if the good angel has visited me when I was asleep or unawares and think how much of a blessing that would be to know of his ever-present care. I think too of Mr Blake and the brightness of his spirits as he is filled once more with ideas and plans and his belief that the sun will yet shine upon all his works and they will be brought into the light of day.

I feel too hot, unable to read my *Paradise Lost*, and I take one of the vine leafs and rub its coolness across my cheek. William is working in the house more contented for the moment to be busy with commissioned work because it brings some of the money that we shall need. And I wonder if the skill of his hands might be able to fashion a crib for the daughter I bear him. It is in the hazy heat of that summer's day that the first pain comes, so sharp that I drop the book and cry out, and the voice I hear does not sound like my own and then the pain comes in waves so I cry out even louder and I have to force myself to break free from its shock to make my lips form Will's name. I scream it again and again and then my hand feels my wetness and I almost faint when I see my fingers stained in red. When he comes I cannot speak but hold up my red-stained hand and he bundles me into his arms and carries me to the house and our bed.

A doctor is sent for but what need for someone to tell me what I already know? And at first Will's care is all for me as I lie in the room that is always too hot and he strokes my brow and dampens it with a cloth. Below my window the city streets boil themselves into a cauldron but I burn with an even greater fire that only fades with each passing day and when I must be on my own for a while I lie and listen to the strange sounds that climb up from the heated confusion that labours there. And then I start to think that it is the foul and poisonous vapours of the city that have killed my child and I call God's judgement on it and hope to see it plunged into the lake of fire. Will attends me lovingly both day and night and then slowly I begin to see that he has come to understand his loss and his spirits sink once more and even though outwardly he tries to continue in his tenderness, soon it becomes a duty that must be rendered rather than a love that must be shown.

I grow stronger in the weeks that follow so he returns to his work but it is as if every bright hope has dimmed and his darkened imagination produces only what is shaped by a sad despair. He works on with his *Songs of Experience* and everything his hand forms conspires to renew my grief. Our 'Infant Joy' becomes 'Infant Sorrow', the Garden of Love becomes filled with graves and briars. And when I think I am well enough to help him once more my first task is to colour a poem called 'A Little Girl Lost' and even though I read no more than the title because my eyes are blurred I cannot bring myself to touch it as I think of our child and wonder where she wanders now and if some angel descending Jacob's ladder will be able to take her by the hand and secure her passage into Heaven. He sees my tears but says nothing and I wonder if it's because in his mind he has started to blame me for our loss. And every waking minute of the day I am haunted by strange and sorrowful thoughts.

One morning just as dawn's light begins to creep into our room I slip from our bed where he is still asleep and go to where we work because I need to look again at the image that accompanies 'Infant Joy' and because my hands need to touch it and feel what answers it may give for what now feels like a terrible mystery and a punishment for something I must have done. But what once I thought was beautiful now offers only a reflection of my own sorrow and the red petals of the womb-shaped blossom that cradle the mother and newborn child are changed into the colour of blood and its very heart is shredded into shards. I want to cry but all the tears are dried up and my sorrow finds a poor release in the shiver of my body and the quickening of my breathing. I go to the window where the first light of day only serves to strengthen the image in my hands and then seeps across the copper plates, the paints and oils and settles on the pile of milky paper. What future will be painted there? Sometimes I see it blotted and stained as if by the soot-blackened hands of the chimney sweeps who parade once more in my imagination like sprites from the gates of Hell itself; sometimes it bears the image of a lost child wandering in dark woods unable to find the safety of home.

'It's a suffering that's difficult to bear,' he says and I look up to see him standing in the doorway, 'but God willing we shall have another child.' I want him to take me in his arms but he turns away and I hold my hand up to the empty space where he stood until the light sifts motes through the splay of my fingers. And because I speak only silent words he does not hear me tell him that God is never willing and that there will be no miracle where Christ blesses the barren fig tree into fruitful life, does not hear me tell him that my womb is withered and closed for the rest of my life.

*   *   *

29

Mr Blake says I must rest and it's true that for a time I take to my bed again but I think the weariness is in my head more than in my body. His pictures are dark now and even the colours seemed edged with bitterness and I can't bring myself to work them or help in the ways I used to. For the first time in our marriage when he is possessed of the spirit and leaves our bed during the night I turn away and try to shut my ears to the graver's scratch and score. Then one morning when I wake he's not to be found and I assume he's gone about his business. The light makes changing patterns on the wall opposite our bed and the room is filled with the clatter of cartwheels, the cries of someone selling fish and what sounds like the distant hammering of iron.

The heat has finally slipped out of the summer and I am glad but never again can I bring myself to sit in the summer-house or see the vine that won't bear fruit. I briefly walk close to the house or in the garden but the emptiness is heavy in me and it seems that nothing has come to fill the space except a sadness that sometimes feels as if it will overpower me. On this morning I stay in bed even though it's long past the hour to rise and sometimes my hand brushes against my womb as if in search of some miracle where the lost child is returned home once more. But there is only the sense of absence and when I gently call her name it returns unanswered. So I don't hear the footsteps on the stairs at first and when I do I realise that there's more than one set of feet. And then he appears and he's looking at me a little surprised that I'm still in bed.

'Can you get dressed, Kate?' he says. 'There's someone I want you to meet.'

'Who is it?' I whisper as I start to do as he requests but he tells me it's best I dress and see for myself.

I try to pin my hair but know it must look slatternly and my clothes are thrown on as best I can. I assume it will be a buyer or someone arriving to commission work, and wonder why he needs me to meet them. But when I come out of the room I see only Will until I realise that there is someone standing behind him and then I catch a glimpse of a dress and know it's not a buyer.

'This is Lizzie, Kate,' he says, smiling at me. 'I have engaged her as a servant until you are restored again to health.'

I stare at the ragged girl who has emerged from his shadow. Her dress has seen better days and her shoes look as if they will fall to pieces at any moment. But her young face still bears the print of prettiness and then I see a little smear of rouge puddled in her cheeks and I remember who she is.

'Greet Mrs Blake,' he instructs her and when she mumbles her response he nods at her until she gives a little curtsey that I have to force myself to acknowledge. 'Lizzie will live with us . . .'

'But where?' I interrupt.

'I thought the back room,' he says, staring at me.

'But I am almost restored,' I tell him. 'A few more weeks and I shall be my old self again.'

'You need to rest, Kate. Lizzie will do the housework and go for what things we need. She can be on hand to be your help and when you are your old self again we can decide whether we shall keep her on.'

I go to speak but I can see from his face that he will brook no further argument so I turn on my heels and walk back into the bedroom from where I hear him tell her to go and bring her things. Her light footsteps echo on the stairs even after she's gone and then he comes to me and his voice is gentle as he says, 'I thought it for the best.'

'We should have talked about this, William. And why this girl?'

'Because it is a kindness for both of you. We can give her a home, help her find a better way in her life, and I think you are in need of someone for a while at least.'

'Have you forgotten all the words she shouted – her curses and her damnations on us?'

'Kate,' he says as he takes my hand, 'that was the only world she has ever known speaking through her. She lives in squalor with older women who with the help of poverty have led her into the ways of sin. We can help her free herself from her chains and I know no one better than you to guide her out of misery.'

'Can we afford another mouth to feed?' I ask, unable in the light of his words to think of any other objection.

'Yes we can. Joseph Johnson has ordered plates for a new book.'

So Lizzie comes to live with us, arriving at the house an hour later with her worldly possessions in a reed basket and which comprise little more than a few items of miserable clothing and a copy of the Bible that she says her mother gave her before she died. There is never any mention of a father. I greet her as I should and in truth feel shamed by the hardness of my heart that I showed earlier. We establish her as best we can in the back room even though her bed is no more at the start than some blankets on the floor with a cushion for her head but I try to make the room pretty by pinning up some of William's pictures of holy scenes and she seems quiet but content, looking about her always as if everything is a great mystery.

In truth her care restores me a little and soon I take her out and buy cloth to make her some clothes as I do for Will and myself, but her eye instinctively falls on what is prettiest and I know she is disappointed by my choice of plainer and cheaper fare. I try also to teach her to read but she's not a good pupil, her concentration soon wandering, and when I look to encourage her she asks, 'What good will it do me?' I seek to tell her that she could read the Bible her mother gave her as she surely hoped but she remains indifferent and I put off the teaching to some future date.

I get her to speak of her life, not out of idle curiosity but because I think it will help me to understand her better. So she tells me her father was a soldier who went off to a war somewhere she doesn't remember and didn't come back. The way she recounts it makes me unsure whether it's the truth or something she's made up. Her mother tried to keep the family together for as long as she could and then Lizzie's two older sisters went into service and her mother had to do what Lizzie calls 'work on the street' to make things meet but she soon got pregnant and died in childbirth.

It's a sorrowful tale and it makes me draw on as much of my kindness as I am able to find. At first as I instruct her on the ways of a home – all of which seem entirely foreign to her – we get on passably well although there are times when I have to sweep the floor after she's finished and if I rebuke her gently she looks at me and then her green eyes that sometimes remind me of a cat's will narrow and stare at me with an unblinking intensity. Once when we sit after work is done and I try to read to her from her own Bible she interrupts by asking, 'Is it true that Mr Blake is given to fits of madness?'

'Who told you this?' I ask.

'I don't remember,' she dissembles.

'Who told you this, Lizzie?'

'The butcher who sold me the mutton chops yesterday. He said, "I hear you've gone to live with that madman Blake."'

'You must not listen to the foolish prattling of such people,' I tell her, silently resolving that he shall enjoy no further of our business.

'But why should he say it?'

'Because Mr Blake is not like other men and when people see someone they don't understand they are liable to make the mistake of calling it madness.'

Her green eyes are narrowed again, this time with suspicion, but instead of instructing her as I should to continue with her work, I find myself trying to persuade her of the truth of my words and so I say, 'Have you ever seen any sign of this madness in Mr Blake?'

'Some of his paintings are strange and not of any world I know,' she says, hesitating at first then growing bolder. 'And sometimes he talks to himself.'

'Perhaps he talks with someone you cannot see. And some day the world will know him as the great artist that he is.'

'His eyes . . .'

'What about his eyes, Lizzie?'

'Sometimes they seem strange as if . . .' she hesitates again then looks at me to see if she herself has said something that is itself strange.

'Mr Blake sees with the holiness of the imagination, sometimes sees worlds that are closed to others. You should not think it strange – it is a gift from Heaven.'

She goes to ask another question but I stop her and think up some work that must be done before the morning and she returns to it with little enthusiasm. As I watch her mope about I can't help but think of her past, what she has seen and done, and it threatens to blot out the kindness I should show her and I am not as convinced as William that she has embraced a new life. Then the suspicion I see in her eyes is also present in me, coiling itself tightly about my thoughts. And despite her questions about William slowly she becomes comfortable in his company, until she likes nothing more than to watch him work, and soon it is clear that he finds some pleasure in her presence in the house.

In a new dress, despite its plainness and with her hair shaped out of its former wildness, she looks very different to the girl we met on the street but perhaps it is my unfair prejudice that makes me think a sense of her former life still lingers in her and she does not have all my trust. There is something about her, and not just in her green eyes, and at times she has the ability to slink quietly throughout the house so she overhears conversations about things that should be private between husband and wife. And there are times when she goes out and is away longer than expected but will say nothing of where she has been and when I put this to William he tells me that she is a servant but not a slave and her life is not ours to own.

Once when I return to the house I hear the sound of their laughter and when I go to the work room he is letting her colour one of the prints and I hear him praising her sureness of hand. I stand silently in the doorway until he realises I am there but when he calls me to look at her work my words are lukewarm. And since I lost our child, even though it is too soon for passion, he has not touched me in love and when I stare at myself in the mirror I think that what happened has taken something of the looks I once had. There are times when she tries to be my friend and taking the brush from my hand will comb my hair but once I catch her gaze on me in the mirror and her eyes are not filled with love. Then it frightens me that perhaps Will wants this girl to be our child, our Eve, to be part of our life for ever, and I cannot bear to think this might be so but I have no means to complain because he will tell me mercy has a human heart and whatever I say will sound as if I am lacking in grace.

He sometimes buys her little trinkets and ribbons that she plaits in her hair and gradually as she increases in his favour she takes less trouble to be in mine. She moves so quietly about the house that I am never sure where she is and slowly I start to believe that she is everywhere and nowhere so her silent steps carry her inside my head. Once I dream she comes into our room in the middle of the night and spies on us but even though I know it was a dream in the morning I look for traces of her presence. And I increasingly think she slips out of the house at night and do not know where she goes, then I start to wonder if she returns to her old haunts. But the one time I get up in the middle of the night and check her room she is there sleeping and I feel a weight of guilt for having doubted her.

She knows I watch her and sometimes under my gaze attempts to give the pretence of quiet industry but nothing she can do will convince me no matter how hard she tries and I become obsessed with finding her out so that once when she goes to the shops I follow her but don't know what it is I hope to see. And apart from stopping too often for idle conversation or simpering and making eyes with the butcher's boy there is nothing that is amiss and I return as if empty-handed. I try to talk to William of my unhappiness but he is working with full concentration and I don't know what words I can find that might persuade him to let her go. And every time I hear their shared laughter it is a blow to my heart and when he says one evening before sleep, 'It is a miracle that has been wrought in that girl,' I simply make silence my reply. And once I think he says her name in his sleep but cannot be sure.

My own child is swept beyond my reach, and in her place has been left a changeling whose presence only serves to remind me every day of what I have lost. And then Will tells me that perhaps I should rest more because he thinks I am still far from my old self and that it would be best if Lizzie did her housework in the mornings and helped him in the afternoon. He believes she has a skill for it and when I look past him she is standing silently in the doorway and her lips are curled into a smile whose sharpness is meant to hurt me and succeeds in this its purpose. So I am pushed aside in my own house and for some days I take again to my bed and feel without the strength or desire to leave it. She plays the good nurse at first and brings me food but there is a smugness about her every movement and then once when I address her as Lizzie, she says, 'I wish to be called Elizabeth. It is my proper name,' and she turns on her heels with the tray and leaves me to the emptiness of the room.

One morning Will tells me that he must journey on business to Highgate and when he says that Lizzie will look after me I understand that it is only I who must call her Elizabeth. There is silence in the house when he is gone even though I strain to hear her footsteps and in time I rise and dress and try to make myself as quiet as she can. The sound of a passing cart and the driver's sudden angry shout from the street below at some obstruction to his passage makes me jump and I realise that I am frightened in my own home. I go barefoot across the landing and stand listening at the half-closed door, hear a little break of gentle laughter and feel the pulse of my heart so loud it seems it must drum my presence. Then I open the door and find her at his desk with the drawer open and the hidden drawings spread on the table. She has at least the good grace to jump when she sees me but makes no effort to replace the drawings or close the still-open drawer.

'What are you doing?' I ask as I step into the room.

'I was looking for something,' she says and already her green eyes are fired with defiance.

'You have no business here. You forget yourself, girl.'

'My name is Elizabeth and I am not a girl,' she answers and her voice is as cold as my face feels flushed with the heat of anger, tempered only by an uncertainty as to what it is I must now do.

'Mr Blake will not be pleased to hear what you have done in his absence.'

'Perhaps what might please Mr Blake would be if you were to do this for him,' she says, holding up a page and pointing with no semblance of shame to one of the drawings. 'But perhaps if you do not know how, I could teach you, or teach you this and this. Better to learn how to please a man than how to sweep a floor or do washing.'

It is beyond my power to suppress my anger any more and I slap her face because I do not have the words I need to force her into a recognition of her shame. She squeals and holds her cheek but thank God she is not much hurt and my hand shakes so much I have to press it into my side. I go to tell her I'm sorry until I see the hatred in her and instead tell her to go to her room but she stands up straight and stares me in the eye.

'You lost his child and in so doing you lost his love,' she whispers and then smiles once more.

I raise my hand to strike her again but she holds up her arm as she shouts, 'Strike me again and I'll be the good angel that brings him the child he so desires. Strike me ever again and I'll work him to choose between your dried-up body and what he can enjoy with me. And you can't be sure he won't choose me, can you?'

And I am filled with fear and as my hand drops to my side I turn and hurry from the room, locking the door behind me, and I stay there until I hear her footsteps on the stairs and go to the window where I watch her walk into the street. But before she has gone more than a few steps she turns and waves up at me and I pull back, then as I sit on the bed I start to cry. I know I am no longer mistress in my own house, or perhaps in his heart, and in that moment it feels she is stronger and more cunning than I am and I know she despises what she thinks is my weakness. And she is right, if I do the wrong thing she will take my place in his affections and she grows daily out of childhood into womanhood and already I have seen how men look at her in the street and how she knows it without even having to turn her head and how she enjoys their inspection, sometimes choosing to reward it with a coy smile or a flounce of her body.

And I think again of his poem and know the terrible truth that the youthful harlot's curse blights and plagues the marriage hearse. But I do not know what I must do to fix things, don't know how to break her spell that holds him ever closer or end the power over me of her curse. She is still gone when he returns, his business successfully completed and a price agreed for ordered work. He asks me where she is but I tell him I do not know and I say nothing about what has happened.

'You're very quiet, Kate,' he says. 'Are you still weary?'

'Just a little tired, but it will pass,' I tell him.

'We are fortunate to have Lizzie,' he says as he stops to remove the shoes from his feet that are tired from walking. 'She's a good help to you.'

'Yes, but I'm getting stronger and I think that soon I will be fully restored to health and then we would have no need of her help.'

'But if we were to finish with her where would she go and then there is always the prospect that she might feel there is no other path open to her than to return to her old way of life? And she's come so far along a better road.'

I give no reply but understand that I must wait my time and find a way of making him know the truth that will not reduce me in his eyes.

'Let's continue with her for the time to come at least and the house is brighter with her in it,' he adds as he tries to squeeze away the pain in his toes.

So the house is brighter for her presence and in his head she has become part of his painted world of innocence. I tell myself that I need all my patience and I must bide my time and wait until opportunity presents itself but as the day slips into night my spirits sink into a lifeless despair and the bed we sleep in seems suddenly bigger and filled with a greater space between us than I have ever known. And I am afflicted by dreams where once more I no longer have the ability to read and when they exchange letters every day their content is hidden from me. It is wakening one night from such a dream that I hear the door of her room open and close and on impulse I rise and put on as few clothes that are needed to render me respectable and then I follow her into the street. The moon is fat and pocked of face and the night feels strange, transformed into something I do not recognise, and there is a throb of life that matches nothing I know from the day but feels almost as if it is a living creature pressing against the bars of its cage.

I stay as close as I dare when she crosses New Road and enters Apollo Gardens where a series of tents and makeshift dwellings offer every type of licentious entertainment that the fallen man might desire. In the light of day it seems a sorry enough place where the rickety shelters look as if they might be dispatched by the first angry storm but at night with their smoking oil lights that throw giant silhouettes against canvas walls and with both the wail of fiddles and human voices it takes on the appearance of Hell itself. Suddenly I am approached by a man who lurches drunkenly towards me and asks me what he must pay for his pleasure and only his unsureness of foot allows me to evade his clutches. The pathways are mucky from earlier rain and in the deeper puddles there is a sheen of moonlight and I am frightened and think of turning back but a greater need drives me on. Two soldiers in uniform stand in the doorway of a tent with tankards in their hands and drink a raucous curse on Bonaparte. I hear their foul jeers as I pass them and then I see her enter the largest tent and she seems able to move through the paths unseen and undisturbed like a shadow.

I start to fear that I am following her into some world from where I shall never return and in every corner of the tent I see faces that look as if they would cut your throat for the meagre contents of your purse. A pile of empty oyster shells glitter like watching eyes. And with every second that passes I feel as if I have entered one of Will's depictions of Hell and the sulphurous darkness smoulders like the very worst of night-mares. And whether real or imaginary it feels as if the colours of this world are painted deepest purple and black then streaked with a violent crimson. I pull a shawl over my head as if this might offer protection and go to the side of the tent where a badly sewn slash allows me to glimpse inside without being seen and she is sitting at an upturned barrel that serves as a table and which is surrounded by a group of men and women who have obviously taken a great deal of strong drink and whose very laughter sounds obscene. Then she is curled in one of the men's laps and garlanding his neck with her arms until he nuzzles his face into her partly uncovered breasts. And I shudder uncontrollably for a second as I imagine that the man who is invited to take such liberties will slowly lift his head and I shall see Will's face. There is a sickness in my stomach and then I watch the man lead her through a narrow doorway at the back of the tent and into the night. I think of following but know it serves no further purpose and so hugging the shadows as much as possible I make my way back home.

When I enter the house Will is standing with a candle and there is apprehension and agitation in his face. He stares at the mud on my shoes and the prints they have left on the floor.

'Where in the name of pity have you been, Catherine? And where is Lizzie?'

'Where is Lizzie? On her back plying the trade that is most familiar to her and at which she is best. Plying it at this very moment.'

'That can't be true,' he says, the insistence in his voice telling me that I have lied to him. 'Why do you say these evil things?'

'Because it's as true as I am standing here – I have seen it with my own eyes. And you would have seen it too if you hadn't allowed your eyes to be blinded.'

'It's false!' he shouts as I have heard him shout about so many other things.

He starts to look past me towards the door and I can tell that even now he is weighing my words for their truth and the continuing doubt in his eyes stirs my anger like never before so when he says, 'I must go and bring her home,' and starts towards the door I lose all control and hear myself shout, 'Go to your little chicken whore and I'll not be here when you return! Bring her again into this house and I shall be gone for ever. I mean it, William.'

He hesitates, his gaze torn between me and the door behind, then says, 'What will become of her?'

'I have no answer for that but I know that if you bring her back into this house what exists between us will be destroyed for ever, so now you have to leave off thinking about her and think about us if you have any care about our life together.'

'But what if she comes to harm?'

'She has made her choice and there's nothing more that you can do for her. What we tried to give her was never enough for her. I knew that from the start and if her plans had been allowed to take root she would have taken my place in your bed.'

'How can that be true, Kate?' he says, shaking his head in denial.

'Look at me, Will, look at me now and tell me that you never felt the impulse.'

He turns his head away and so we both have our answer. The house suddenly gives one of those inexplicable groans where everything seems to shift a little as if burdened with too much weight but I feel no mercy for him even though I see the anguish in his face.

'It's a poor prophet, William, that can't see his own future, that lets his will be bent to that of one so unworthy.'

He stands like a child and the candle flutters a little from the door's draught so his face is shadowed and flecked.

'What must I do?' he asks, looking at me for the first time with the spark of love in his eyes.

'Lock the door, Will. That's what you must do. Lock it and don't open it no matter how loud the knocking. In the morning she can collect her things. Now come to bed and hold me tightly so that all my doubts fade away and everything is mended and made new.'

He does what I ask and when the hammering starts he tries to press it out of his senses by burrowing his head into my empty womb and after a while the knocking is replaced by curses that seem to flap about our heads like bats until eventually silence settles and there is only the steady beating of our hearts.

I do not know what happens to her – in the morning he tells her she must go while I stay in our room and it is only years later that he tells me he tried to find a place for her in Lambeth's Asylum for Girls where such as her are trained for domestic service or to work in some of the new manufactories that need labour. I do not think it is a place where she would take kindly to the discipline and in my mind at least, and although I never say it, I consider it more likely that she joins with others such as her at Charing Cross. And that is a place I never venture for fear of encountering her.

But even then things are not fully mended between us at first and I cannot so easily forgive him for all that has happened so our bed is cold even when I am mended and although he is solicitous and kind he gives his passion to his work and during this time I do not help him so often and he does not choose to show me what he has done except one morning when I am slow to rise there is a poem on the table and I know he has left it for me to see:

My Pretty Rose Tree

A flower was offerd to me:
Such a flower as May never bore.
But I said I've a Pretty Rose-tree,
And I passed the sweet flower o'er.

Then I went to my Pretty Rose-tree:
To tend her by day and by night.
But my Rose turned away with jealousy:
And her thorns were my only delight.

I take it and read it again and then I go to the window and look out where the river glides between houses. At first I am angry because I should not have had to turn away with jealousy and what thorns prick him now count as nothing to the pain inflicted on me. There are fishing smacks and cargo boats crowding the river that every day grows busier with the city's business. I wonder what distant sea it flows to. I have never seen the sea. Then I set the poem back exactly where I found it and go about the business of the day.

All our long future days together are filled with his visions and wondrous revelations and surely this is a portend to some miraculous event. I ask Mr Blake in a whisper if he thinks it is a sign that we are in the final days but he doesn't reply and stands as if mesmerised as all around us people are halted motionless, their upturned faces struck by a sense of wonder. And it is as if one of his pictures has been made real and engraved on the night sky and the very colours are like the ones he favours and for a moment I wonder if it is possible that the Divinity of his imagination has rendered this real. Or perhaps it is God's punishment on a people who have turned their faces away as they do from all those who are prophets. The city's dogs are barking and whimpering and those children still at play in the street are frozen into stillness and some are crying with fear.

Seemingly almost motionless at first then a ball of fire tinted with blue and red so intense that it almost burns the eyes as it moves across the night sky. And its brightness makes shadows of us all as in its wake trails a great flaring tail of orange flame that breaks into smaller pieces to a rumble of thunder. And when it is gone people are left confused and silent for a few moments before they burst into animated argument about what they have seen. And some of them call to Mr Blake to explain but he simply smiles at them and says over and over again, 'The stars throw down their spears,' and no matter how hard they press him he answers nothing else. Then when we return to our home he dances a little jig of joy and takes both my hands and makes me dance with him to some music that only he can hear and I try to follow the rhythm of his steps until eventually he collapses on his chair.

'You're right, Kate, surely it is a sign,' he almost shouts and his eyes burn bright and he tells me of all his ideas and plans for another new work that he must undertake and he is filled to the brim with excitement and some of his words I follow and some are lost to me but I believe all of them have the deepest meaning. And that night he labours through all the hours as if the Holy Spirit is upon him and I sit by his side and watch what energy and passion shape everything he does and he speaks little but sometimes stops and with his inky hands takes mine in his and then raises them to his lips. And in the morning when he is spent I bring him drink and bread and when he lays his head down in slumber on the engraving table I make him stand and then lead him to the bedroom where I undress him and as a mother with a child help him into his nightshirt and then leave him to sleep, going about the house for many hours on tiptoe so as not to disturb him. Then after a while I hear his voice call my name and when I enter he beckons me to him and it is the richest and most wondrous of times and his words that whisper about fire flowing through the sky and distant stars hang like pearls from my ears and when he tells me I am his heart's desire he burns so bright that I am almost frightened I shall be consumed by the flames.

In the days that follow he is tender but quiet and I do not know what spins inside his head but then in time he grows restless and wanders about the house and sometimes he is in conversation with those I cannot see. And once he gets into a fight in the street with a man who is beating a horse and claiming his ownership allows him to do whatever is his wish and for a moment I think that William will tear the stick from his hand and turn it on the man. I have to drag him away and then everything that the city has to offer seems destined to anger him, such as when we pass a house that has songbirds held in cages attached to its outside walls. And on Blackfriars Road he rails against Albion Mill and exclaims in a loud voice that all can hear that man is not a machine. As we walk he speaks of Christ going into the temple and clearing out the moneylenders and I fear he will do some violence to anyone who runs counter to what presses so hard upon him. I try to calm him but it feels as if the earlier joy at what we witnessed in the sky has dissipated and in its place has slipped an aching dissatisfaction with everything the world has to offer. It is then that I fear his dark star will be what shines most brightly in his firmament and he asks me constantly to be with him, either when he sits at his table but where he does little work, or when he walks the city at all hours of the day and night. And there is a restlessness that will not give him respite except when I read the Bible to him or force him into a stillness through the tightness of my embrace.

Once in an attempt to divert him I persuade him to view an exhibition of mechanical toys and curiosities and in the back room of a shop we see a soldier marching, a bear playing a drum, a fiddle player, and a trickster playing hunt the dice but in truth all are a little tawdry and their cleverness of invention makes little impression on him. Then one day as we take the bridge across the river a man hands us a bill that we think is for some miracle cure or foolish entertainment that springs up everywhere as if the city must constantly entertain its citizens with what is base and ignoble. But Will stops to read it and it invites 'those desirous of beholding the wonders of nature' to view the Royal Menagerie at the Tower of London. And for a second I think Will might remonstrate with the hawker of these printed bills and tell him, as I have heard him tell others who imprison a creature which has the right to live unchained, that they commit a crime against Heaven. But instead of rage he says nothing and hands me the paper to pocket and then we proceed with our walk and we pass the Royal Academy school where Will tells me about his student days and then journey to Westminster Abbey where not much more than a boy he practised drawing amidst the tombs and effigies. He grows quiet again as he looks about his old haunts and shows me the things he drew and I start to believe that he is considering the path his life has followed since those days and I do not know whether those young dreams he harboured are replaced by better ones or if it feels to him as if they are broken into fragments and trampled over. The Abbey is cold to the eye and to the body with its marble and stone and neither candle or gilt can stop me shivering and I am glad when he takes my arm and we return to the sunlight.

It's an impulse that I think he will deny when I ask him if we can go and look at the menagerie and I suppose my request is a foolishness that will offend him but I am desperate to find something that will distract him and I am frightened, because already I have seen the signs, that he will slip away from me into despondency. And I think even his anger is better than the state where nothing can prompt him into feeling and all is governed by a heavy lethargy. But I am surprised when he makes no objection. And when we pay our admission money I worry that as Christ did he will think of throwing over everything he considers wicked and an abomination of life and all that is holy. He is sullen as we view the strange creatures that have been brought from distant countries and the excited chatter of the other spectators is an irritant to him and when he sees a great hulk of a bear chained to a wall he compares it loudly to the toys we viewed and then to those unfortunates who once were held in this damp and dismal place. People are looking at him and so I try to calm him and tell him it was a mistake for us to come here but as we are about to go he breaks free from the gentle link of my arm and wanders to a cage under the high walls where ravens blacken the ramparts.

I stand at his shoulder as he stares at it but says nothing. The creature unlike anything I have ever seen is all sinewy strength and its brindled tawny body is coloured like the tail of the comet. It prowls from one side of the miserable cage to the other and then it turns and looks at us, its eyes burning with a yellow fire that speaks of some hidden fury, some intense hatred. Every one of its movements frightens me, a fear that is made worse by my sense that the cage that holds it looks makeshift, so when William takes a step closer to the bars I try to pull him back but he agitatedly motions me away and I release my grasp. And it's not like any of the other creatures, whether the monkeys who sought to ingratiate themselves for whatever scraps they might be given or the other dismal animals each as abject and lifeless as the other. I look at the creature in front of us and know it has not subjected itself to its fate, see in its restless prowling a hunger for what it doesn't have. I say something of what I'm thinking but William doesn't reply and he stands perfectly still in seeming absorption of everything. He goes a little closer again despite my caution and the creature turns its head slowly towards him as if deigning to look at him for the first time. And I am frightened as he stares at its amber-coloured eyes where seems to smoulder something which I have no words to name.

Then the spell is broken as a group of young men approach the cage, their oath-filled voices blending with the croaks from the sooty ravens nesting above. They crowd in around the bars and jeer at the beast and in the throng William is pushed to the side as one of them tries to draw his friends' laughter by going closer and speaking to it as if it were some house cat. And when they cheer him on he grows bolder until he finds a little stick and pokes it through the bars while making a shrill whistle. It's then that the tiger springs and roars such a sound as I think once more of the comet's thunder and the youth jumps back so fast and shocked that he falls on his friends with such force that they scatter like skittles before they retreat. Then there is only William standing as close as he was before and just the bars separate him from the creature that stares at him with fire-filled eyes for a few seconds before it turns away and walks to the shadows at the back of the cage where it rests on the floor with its head turned to the wall and will no longer deign to look at us.

As we walk away one of the youths who are still dusting themselves off but who have assumed a new attempt at bravery shouts out after us, calling William a Daniel.

'It shouldn't be in a cage,' he says in a quiet voice that I have to strain to hear and when I tell him that I'm glad that confinement separates it from us he replies, 'More than anything I've ever seen it shouldn't be in a cage.' And when I tell him that only the cage prevented it from devouring us he says, 'It is the way it is and nothing more.'

When he stops walking and glances back for a moment I think he's considering returning and doing whatever must be done to set the creature free and I'm frightened by the intensity of his expression when what I crave is gentleness and calm. I tell him that I feel faint and in so doing make him turn his attention to me and we stop at a tavern and he goes inside and brings us something to drink and we sit and watch the ceaseless life of the river.

After a while he asks me if I would like to see the sea and when I tell him that I have often dreamed of it he says that I can have the chance if it's what I wish because he has important news to share with me.

Perhaps I was slumbering here by the fire and so didn't notice his arrival. When I look up he's smiling at me and his face is calmer and more at peace than I have ever seen. His clothes still wear the sheen of light and I want to go to him but am frightened that my arms will embrace only what dreams and memories exist inside my head. So instead I ask him as I always do, 'How much longer, William?' and he answers, 'Soon, Kate, very soon,' and his words make me content. Then we sit in silence for a short while and although nothing is said it is as if all the days of our life pass again between us.

So now he's giving me again his important news that he's been offered work and patronage by William Hayley who is a great admirer of his art. We are to leave London that has become as a desert for us and full of anger and discord and rent a small cottage in Hayley's home village of Felpham in Sussex and be under his generous auspices. William shrugs off his despondency and enters excitedly into the necessary preparations and I am glad to be leaving the city and hope that in our new home there will be less to agitate and distract him from his work.

'It seemed like a good idea,' he says as the light from the window breaks then flows through him. 'Do you remember the journey to get there?'

I tell him yes and recall just before we left he said his fingers emitted sparks of fire with expectation of his future labour. I look at those same hands and once again wonder at their whiteness, the absence of any trace of ink that no amount of scrubbing could ever fully remove. Everything of his past struggle now seems stilled and washed away so he sits as if bathed in some waters purer than human eye can see.

Seven changes of coach to be made before we got there and each time the laborious loading of the heavy boxes containing all that we possessed in this world, arriving just before midnight, but still able under the bright moonlight to see our cottage looking as good as any home could be and a seeming haven of tranquillity and hope. And as we stand in front of it we hear what we have never heard before but which we tell ourselves must be the sound of the sea and the very smell of the city is replaced by something briny and fresh. Early on the first morning he wanders outside to the song of birds and in a field beside the house hears a boy call to the ploughman working the field, 'Father, the gate is open,' and he rushes in to me to tell me that it is a sign and we are excited as children and go about getting everything ready with great strength of purpose.

Then when our day's work is over we walk across the field that separates us from the sea and while you hurry in anticipation I am hesitant, nervous about what it is we shall find, and with every step the noise grows louder until it drowns everything else. And there it is stretching as far as the eye can see and we suddenly clasp each other's hand as if in need of protection from both the vastness and its unceasing motion that rolls towards us driven by some unseen force. The wind blows strongly and the waves rise up as if in anger then break their fury before being replaced by those that come behind. Will starts to make his way on to the shingle and his face is held towards the sea but when he signals me to follow I hesitate at first, frightened that we might be snatched from the shore and borne away to its hidden depths. But he turns and holds out his hand and I take it and we stumble a little as our feet sink into the deep shingle and the wind whips at our clothing and streams my hair. Closer and closer we go until we are at the very edge of where the waves shuck and steal the shingle and then he releases my hand and opens his arms wide and he signals me to do the same and so we stand windblown, offering the vastness our embrace. Then he lifts the shingle in his hands and holds it as if it is the world's most valuable jewels and he stares at them so I do the same but cannot see what he sees and when I ask him he tells me we hold the whole world. And everything in him is filled with an extremity of wonder and excitement and for a moment I think he is going to wade into its depths but I rest my arm on his shoulder and tell him I grow cold and we must go back to the cottage. And with reluctance he turns away and we retrace our steps over the shingle but all the time he returns his gaze.

That night he rises from our bed and dresses and I watch him from our bedroom window go outside and I know he has gone under the waxing moon to look again at the sea and as I wait for him I grow frightened that he will be sucked into its darkest depths and swept to eternity in an instant. And I lie in a strange bed in a strange house with the sea's low moan breaking about it and suddenly feel a terrible loneliness and not just because I am alone, but because I know there are worlds inside his head that I have no path to and whose very nature and colours seem always beyond my grasp. And that night I see most clearly what I have always known which is that I possess part of him but only part and although I know that he both loves and needs me, his 'shadow of delight', I am never to have all that is my full desire. I am a wife and a help-mate but want to know what he knows, see what he sees, and for a second I think of following him except my fears prove stronger and so instead I go only to the window and hope and pray for his safe return. And in time he appears out of the cornfield and his face is moon-washed and his hair is blown jagged and stiff like the stubble of the field. Behind him is the sea and he strides towards the house like some creature broken free from its secret caverns and when he holds me in the bed and kisses me his body trembles and his skin tastes of salt.

After the third day he won't be put off any longer and I know there is no point resisting so in the early light and accompanied by the sweet song of the larks we walk the short distance to the sea and I am thankful that it's calmer now, cradled in the morning light with the waves less angry and wind-tossed than they were the first time I saw it. The light sparks the shingle so it glitters like a swathe of precious stones and it is sharp on my bare feet and then we take off our clothes and stand naked at the edge of the vastness. I am frightened again but William goes first and walks into the waves, his arms stretched out by his side, and when he calls me to follow I step into the ripples that froth and foam about my feet. He calls me to be brave, that it is the sweetest baptism that we can ever know, and encouraged I wade after him to where he stands with the water breaking round his waist and I gasp at the coldness but to which he seems indifferent. The shingle under my feet shifts and presses itself between my toes and I am frightened of losing my balance but he takes my hand and we stand side by side and face the waves that buoy us up briefly while the water breaks white against our bodies. And then suddenly he isn't there but ducked under the waves and vanished from my sight for a moment before he reappears, the sea sluicing and dripping off him, and he is washed in the morning light so that everything about him is gleaming and newly made and he tells me to do the same, to baptise myself in the purest light. But I am frightened and so he takes my hand again and I dip myself under the surface and it gets in my eyes and mouth and so I emerge spluttering and coughing and he takes me in his embrace, bears me up and pushes the wet plash of my hair from my eyes.

We stumble back up the shingle and dry as best we can and dress, then sit facing the sea that seems as if it's stirring itself into quicker motion and whose waves gather size and power. William sits silently in the morning light and then his lips begin to move wordlessly and he holds his face skywards as if to receive a blessing and he turns to me and asks me if I can see it and when I ask him what, he says, 'Each grain of sand, every stone on the land, each rock and each hill, how the sea itself all take on a human form,' and he stands and looks about him entranced by what he sees and I desperately look about me because I too want to share this vision. 'The whole earth is become as one man made up from shining particles of light,' he says as if it forms before his eyes and might be touched by the very stretch of his hand. He tells me he 'stands in the streams of Heaven's bright beams' and his rapture is engraved on his face. I look about me again and try to see this world but all that is visible to me is the wet gleam of the shingle and the sea that stretches to the sky. I close my eyes but nothing comes to my senses except the rising wind that blows against my face and the shingle that shifts no matter how still I try to stand. In sadness I turn away and start the slow climb to the house, pausing once and looking back to see him standing as if transfixed before what looks to me only like the great vastness of ocean.

In Felpham here beside 'the sea of time and space' he has many visions. He sees his dead father and brother and once a thousand angels upon the wind, then when walking along the sea's edge the faces of ancient poets and prophets. The wind rustling through the cornfield seems to him the noise of souls. It is as if freed from the chains of London with all its fog of dirt and chartered streets he is able to see the gates of Heaven. And for the first few years he works steadily and is contented but eventually things begin to change for the worst. The cottage that we rent and which looks so homely soon reveals itself to us as damp and cold – it is there that my pains start and there are times also when we both get laid low with fevers. And gradually Will falls out with Hayley who binds him to the drudgery of his commissions and he comes to believe that he should be exercising his talents in pursuit of his own work. It is then that his thoughts turn to London once more.

William has gone again, his chair that faces me empty once more. There is no knowing or predicting his coming or leaving. But the room itself always feels different, coloured and printed with his lingering presence, so sometimes I talk to him even in his absence. And I tell him that after all these years I think I too see visions and am visited by fleeting glimpses of Paradise and sometimes too hear the songs of angels. And then I journey back and question again why when I was with child no good angel came to bless her and wonder was it because of some sin of mine where I like the first Eve yielded to temptation and so was sent out from the Divine garden. But what sin it was I don't know except perhaps that of binding myself too much to earthly things – the cooking of our meals, the making of our clothes, the constant shuffling of money and all the other services I tried to render – and in so doing neglected to lift my eyes often enough to the salvation of my soul. And I think much about our lost child and wonder if she now is cared for in Heaven and does she remember me as her mother as she plays in the fields and by the sweet streams of Paradise. The tormenting thought that still visits after all these years and which I try to vanish is of her lost, wandering in the forests of the night and calling out to me to find her and lead her home. Sometimes when I'm in the street or looking down at it from my window I see a solitary child and for a moment wonder if somehow it might be her and then it feels like a bitter hurt to think that there are those who are given a child and then show it such indifference and neglect.

And although his chair is empty I ask William if our child is safe and cared for by the angels and he tells me that he has seen her and she is well and waiting for me to come and then my heart almost overflows with joy. And I grow impatient for that time and find little other pleasure to embrace in these days that linger slow and unwanted.

Not all things can be blinked away and darker memories insist on their too being coloured. And before we could return to London from Felpham, Felpham that at the start had seemed to hold nothing but promise, a disaster befell us and threatened William's freedom and our future life. Even to this day it remains a black stain lurking in the memory and which caused us also to be separated for the first time in our lives and was in truth I think the reason I fell so ill.

In our lives together there were many times when William's head was filled with fire and fury at the injustices of this world and its treatment of him but never, never did he ever show anything to me except gentleness. The fire was always there, caged like that creature, but capable of breaking free when he witnessed the world's cruelties. However on that August day when there were butterflies embroidering the edges of the cornfield and the sky was a deeper blue than the city had ever revealed nothing seemed able to disturb the calm of our existence.

It was a stranger's voice complete with oaths and foulness of expression that first alerted us to the presence of someone in our garden. How strange and terrible it sounded remains with me still and how in that moment it felt as if the world that was ours was under assault. When we looked out there was a soldier – one of those from the Regiment of Dragoons – with his tunic unbuttoned and careless and it was soon apparent that he had drink taken. There were soldiers billeted in a nearby inn and disliked by all for their coarseness and intrusion into the quiet life of the village. When William went out and asked him to leave he was greeted by insults, disgusting oaths and an angry refusal. In that moment the fire in William took flame and grabbing the soldier, although the scoundrel was much bigger, pushed him out of the garden despite the blows. In the road more insults and threats were issued with a vile tongue and then boiling over William took him by the elbows and, turning him round so that the soldier's back was to him and oblivious to his flailing arms that tried to rain down blows, forced him to the inn where others soon appeared and the soldier was persuaded to go in.

Afterwards in the cottage William trembled as if all the strength had suddenly gone out of him and at first claimed he didn't know how he had managed to move such a stronger creature but then proclaimed it due to the power of the Holy Spirit. As I gave him drink my hand also shook so that I spilled a little on his sleeve. But even in what felt like victory the scoundrel that was Private John Scofield was plotting his revenge and three days later swore in front of a magistrate that William had used seditious language, attributing to him all kinds of treasonous utterances such as 'Damn the King, damn all his subjects, damn his soldiers, they are all slaves,' and if almost all of these accusations were false, in his risen fury I cannot deny that it's possible Will did utter some imprudent sentiments in the face of the great provocation.

Before the trial takes place we return to London and take rooms in South Moulton Street. And there in the greatest trepidation William begins to brood that he is the victim of a conspiracy because of his association with free thinkers and his previous support for the revolution in France and because everywhere in England the country is preparing for war against Napoleon and fearful of an invasion. I think it is my anxiety and fear that they will send him to prison that makes me ill and I take to my bed and am very low. The days when he goes away alone to the trial in Chichester are the longest and slowest of my life and I am tormented by the dread that he will not return. I want to sleep to make the time pass but am afflicted by fears that seem to multiply and grow greater the more I try. Outside the tumult of the street grows ever louder as my heart turns ever more silent. It is a January day with the light coming into the room rising and falling as the sky clouds and then frees itself again. It grows colder too, but I am too ill to light the fire and so I shiver in the bed that feels like my future grave.

Terrible images form in my imagination springing from the pictures I have coloured. And in my delirium I see a great monster rising from the sea to ensnare William, fettered figures forlorn and crestfallen, and the great serpent coiling itself around the body of Eve. Nothing is coloured by joy or future hope but by the darkest hues of despair. Strange thoughts trouble me such as we have been cursed by evil for all our efforts to portray the light of Heaven and in my memory the procession of blackened chimney sweeps bursts anew full of clanging noise and the children's faces are changed into those of devils and everyone who looks on them is afflicted with a curse that will only unfold itself at an appointed hour and in unexpected ways. I try to ward off these thoughts by turning to my Bible and I let it fall open so that the Spirit can guide me to what I must read and it falls at the tribulations of Job and so I know this must be a test of faith. But my faith feels as weak as my body and I am tormented by a new and terrible thought that fills me with shame to recall and which I now claim must be the product of my illness, the fever that burns my brain.

And it is whether Mr Blake has been deceived all his life and the voices he hears and the visions he sees come not from Heaven but from somewhere and something else. 'Poor Blake' is what they call him and it's true that, despite what I told him, I've often heard it on their lips, seen the way they laugh behind his back and know they think he suffers from fits of madness. And if it's true then perhaps I too have fallen under the spell of his madness so that I no longer know how to tell what is of Heaven and what of Hell. And are there two creatures living inside his brain? So sometimes it's the lamb and I remind myself happily of all his gentle tenderness but at others it's as if the tiger lurks there and his fury roars against everything the whole world holds as true and he's like some caged creature desperate to break all the bars that limit him. I think of the tree full of angels he encountered as a child and wonder if what he saw was the fluttering of autumn leaves turned red and gold as the wind quivered them into life. And in his childhood home in Broad Street when God appeared at an upstairs window was this the Divine image or merely the reflection of a boy's loneliness and desire for the holiness of a different life? These are shameful thoughts but they flit around my head like living creatures and I cannot beat them away.

Something brushes against the window and snow has started to fall and with it comes a sense of shame for the coldness of my heart, the treacherous doubts that swirl so deep about my thoughts. And suddenly I have a vision of him in the court and his voice disclaiming 'It is false!' with all his passion of truth at some lies told by his accusers and in that moment I know that my serpent doubts are the temptations of the Devil. And with that knowledge they clear and scatter for ever and in their leaving I feel the fever ebb out of my body and a new calmness flows over me and I read my Bible where Christ stills the storm that makes the disciples so fearful and His peace that passes understanding spreads slowly through my whole being.

I leave the bed and dress and am smitten by a desire to escape the confinement of our lodgings where these despicable thoughts first came and it is as if I must see the world anew and know it in all its truth to cast off the oppressing world of dreams. And as I think of William in the court facing more danger than he has ever known or deserved I want to walk those paths I have shared in his company and the snow will not prevent me. It has fallen thinly but enough to whiten the city and so with a shawl covering my head I venture into the streets where already the carts and carriages press their tracks. Carts carrying whitened coal trundle past, the horses' heads never raised from their plodding step, and everything I look at seems held in a balance that might tip into either the holiness of justice or the despair of defeat. So here is a shivering woman wrapped in rags with a child held in her embrace begging charity from indifferent gentlemen of plenty whose hats are crowned in circles of white and here is a blind man with a whip who makes his dog dance to his whistle. But here too are mothers holding their child's hand as they seek a passage across the busy street and I see the care they exercise over their loved ones but the greater heart of the city seems quickened only by the beat of money and everywhere it is commerce pursued with a passion that exceeds all else. Some of the children hold their hands to the sky to try and catch the delicate flakes that continue to fall but in every street and shop there is the ceaseless clamour for the making of money. And here is little more than a child barefooted in the snow who invites me to choose from her gimcrack array of beads and trinkets draping from her arm or another who offers me a choice of combs and scarves that look spun as thin as she. And in the busy street the city won't let the snow hold it in white and its ceaseless torrent of feet tramp it into nothingness.

I look into the faces of those who hurry past me and know the truth that each bears the marks of weakness, marks of woe, and it frightens me that these are the people who now sit in judgement on a man who is not of this world but who walks in Heaven's highways. Voices ring out across these thoughts calling attention to their wares and people try to press my hand with bills announcing all sorts of supposedly wondrous exhibitions and entertainments but no sooner are they handed to passers-by than they are thrown to the ground to be covered by the still-falling snow. A troop of soldiers march past with their red tunics snow-spotted and it reminds me of the scoundrel Scofield who spins his lies in the face of all decency and truth and I know that if I had to answer truly I could not swear loyalty to any King or priests in black gowns and think that in those like Tom Paine a greater truth is to be found. And I feel an anger that a court might deprive William of his liberty and if that be so then there is no justice or power that deserves to be protected from whatever force seeks to overthrow it. I want in that moment to wave a banner engraved with his words 'the fire the fire is falling! Look up! Look up! O citizen of London enlarge thy countenance ... Spurning the clouds written with curses, stamps the stony law to dust, loosing the eternal horses from the dens of night, crying Empire is no more! And now the lion and wolf shall cease.'

So let strength be given to the hand that ends the tyranny of lion and wolf. But I have already wandered too far and feel suddenly the foolishness of replacing my fever with this coldness. The snow has stopped but lies in runnels along the sills and roofs of buildings, momentarily changing them into strangers to their familiar selves, and gangs of boys give themselves to mischief by throwing snowballs recklessly at passing carriages, cheering wildly when they score a hit or provoke the curses of a driver and the threatening shake of his whip. I make my way home but conscious with every step that he won't be there and am tortured to extremes by the thought that even at this moment he might be borne away in fetters to some place of imprisonment. I feel as if I might faint and frighten myself into wakefulness by thinking of falling into the snow, a cause of indifference to those passing by, and then be covered by new and heavier flurries until I am cold and stiff with death. So I hurry on shrugging off these forlorn imaginings until I find our lodgings and there I light as good a fire as provision will allow and wait in ceaseless prayer for his safe return.

He is here now sitting as always in his seat by the window and there is neither winter or snow in his countenance but only a bright and tender affection that has need of nothing that the world can offer. He comes to watch over me and help me with his presence and I am grateful for it and tell him that it makes our separation easier to bear. He asks about my days and how I keep my spirits up and he tells me that he knows no longer the shadow of night and there is no darkness moving on the face of the deep but he abides in a light that is never extinguished and that burns bright. And then he asks me to read to him and requests that it be from the Song of Solomon and I choose the chapter in which the beloved is gone in the early morning into the garden and picks the sweetest choicest flowers and he tells me that soon I too shall be plucked from the trials and tribulations of the flesh and taken home. And when I am impatient to know when this shall be he gently hushes me and tells me it is not for me to know the day or the hour but only to trust and hold myself in readiness.

And then he comes and takes my hands in his and it is as if he can see the pain in them so he tells me that old things will pass away and all things will be made new and soon there will be no more suffering of the flesh because I shall exist only in the freedom of the spirit. I want him to hold me, to embrace my loneliness, for after almost forty-five years of marriage it is a strange and difficult thing to be separated in body if not soul, but he never comes closer than to hold my hands or fleetingly kiss my brow and I know I cannot press for more. Once I ask if I can draw him and he nods and smiles and I try to capture him with all the light in his eyes but although I work at it, the pencil gripped awkwardly in my hand, when I glance up at him he is gone and the page on which I thought I had captured him is blank.

When William comes through the door I know without words being spoken that he is acquitted and as I hurry to him he holds me tightly then lifts me off my feet and spins me so hard it makes me dizzy and when he puts me down he has to hold me upright as I stagger away from his arms and with a playfulness he asks me if I have taken strong drink in his absence. And Scofield is shown to be a man not to be believed, a soldier who lost his rank through drinking, and the blessed testimonies of the villagers clear Will of all charges of sedition. So together we sing a hymn of praise and thanks and then he grows thoughtful as he takes a seat at the fire I have kept lit for him and as he leans towards it to warm his hands the ridge of snow on his shoes begins to melt and dampens the floor. He stares into the flames, his face suddenly pale and drawn, and it is as if he sees in it a different outcome. Then he looks at me and I hear him say:

> And because I am happy, & dance & sing,
> They think they have done me no injury:
> And are gone to praise God & his Priest & King
> Who make up a heaven of our misery.

I nod my understanding and after I have found him simple food and drink he appears replenished in both body and soul and as his custom when in good spirits he starts to talk of the work that he must do and how he will 'labour upwards into futurity' and he shows a renewed belief that we have overcome the dangers that have beset us and so are free to venture towards new and greater things. Even the fire itself seems to flicker with renewed strength as the words tumbling out of him are set free on a wave of excitement and anticipation. I like it much when he talks like this and it feels as if it is when he is at his most happy and unencumbered by the world's indifference. He drinks the wine I have given him and the fire deepens its redness so that its cheapness is turned in appearance into something richer.

Something flecks across the window and we both turn our heads to see that it has started to snow again and the wind feathers it against the glass. He goes to it, the wine still in his hand, and calls me to come and look and while the fire flickers we watch the snow falling in heavy squalls on the slumbering city. It seems to sense us behind the glass and flurries again as if desirous to cover us as it does the city's streets. And all the world outside seems to fall silent as we stand watching it being slowly lulled into some long sleep in this midnight hour and then he turns to me and whispers, 'It is a mystery,' and his breath is warm on my cheek and when he kisses me I taste the sweetness of the wine on his lips.

There's something I've never told William about because the memory causes me shame but although I don't know why, it too demands its time and will not be denied even though it happened a lifetime away when I was a child in Battersea. It concerns a traveller who came to the district at intervals and it was said that he was the seventh son of a seventh son and that he had healing hands. He travelled in a covered wagon that served as his home and in it he carried all manner of goods for sale

– cloths and beads of coloured glass, little mirrors and purses, bottles of perfume and medicine that he claimed could cure all sorts of maladies. He'd take the covering off the wagon and set up his stall on the green opposite the tavern and at night he'd sing and tell stories for the price of a drink. And he knew how to play a crowd better than any preacher or those who stand for election and he could make them laugh or cry with equal ease. There were those too who were ready to claim that by the laying on of his hands or by taking some of his medicine they had been miraculously cured of some illness so it was said abroad that Mary Clark had conceived a child after many years of barrenness and that Henry Smith had been healed of the ague. It is also true that in the fullness of time there would be those who whispered that Mary's child bore a singular resemblance to the traveller rather than her husband.

In a place where nothing much happened his arrival was welcomed and he had a handsome charm for all the women and friendly good humour for the men and was able to tell them stories of foreign countries and their strange customs. He wore a leather waistcoat and a spotted handkerchief at his throat and in his swarthy skin there was much of the gypsy about him. Although many sneered he claimed he could tell fortunes and at night a succession of women made the journey to his wagon to have theirs told. My own mother went secretly, instructing me to tell our father that she was gone on a message to her sister if he enquired about her absence. When she returned she was breathless and on my persistent questioning claimed he knew everything about her and told her things about her situation that none without a special gift could possibly have known. But when I asked her what had been foretold she grew flustered and said she couldn't share it with me or anyone and I wasn't to ask. And she'd bought a little cloth purse embroidered with coloured beads and so pretty I always desired it and when possible I liked to touch it and think it mine.

As a girl I suffered from cramps and sore pains beyond what might be expected when it was my time and I was always frightened that something terrible would happen to me and that the bleeding would never stop. None of the old remedies seemed to bring any relief and it was one summer when everyone worked the long hours of the day to bring in the harvest that I fainted and had to be carried home on my father's shoulder and put to bed. We told my father it was just the heat but my mother knew better and as she pressed the damp cloth to my brow she asked me if I wanted to try a cure from the traveller. And somehow I hoped that from such an encounter I too might get a pretty purse. I was no more than thirteen or fourteen then and foolish in my thinking. When I agreed my mother told me that it must be my secret because my father would not approve the cost and had expressed no faith in what he called foreign scamps.

That night my mother told him she was taking me to her older sister's house who had girls of her own and would know what was needed and we left him sitting drinking in the evening sun after his long day's labour. When we got to where the wagon was settled for the night under a hedgerow flecked with white blossom and beside a bank where foxgloves lolled in thick swathes, rabbits scattered at our approach. The covering was up and at our call there were whisperings and then a sudden hush for silence before we heard his voice asking what was wanted and when my mother explained, also in a whisper that I couldn't hear, he said we must return in an hour but that I must come alone.

My mother asked me if I was willing and in truth thinking of nothing more than I might gain one of the purses or have my fortune told I said I was and so when the time was up I stood before the wagon once more. He let me wait there for a few moments then opened the flap and helped me inside. I was struck by an intense curiosity about how he could live in this little space with not much more than a straw-filled pallet and pillow along one side of the cart and a chest that I assumed contained all his possessions and wares along the other. He beckoned me to sit on a stool and although not tall my head was not far off touching the canvas canopy. He had an oil lamp but the summer's evening had no need of it yet and behind his head hung a mirror and a ring of silk scarves.

The first thing he asked me was my name and the second if I had the money. As I gave it to him my fingers touched his hand briefly. Then he told me I had a pretty name and a pretty face and he asked me my age and when I told him he said why I was almost a woman and no longer a child. Then he talked of how I must trust him for the cure to work and if I didn't trust him or questioned him then I could never be made well. And when he asked me did I understand I nodded, my eyes all the time looking at the chest where I guessed he kept the purses and wondering if the few coins I had would be enough to buy one.

Abomination to use a child so and I have often prayed that he will find his just reward either in this life or the next. And I see him now standing so close to me that there is less than an arm's length between us and I stare into the darkness of his eyes and hear him say he must touch where needs healed, feel the breath of his speech on my face. Then he places his hand where none has ever been and when I flinch then squirm away he tells me that I must trust him if I am to be made well and his other hand touches my hair and I am suddenly frightened that he will grab it tight and hold me there so I stand motionless and shamed until a few moments later both his hands drop away and he smiles at me and tells me that I have the cure. I am shaking a little but when he tells me to go I show him the coins and ask if I have enough to buy one of his purses but he only smiles and shakes his head and I rush away as quickly as I can and find a place to cry where no one will see.

I have never told William of my shame and even then I said nothing to my mother or anyone else. The shame is my secret but there are times when I think that Will sees and knows everything that has ever happened to me and there are times also when his words salve the pain as I recite over the bitter memory,

Cruelty has a Human Heart
And Jealousy a Human Face
Terror, the Human Form Divine
And Secrecy, the Human Dress

The Human Dress, is forged Iron
The Human Form, a fiery Forge.
The Human Face, a Furnace seal'd
The Human Heart, its hungry Gorge.

What evil hunger the traveller's heart sought to satisfy through the rest of his life I shall never know but we never saw him after that summer. The village gossip said some cuckolded husband had sworn death to him if he ever showed his face again but I cannot say if this is true or merely tittle-tattle. What I do know is that time and God's providence cured me.

And I want to tell William that these might do so again God willing but I am unwilling to hurt his tender care so that now in my old age I submit myself to this strange treatment that his friend Dr Birch has developed and my rheumatism is to be helped by electricity, something that I don't fully understand but that William avows his confidence in and I have no wish to be ungrateful for their ministry to me. We go to his medical rooms that are full of strange items and machines such as I have never seen before or since and William takes a deep interest in everything, and then the doctor, who is small and bird-like but kindly in his manner, tells me that there is nothing to fear and that I shall come to no harm. There are jars and cylinders, a glass-mounted object with a wooden handle to the end of which a brass ball and wooden point are fitted. I am placed in what he calls the insulated chair and then he applies the ball of the glass-mounted object that has been connected to what he names as the prime conductor by a wire to the parts of my body that are afflicted by the pains, and then as I gasp there is a stream of electric sparks and Dr Birch asks me to trust him as he applies the brass ball to my spine. He tells me that passing these gentle shocks through my body will serve to free it of its malignancies and William comes and stands close to me but at the doctor's orders does not touch me and I feel no pain only a curious creeping sensation and the sparks still flicker across my eyes even after they have faded into nothingness. I think it helps and I tell William so but mostly because I don't want to disappoint him and as we walk home he talks of the sparks and there is an excitement in his voice and I think in truth he would like to experience the sensation. Then as we pass some street-sellers, their wares spread out under the shelter of arches, on impulse I make him stop and I buy a little purse all embroidered and shiny with beaded glass.

What have we to fear in death, William is always saying, when it is nothing more than walking from one room to the next and his words make me remember the death of his younger brother Robert. For fourteen days and nights in the exercise of the utmost faithfulness William sat at his brother's bedside and ministered to him both in body and spirit. At the final moments William saw his beloved brother's spirit departing his body and ascending skywards with a joyous clapping of hands to be with Christ. Afterwards William fell into a deep slumber and slept for three days and nights.

When it is our appointed time he tells me we must also rejoice but I am fearful when I think of him being called before me. And so I do not like this life mask that Deville asks to make because although he calls it a life mask I know that he's thinking of preserving Will's image in anticipation of his death. So Will sits with his face covered in wet plaster until it hardens and two straws are the only means by which he breathes. It becomes increasingly hot and unpleasant and when in the fullness of time it is removed the plaster pulls out some of his hair. I am not much in favour of the final head – it makes Will look unnaturally stern and because his eyes are closed it shows none of the light that burns there and the tight press of his lips transport him into the realms of unresurrected death. Afterwards I bathe his face with warm water until it soothes away the mottled redness but even when he smiles at me I think of the mask with its closed eyes and then when I shiver a little turn away so that he doesn't see.

And this is also the shiver of what must inevitably come as creeping up silently like a hunter there arrive the years when time's hand begins to rest more heavily on him and wound with longer periods of illness. Then in the knowledge that his race is almost run he gives himself to his final watercolour illustrations of Dante with renewed vigour and concentration and the colours are as bright as anything his hand has ever made. And I give him back his own words and tell him that everything he has created from the world of the spirit will live long after he has gone and that pleases him. He has reached three score and ten, the allotted span, and we are married almost forty-five years. So many years; the days rush in against each other until it feels a lifetime is but a single day shaded in a host of different colours.

I think of it all now in this my final house – sometimes I get confused about the houses and what took place under which roof. I do not think of it as a home but somewhere I must wait and hold myself in readiness. This is not a house he ever lived in so at first I worried that he wouldn't be able to find me but he is surely guided by love and there is scarcely a day when he doesn't come and then it feels like all the homes we shared and everything in the past is somehow here in this one place. The pages of two lives that are one life and sometimes

I am that young bride again in Battersea with flowers in her hair and sometimes I am the learner of words stepping into what seemed like a foreign country that I thought was forever barred to me but which opens itself until I step into its open garden. I like to think that it is the garden of love in which I have lived and while all things wither and fade, my hair brittle and grey, my body shrivelled, my heart is able to sing that there is no diminishing of love, no fading of the light.

He still ventures forth as best he can and continues to draw and work with all the strength he can muster and I watch him and see that what burns there is untouched by age and ill-health. There is a miracle in that and it makes me think of Moses seeing the burning bush and there are times when I think I too stand in a holy place. It is the world's loss that they do not see what I see and a prophet is always without honour in his own country. I try not to think of the hardships that accompanied all our days, how many times we had to scrape and struggle to live, but can't stop recalling with both a smile and a little shame when as a young wife I once served him an empty plate for his evening meal and told him that while his head was in Paradise our bodies needed food and the wherewithal to buy it. I was angry then, telling him that none of the shopkeepers would accept payment in dreams and visions. And so for a while at least he turned his hand more fully to making the money we needed to live.

His body grows ever weaker and he has to take to his bed but continues to work. These are dark days to recall and the colours I paint them are muted with sadness. I am increasingly filled with a dread of him leaving me, the selfish thought leading me into a fearful confusion about how I shall be able to live the first and every following day without him. He likes me still to read to him and sometimes I think he feels a pride in it as if I am his best pupil. And sometimes too I sing a little and all the old agitations and furies seem to have worn away from him so what is left is a calm, the still small voice of holiness.

On the final Sunday evening, the weather mild and the city itself as if becalmed into a final rest before the returning world of labour, he continues propped up in bed to work on the Dante drawings. When I ask him how he is he speaks of being 'very weak but not in spirit and life, not in the real man' and he smiles and reminds me again of the imagination which 'liveth for ever'. I look into his eyes and see the light flicker and am afraid, think of turning away because it is more than I can bear, but then he stops his work, all the brightness flooding back, and says, 'Stay, Kate, keep just as you are – I will draw your portrait – for you have ever been an angel to me.' He draws me as best his trembling hand can manage and it moves and quickens my heart more than anything else to know that I am his final image and as he works he tells me we shall never be parted and when he's finished he holds my hand and tells me not to cry because soon he will throw off all the fetters and cares of this world that is not our true home and exchange it for the gardens of paradise. His voice holds no fear even though it slips slowly into a whisper so I have to lean in close to hear him and as I do so he lays his hand briefly on my cheek before it falls away again and then he is gone into glory.

I am a ghost to myself, barely existing at first, moving through the house as if I have no corporeal presence and without need for food or sleep. Sometimes I get up in the night and sit at his table and wait for him to come and start his work but there is only his empty chair and the unused press. Soon he will tell me to sell everything, give me instructions on what I must do with all that remains, but during these first days there is only a solitary emptiness that nothing seems able to end. I feel shut out from him just like all those years ago when I held his letters I couldn't read and just as I felt that time by the sea in Felpham when he had his visions. I try to find comfort in telling myself that he will find our lost child and together at last they are waiting for me to join them. But in truth there is nothing that can salve the sorrow that feels as if it will crush what is left of me so that I breathe and move only through what feels mechanical.

Sometimes I spread what remains of William's pictures carefully on the floor under the window and look at them even more closely than ever and there are so many questions that I regret not asking. I like too when the sun streams through the window and makes the colours freshly new but not even the light can reveal the full mysteries of these worlds and yet I have to believe that in time all will be known to me and the dark glass through which I view them now will be removed for ever, my immortal eyes open, and I shall see the eternal world in the way he saw it. I know that only in that moment shall I stand beside him as his equal.

At intervals there are those who arrive to buy his work and although reluctant and wanting often to say they should have come when he was living I have been told by William that I am to sell everything but when they ask me the price I tell them they must return in a day or so after I have had a chance to consult with Mr Blake. And if there are those amongst them whose manner or character are not to my pleasing I refuse their money. And the sketches he did of me are not to be bought for any price but are destined to stay close to me as long as I breathe.

I stand and watch the light illuminate all the holy images carefully spread on the floor and for a moment the world seems to fall silent and the noise from the street below is stifled and borne away to some distant place. Then by the rustle of some watching angel's gossamer wings the paintings stir a little and raise themselves as if touched by celestial hand and I hear the still small voice of the Divine and everything is burnished brighter than earthly colours could ever fashion. The whole world turns silently and there is nothing but my breathing and then to shield themselves from the bright intensity of the colours my eyes blink and in that moment the noise of the street flows back into the room and all is changed once more.

The first time when he returns to me is when I am at my lowest and he comes one morning without warning, as if made from particles of light, his black suit shining, and he takes his seat once more as if he has returned from one of his walks through the city's streets. I blink and wonder if I am still in some dream but when I open my eyes he is there and the light from the window shines both around and through him and when he speaks his voice is gentle and full of love. He tells me I must be patient and that soon he will come and take me home. But as he will do so many times in the future he answers my impatient questioning by telling me that it must be in the fullness of time when everything is ordered and ready.

He talks to me of the past and then he reminds me of that morning when we first baptised ourselves in the sea and how I was frightened that it would swallow me up. And I try to tell him that a lifetime later grief threatens to do the same. When I look up he has slipped away but I speak to him anyway and try to find and colour the words so that he will understand. Gradually the sharpness of the pain is replaced by a dull ache that is only made bearable by his frequent visits. And the pains are in my body as well as my heart and increasingly as the years slip by I feel the slow fade of my strength and am grateful for it, glad that the long struggle is coming to an end. I venture out only as is necessary but am mostly confined to this place that sometimes seems like Green Street, sometimes Fountain Court and at others like Lambeth. So there are times when I look from the window and imagine I see the Thames in the morning light and others when I look out on the courtyard where children played and it is as if I hear their voices rising up again and darting across the glass like swallows.

It is four years since he first departed, each one the longest expanse of time, dragged out as if by the tardy hands of a slowing clock. I am consumed by a great weariness and then at last there is the slow beginning of letting go and everything in anticipation finally given its truest colour, but for a moment, just for a single moment, I am frightened that I shall be swept into the eternal forests of some distant, starless night until my soul lays stronger claim to its inheritance and my eyes are clear enough to read, my heart strong enough to rejoice in Solomon's words:

> Whither is thy beloved gone, O thou fairest among women?
> Whither is thy beloved turned aside? That we may seek him
>   with thee.
> My beloved is gone down into his garden, to the beds of spices,
>   to feed in the gardens, and to gather lilies.

I was married with wild flowers in my hair – rose, daisy and the sweet scented honeysuckle. For my posy I carried bluebells – I have one still, its faded blueness pressed between the pages of my Bible. Now this poor bed with its threadbare blankets is no longer of this world but that bed of spices and soon my beloved will come to gather what is finally his and then I too shall be dressed in light and all the infirmities and afflictions of old age shall surely fall away. Such colours then, already spreading in wonder across new worlds, and I shall see the visions that were denied to my mortal eyes, my head and heart freed for ever from their earthly limits, and I shall be as the woman clothed with sun, no longer 'the shadow of delight'. And as we did when we walked in the lanes and field of courtship I shall teach him the names of what grows in Paradise.

But how will I know he's come and will my going be like that sphere of fire we watched burn itself across the sky or will it be in the slow unveiling of early-morning light as the city stirs and wakens, this city that is the human awful wonder of God? As always impatience makes me restless and I calm myself by thinking of Eve who is waiting for me and how he will take me to her and she will be safe inside my embrace and never lost to it ever again. And now it's as if all the city is singing with the voices of angels echoing through every street and stilling the clamour and chaos into one holy song and then as it falls silent again he's standing there at last and he gently calls my name. The Bible slips from my grasp, the bluebell falling out into new colour in the light that flows about him, and he's whispering my name and holding out his hand. His hand that has no stain or mark. He's telling me that the pure soul will cut a path into the Heaven of glory, leaving a track of light for men to wonder at. He's calling my name. I can barely raise my arm but I reach out and take his outstretched hand. Then we step into the other room together.

Nadezhda

You took away all the oceans and all the room.
You gave me my shoe-size in earth with bars around it.
Where did it get you? Nowhere.
You left me my lips, and they shape words, even in
silence.

Osip Mandelstam

1939

T HE LONG QUEUE ON Moscow's Sophia Embankment
consists almost entirely of women. A few have brought
their children whose faces sullen with impatience at the hours
they must spend in line are tempered by the drilled knowledge of the way they should behave, and above all how they
must avoid the danger of idle speech. Because the children
know as well as anyone that nothing opens the cell door like
a prattling tongue. Perhaps it was such a careless tongue that
made them come in the night for their father. But there are
also children who have denounced their own parents. So not
to put yourself, or them at risk, never talk in front of a child.
Never talk in front of a stranger. That's the rule.

Their clothing damp and spangled from the earlier fall of
snow smells like old sacking and seeps into their collective
misery. The woman who stands behind her reeks of onions
and cheap scent. It inveigles itself into her senses and every
time the queue shuffles forwards it follows and releases a new
pungency. Of course there are always those who cannot hold
their tongue whatever the danger and so one or two lean in
closer to whoever will listen, to whisper no doubt that it was
all a mistake and say they're hopeful everything will soon be

sorted, and they'll speak of the letters they've written, the appointment with the Prosecutor's Office they're seeking, but which even if it is granted will seem like an eternity away in comparison to the mere three or four hours required of them now. She thinks it strange how everyone considers their own loss a mistake while instantly believing the guilt of others, no matter how fantastic the charge. On a tram she has even heard a woman proclaim with confidence that Stalin didn't know what was done in his name and that if she can only get a letter to him everything will change. Foolish woman – if ever she wrote such a letter it would secure her a passage to the camps before the ink was dry on the page.

She looks at the forlorn children leaning in on their mothers' hips, trying to find some fleshly cushion for their weary heads, but they are out of luck because none of the women carry anything surplus other than the weight of their despair. Their husbands are denounced as counter-revolutionaries and not to join in the denunciation is to embrace the shame spiralling about them and to risk their own arrest. And then what will happen to their children except that they too will be branded with the mark of the traitor and dumped in some far-off orphanage. No little red Komosol scarves for them, nothing hanging round their necks except humiliation and future lives lived in constant fear of exposure. She wonders why they brought them to this place and so subjected them to public gaze. Perhaps simply because there was no one willing to help look after them, perhaps because they didn't want anyone to know where they were going. She is glad that despite everything her marriage brought her it never gave her children and she thinks there is enough suffering in the moment they take the man you love without adding their cries into the loss. And soon they will come for her. She thinks it is only a matter of time, sometimes is convinced that the delay is because they are enjoying the pleasure they derive from exerting their power, like a cat playing with a mouse.

She has come on the day of the month that the clerk deals with the letter M. Mandelstam. Osip Mandelstam. It makes her wonder about the enormity of the lists that this alphabetical arrangement has to be applied. The queue that slithers its way to the small, wooden-shuttered window falls into a silence disturbed only by the stamping of feet in vain attempts to generate warmth and the angry barking cough of an old woman. Occasionally at the window itself voices are raised but almost as soon as that happens there is the sound of the wooden shutters being slammed shut. She knows by now that the head that sits there does not enter into discussion and has no use for argument. The vastness of all their inner worlds, their loves and secret memories, the enduring intimacy between man and wife that is called marriage – all are drawn inexorably into this tiny space and this one head whose voice snaps at any hesitation as they give the prisoner's name before handing over their little parcel or small amount of money. In return they receive only a scribbled receipt. Sometimes the window summarily shuts and although they go on standing they do not know if it will open again or if they must come back another day. There is a soldier on hand to deal with any recalcitrant or someone who loses possession of her senses and tries to make an appeal to this doorway into the void where their men have fallen. Fallen into a world that can only be imagined in the dark sleepless hours before dawn or partially constructed from the broken, reluctant witness of those who somehow manage to claw a way back. It stretches out behind the high walls of the prisons and into the snowy wastes far beyond the reach of love except through the tenuous, uncertain possibility of what they hold so tightly in their hands. Appeal to the window? As much point as howling at the wind.

The age has declared her a fool for thinking that anything that happens to an individual has any meaning. So she is on her own and soon there will be a knock at the apartment door and they will be there telling her to get dressed, all the time speaking in their calm, almost weary voices, unwilling to panic her any more than they already have. Speaking as if everything is matter-of-fact, a mere piece of administrative procedure, a question simply of having the right paperwork. She is supposed to be satisfied with the charade that everything is being done under correct legal process. It's said that some sleep with their things already packed but they'll always be told there is no need to bring so much, as if a safe return is guaranteed and imminent. A few questions, that's all, and then everything will be done and dusted. Done and dusted, true enough, and she with all the countless others turned to camp dust and their remains scattered to the winds or buried in the frozen earth in the tundra's unmarked graves.

As a weak wash of blue-edged light suddenly sheens a momentary definition into the greyness crowding in on her she sees the small drops of moisture beading the sable strands in the hair of the woman who stands in front. She can't be more than thirty and still thinking it important to try to turn herself out well, to mend her clothes carefully so that it isn't obvious except to someone who has stood close behind her over the space of three hours. They say that often the prosecutors tell such women that they are free to marry again even when their husbands carry a ten-year sentence. The price of divorce itself has been reduced. Perhaps these officials know the husbands will not be coming back, or if they do it will only be to enter the revolving door of re-arrest. Sometimes in love men have made their wives divorce them, broken off all contact just to give them a chance of survival.

That will never happen to them. They are together for ever, she believes. And then beyond. As she stamps her own feet she tells herself that he will not live long, that he isn't strong enough to survive the camps, and she finds a kind of comfort in that. His heart is weak – already he has taken on the physical appearance of an old man so she shouldn't be surprised by these few sable strands that streak the black sweep of this young woman's hair. Once after his first arrest in '34 for reciting his poem about Stalin and when they had been banished first to Cherdyn, then to Voronezh and compelled to become wandering beggars, she had offered him the thought of suicide but he had rebuked her with, 'Life is a gift that nobody should renounce.' He had the unfailing capacity to live life-glad in the moment and absorb fully whatever pleasure could be found despite their circumstances. Now it is the boarded-up prison trains and the weakness of his heart that will hurry him towards his death and she is glad his suffering will be short. What she hopes is that it will happen before fear is able once more to contaminate his mind, his poet's mind that is the very best of him, and even now in the rigid order of the line she bridles with anger that such a man's fate can be in the hands of those not worthy to breathe the same air.

But almost at once she is frightened by her anger because it above all things must be held in check. Her scream of rage can be heard by no one except herself. Fear is what they deal in. It is the only thing that exists in abundance. When everything else – food, clothes, bread itself – has shrunk to the margins, fear multiplies and flourishes. It is the currency with which anything can be bought, able to take someone else's apartment, someone else's wife, a reputation gained through a lifetime of exemplary service and sacrifice, and of course a life itself. It can even wipe away all memory and rewrite the past. In the Lubyanka the interrogator told Osip that he would experience 'fear in full measure'. It is the only full measure they give so perhaps he expected his victim to be grateful. The fear is all around her now, coursing through the bowed heads and hunched shoulders, so real that it can almost be shivered on the skin or tasted in the mouth. She thinks again of the time she hesitatingly suggested they might together escape the fear, the terrible drawn-out waiting for the inevitable and his refusal to countenance it.

There is a short outburst at the window. Heads raise surreptitiously and lean out of the line to see what's happening. An old woman is wailing, her cries fragmenting in jagged breathless shards. Her arms flail in the air and her hands pluck at her hair. Then the soldier has her by the shoulder, bunching up her shawl in the tight knot of his fist as he marches her away from the closed window. Passing along the queue they glance at her distorted face, its furrowed tracery of lines and creases that look as if they will crack open and allow her molten grief to pour out – the small parcel tied with string that she clutches to her heart confirmation that her child or husband no longer needs whatever it contains. Her wailing unsettles the waiting women and there is an unmistakable murmur threading its way along the length, momentarily linking them before it fades away almost as quickly into separate silences again. A child is asking a question of his mother but she hushes him and pulls his face into her side and holds him so close it looks as if she has an extra limb.

The line moves forward to occupy the vacated space. Somewhere behind her there is a whispered sibilance as if someone is praying but she cannot make out the words. She has no faith in prayer. The night before they came for Osip in the final arrest at Samatikha she had a terrible dream of icons. She thought it a bad omen and she was right because in the morning they took him away. That moment had played out and rehearsed itself so often in her head that at first it was as if she was acting out something already scripted for her. Everyone playing their allotted part. Two men in uniform and the doctor from the centre. Their knock at the door is soft, unthreatening. The two men complain about having to work over their May Day holiday. The doctor looks apologetic for his role in helping trapping them in Samatikha, which has been offered as supposed respite from their impoverished wanderings, but they realise at last that it was granted because it was too far from anywhere to effect an escape. He hangs back in his white coat, physically positioning himself at the edge of what's happening as if some part of him – his conscience, what's left of his self-respect – needs to be removed from the damaging reality of what's taking place. They realise they've been sent to this dead-end to make it convenient for them when the appointed time arrived. But already she is thinking of preserving the poems and gives them the lie that all their papers are in the Moscow apartment when the truth is that many are still in Kalinin.

And this moment has played out so many times in her imagination but now the script slips from her hands and she struggles to play the part for which she has prepared herself. Osip gets dressed, she puts on her dressing gown and gathers up his things but hears the uniforms ask why she needs to gather so much stuff when he'll be back after a few questions. There is a coldness opening inside her that paralyses her speech, weighs her limbs so that she has to sit on the bed as if turned to stone. Through the open door she can see the rear of the truck. In a matter of minutes it's all over and when he asks her to come with him as far as the station they tell him it isn't allowed. They're taking him now and the script is dissolving in her head so that as they lead him away she gives him no proper words of farewell. This man whose whole life is built on the beauty and power of words she gives nothing of worth to carry in his head on the coming journey. Those words that have been prepared in her heart are frozen mute and as they put him in the truck she sits on the bed unable to move or cry out. She stays there as it pulls away and the noise of its engine roars in her ears long after the platitudes of the doctor who still lingers have faded into silence. Then when he quietly closes the door the frozen mask of her face is broken by the slow movement of her lips. Over and over, her lips reciting the poems, engraving them into her memory.

It is what she must do now. Right from the start of the process of making him a non-person they wanted the poems to disappear and she will not let that happen. Every remaining fibre of her being will not let that happen. And there is no place that is safe except her memory. The manuscripts sewn into cushions, hidden in saucepans or shoes – anywhere that might evade the searches – all of them vulnerable. Sometimes copies of the poems were given to others for safekeeping but who to trust? Always there are informers, sometimes because they believe they do good service for Mother Russia, others because they have been bought or pressured. Because the fist of fear has gripped their heart. Sometimes wives of those who were entrusted to hide some poems for them discover their hiding place and destroy them out of fear. There is nowhere they are safe but with her and that is why she must go on living, must stay one step ahead of them. 'Let them forget about you, Nadia, make no stir,' is the advice she was given after his arrest and so it is dangerous to come here with her pathetic parcel that her hands grip so tightly, as if at any moment she thinks someone will try to rip it from her grasp, but love compels her.

The queue shuffles a little closer to the window. Even before his first arrest his fellow writers, his so-called comrades in the Writers' Union, had cast him into the wilderness. She recalls with fresh bitterness how no one would publish his work, no one would accept his contributions to their magazines, how people snubbed him in the street. The only work he could find was a few poorly paid bits of translation. There are those too who insist on describing him as a former poet and refer to him as a translator. But the poems exist and in those years of exile in Voronezh the knowledge that his time was short spurred him on to write, the words tumbling out of him so that she could hardly keep up with their transcription. From under the shadow of death, out of his mouth and out of his heart and soul, a whole other world spinning through the excited but careful accuracy of her hand and on to the scraps of rough paper that were their only manuscript. Written on scraps and then written on the heart.

She stands in the queue that appears to move ever slower the closer they get to the window. The old woman's wails have disappeared but seem to echo and linger in the renewed silence. It is what they all fear and fear it more with each step that brings them towards the moment when the clerk will look at his lists of names – something that always takes a long time until the wait becomes almost unbearable. Sometimes the wait and the fear reduce the woman's voice to a hesitant whisper, or even drain it completely, and then he will snarl at them to speak up. Perhaps the clerk enjoys this power over them. But does he feel nothing when he bluntly tells them their loved one is dead and then is unable, or refuses, to give any further information? Perhaps he experiences only satisfaction that another enemy of the people has perished for their heinous crimes. The inevitable stream of questions about where and when and how are dismissed by the shout of 'Next' and she has seen more than once the suddenly bereaved shouldered out of the way by the person behind her in the queue. In these times the living always take precedence over the dead.

Everyone believes she is watched, perhaps even here in the midst of this long line. In every apartment block there is at least one police spy who seeks to ingratiate him- or herself with their masters by supplying information, or by denouncing someone on whatever pretext is available. Sometimes in Moscow they were visited by strangers who made little attempt to disguise their official employment while others purported to be admirers, lovers of literature, and sought to entice Osip into saying something that would incriminate him, or ask for a copy of a particular poem that they supposedly loved so much. On occasions the flat was searched in their absence and such was their sense of power that they were happy to leave their calling cards – cigarette butts in the ashtray, a drawer pulled out but deliberately not closed. As she stands in the queue she tells herself that they cannot search the hidden folds of her heart.

The sky is opening itself as if it might snow again and as she turns her face to it she wonders what these women have had to sell as they desperately seek to find some money to make the parcel. She herself has become a beggar, going in desperate hope from friend to friend, from family member to anyone who might be able or willing to give something. Sometimes doors were closed on her – in one place she was told to wait but no one returned as they had suggested they would. Despite Pasternak's kindness and his intervention on Osip's behalf, soon his wife will tell her not to come to their house. Others scrape together whatever they can spare. Once someone silently slips an envelope into her pocket. Perhaps there are even women standing in the queue who have had no recourse but to sell themselves and she knows already that there are some who having lost their husbands have sought protective shelter in marriage or relationship with some Party official. She does not judge them. There are enough others whom she does.

She thinks of those fellow writers who refused her husband clothes after his return to Petrograd from the Crimea and when he had nothing to protect him from the winter. The only means of getting clothing was from the exchange of vouchers and it was one of those at the top of the Writers' Union who authorised their issue. When Osip had asked for a jumper and a pair of trousers someone had scored out the word trousers on the voucher. 'He'll manage without,' was what he had said. So Osip who was reduced to such a level that he had to ask for a pair of trousers was refused while the Union of Writers could find dachas and apartments and who knew what other luxuries for those so-called writers whose talents didn't merit being mentioned in the same breath. It angers her again that he has been subjected to such indignities, angers her more than he ever showed, so she takes his and adds it to hers. Then as the queue shuffles a few feet forward again she finds comfort in telling herself that the judgement of history will pay them back. It's what she has to believe. Their work is dead, withered on the vine, and she takes pleasure in that. So now there will be no poetry as true and beautiful as that her hand transcribed but only the doggerel that they justify by calling it proletarian art. Perhaps if he could have done it he would have survived but it wasn't in him. Even when Lakhuti organised for him to see the construction of the White Sea Canal and write something appropriately celebratory about the revolution's power to transform and master nature, Osip couldn't do it. It was an abomination to him, the poem he produced feeble rubbish, and nor could he ever bring himself to disavow what he had written in the past.

So it's one of the poems that she recites now, recites over and over until the words seem to become part of her, flowing along her consciousness into the quick of her being with no longer any need for memory or the imposition of her will. It feels like they suffuse her breathing and her consciousness and for a second she worries that the words will print themselves on her face and force themselves into the light. If she had a mirror she would look to reassure herself that her imagination is playing tricks on her. And there is the deep pleasure of listening to his voice again because it is not hers that she hears and she knows she will never let it stop speaking. As long as there is breath in her body the words will exist. So during the long wait in the queue she uses the time to recite the poems until she has little understanding of how many hours have passed and how close she is getting to the window. But something suddenly disturbs her and makes her look up and frees herself from the silent incantation.

She stares at the woman in front. The droplets in her hair and the little blisters of snow on her shoulders have dried but the silver strands seem to have been polished brighter. It must be the changing light. There is something wrong. She sees that in the almost imperceptible rise and fall of her shoulders, the slackening of her neck muscles and the way her hand moves repeatedly to her face. And then amidst the shuffling feet and stifled coughing she hears her breathing begin to quicken and deepen. Instinctively she reaches out her arm and rests it on the woman's shoulder but drops it again as she feels her whole body start under the touch. In that second she had also felt the woman's thinness, her shoulder blade pressed up tight against the skin as if trying to break free. The woman turns her face to look at her and reveals dark rings under her eyes, the hollowed cheeks that make-up has been unable to disguise. Her eyes are closing as if succumbing to an overwhelming weariness and she is about to fall asleep on her feet.

'Are you all right?' she asks.

'I feel faint.'

There are no chairs, nowhere to find her a seat, and anyway after three hours in the queue she knows that neither of them will want to give up their place so close to the window. She looks around her but sees nothing that can help so she steps forward and puts her arm round the woman's waist and feels her lean the little weight she has into her. The smell of onions and cheap scent quickly occupies the space she has just vacated. There are tiny beads of sweat on the ailing woman's forehead and her face is drained of all colour. She gives her a little handkerchief and watches her use it to wipe her brow then dab the corners of her mouth. They move forward a couple of steps in tandem. The young woman holds her head up and breathes deeply, desperately trying to inhale fresh air. After a while her breathing becomes more regular and she is able to straighten herself a little.

'I'm pregnant,' she whispers as she wipes her face again.

'How far gone?'

'About four months.'

'Is there no one you can get to queue for you?'

'Who can I ask? Who wants to risk themselves for someone else's husband?'

She understands so says nothing in response. There are only half a dozen people ahead of them now and she is momentarily distracted from the young woman who still leans against her by a rising pulse of fear. Already she has caught her first glimpse of the clerk's face and felt the dryness in her throat.

'A child who will never see his father,' the young woman says.

'He will come back,' she says and then wonders what right she has to comfort a stranger with a lie.

The woman slowly shakes her head in silent denial before saying, 'A father who will never see his son.'

She says nothing in reply but instead asks her name. She tells her that it is Marta and then confesses her shame at the paucity of her parcel's contents.

'We're all the same,' she tells her, 'scraping and borrowing to find something to send.'

'How will we survive?' the young woman asks.

But she has no answer for this and she listens as the young woman takes deep breaths. Somewhere on the other side of the wall a man's voice laughs. She feels her slowly ease her body away as she tries to refind her own balance. The young woman glances at her and whispers, 'They took him a month ago. My husband is a good man. He would never do what they say. He is an engineer . . .'

But she gently hushes her then whispers, 'They are all good men. Be careful what you say.'

'We quarrelled the day before he was taken – about something so stupid that I cannot even bear to remember it,' she says as she holds the handkerchief to her eyes.

'He will not think of it, he will think of only you. Your love will keep him strong,' she says. 'And you must be strong for the child.' Then she steps back into line and the young woman without turning round lets her hand move behind her and she takes it and clasps it briefly before they release their grip again.

She holds the sensation of another's hand in hers long after they have let go. There feels a momentary strength in it that contains the promise of endurance, the possibility of survival, that each of them is not alone in the world. The queue shuffles forward. Almost there now. She recites his words, believing they will exert their own protective strength, and it is important the closer she comes to the window that all he has written and all that is him in each of the poems will stand resolute. She layers the words across her heart, a dancing line about pear and cherry blossom. There is a sudden synthesis of voice and scent and colour that breaks and shudders through her senses. A mother and her child walk past her having delivered their parcel. How many millions of parcels tied with string or sealed with wax? How many ledgers of names? She finds the strength to smile at the child but she stares back with expressionless eyes. She hopes that despite her eyes she too carries words in her memory – a favourite story told before sleep, a simple expression of love, or a father's sentimental song from better days. She recites again, the power of the words involuntarily making her lips move. The young woman in front has reached the window and eventually after the drawn-out bureaucratic requirements she hands over her parcel so a slender possibility of hope still exists for her. Then she turns away tightly gripping the receipt that means her husband is still alive somewhere in the world. As she passes their eyes meet for a fleeting second, a slight bow of the head offers a final thanks and then she too is gone.

So now it is her turn and she tries to clear her throat so that when she says his name her voice will be clear and strong. The clerk's head is still down, writing something that is hidden from her. His white papery scalp is visible through the thin gauze of his hair. She stands perfectly still, invisible to him. She tries to tell herself that she doesn't feel sick but everything is tightening inside her as she finds herself inescapably drawn to the void that stretches beyond the window. He looks up, his eyes blinking behind his pince-nez. There is a smear of ink staining his fingers. He is a little hard of hearing so it is his good ear he angles towards her. Then at his demand she raises her head, gives the poet's name her voice.

1936

AFTER THEIR BANISHMENT IN Voronezh has ended,
they risk a journey to Moscow hoping to raise money
and speak to those who might help their situation. On the
train they do not talk much but stare out at landscapes that
have finally been surrendered by winter and are slipping
into the first full flush of spring. No one makes eye contact
with anyone else. They say there are some who ride the
trains simply to listen for those whose tongues have been
loosened by the illusion that they have been afforded the
privilege of a private world momentarily separated from
the rest of their lives. Everywhere white-barked birch trees
quiver into loose-limbed leaf. Thick collars of pine tighten
around tiny hamlets so it looks as if they are choking the
life out of them. They pass ragged ribbons of villages that
outwardly look as if history has left them untouched but
she knows that this too is just another illusion and remembers the dispossessed kulaks and peasants who beg for food
in the streets of Voronezh.

The money she had been given by the women who turned
up at the apartment after his arrest is now exhausted. There
is no work despite Osip going on a regular basis to the local

Writers' Union. Even the translation has ended. In the winter they will stop his pension. They live on cabbage soup and eggs, manage when they're lucky to acquire tea and butter, some cigarettes. She has made earlier trips to the Moscow offices of the Writers' Union where she sees Marchenko or Shcherbakov but their faces are blank and stony, their eyes hard, and she knows they have no help for her. At first she thinks her words can be sharp flints that will chip away at them until she carves out the human beneath the surface but their impassive faces blunt her pleas and she goes away empty-handed.

In Moscow outside the railway station they see Petrov who once loved nothing better than to come to the flat for supper and debate. Osip raises his hand in greeting and she watches it freeze in the air as Petrov turns on his heels and crosses to the other side of the road. They are plague carriers, marked as infected, contagious to all who come in contact with them. Only the strangers rushing through the crowded streets or piling on to the overcrowded trams are able to brush against them, briefly share the air they breathe. But even then the protective shield of anonymity feels paper-thin, able at any moment to be torn asunder, and so they huddle closer together as each moment torments them with the possibility of denunciation. She listens to the struggle of his breathing and is frightened that the journey will prove too much.

'Let's not judge him too harshly,' he says suddenly.

'We were always good to him,' she replies. 'Why must you always be like Christ, offering your cheek to the betrayer?'

'Because he's a weak man and who knows what fear has worked in him.' And when she doesn't answer, 'Put your sword away, Nadia, he needs his ear if he is to survive.'

She goes to reply but reluctantly stops – they have no energy to waste in arguments about Petrov – and tells herself that perhaps it is because he has tasted fear he is not so quick to judge.

It was one of those who came to their home and was present at the reading of the poem about Stalin who betrayed them. Petrov had not been there that evening. She sees the circle of listeners in the faces of the strangers who stream all about her and wonders who it was and knows it is the curse of the age to suspect even those whose heart bears nothing but love. There is a sudden commotion on the pavement. A woman is shouting and waving her arms, berating a younger woman who is bending down to gather up carrots that have fallen. A page of newspaper flaps on the ground. Her crime in the absence of paper bags in the shop is to wrap the carrots in a newspaper bearing Stalin's photograph. As she bends down to retrieve them her face is curtained by the loosening fall of her hair and she has to pause to push it out of her eyes. The accuser towers over her, her face a burning red as she angrily denounces this act of criminality, and then stamps on a carrot that has rolled towards her with a repeated rhythm that makes it look as if she is doing some crazy dance. The younger woman scampers away desperately trying not to spill what's left of her purchase as shouts pursue her. Then the shouting, stamping woman is transformed, carefully cradling the newspaper as if it is a young child she has taken into her arms to suckle.

'So this is what we've come to,' Osip says as he stands motionless but she encourages him to move away with a sharp pull on the sleeve of his coat. They have places to visit, information to seek, money to try and borrow. After the countryside the city's waves of noise and movement seem clamorous, making her feel as if they are flotsam on its crowded currents. She thinks it strange that during the day life flows like this and there is little that signifies what goes on under the surface. It is at night that the fear emerges as families whisper, anxious that none of their voices carry through the thin makeshift walls that divide their living spaces. So the sound of a car stopping outside or the rise of the lift is enough to make them think their time has come. To die in your own bed becomes the unspoken dream. But what chance of such a welcome end when now there are quotas that must be met? So who can tell when the knock at the door will summon them to a different fate? Once it was thought that living quietly and guarding the tongue would ensure safety but now there is no way of knowing in advance or understanding what crimes they have supposedly committed. All around them there are sudden spaces like a wood where each day the axe comes to cut down more trees. Cuts them down supposedly to allow more light and air, to give the rest the chance of future growth, but in each of those spaces stretches a shadow that grows longer until it encompasses all of them.

They find a seat in one of the parks to allow him to regain his breath. There are children at play under their mothers' watchful eyes. The weather is warming and in the lake some young boys sail a model boat. On their journey into exile they had transferred to a river steamer at Solikamsk and the kindly leader of their three guards – simple peasant soldiers more used to transporting those convicted of spying or sabotage – had helped them to gain a cabin where Osip could rest. They had stayed on deck – the greatest distance they had permitted themselves – obviously having decided that his physical condition and his crime of poetry rendered him unlikely to present the possibility of problems. Psychologically he was in a bad state then, the worst she had ever seen him. She had tried to calm him, soothe away the reverberations that echoed discordantly in his head. All those things that allowed him to be a great poet – heightened sensitivities and senses, the sharpest perception – now conspired against him to flood his mind with what he didn't want to remember in all the starkness of their horror and gave him no peace.

A breeze catches the sail of the boys' boat, sending it curving through the water, bisecting the shadowy surface with a bevelling white. The boys' cries of pleasure accompany it even when it seems to lean precariously close to the surface. Suddenly he gets up and walks to the edge of the pond, each step accompanied by the piping, wheezing descant of his breathing. She watches him stand with his back to her and yet is still able to see the pleasure he takes in the boat's untrammelled flight as it runs before the wind. He takes a child's delight in it, even holding his hand up in alarm as it finally slips sideways and its sail flops into the water. There has always been something childlike about him but she isn't sure if it's something that she admires or is irritated by. He turns again to resume his seat beside her. Even that short exertion has tired him and when he takes her hand she isn't sure whether it's from affection or merely to assure himself of her presence and support.

They watch the boys squabble amongst themselves until the tallest takes off his shoes and rolls up his trousers before carefully feeling his way, stepping with exaggerated caution. One of the other boys picks up a small stone and gently throws it to make a splash but is rebuked by the others and he wanders off shame-faced.

'Children still play,' he says. 'Whatever happens in other places children still play.'

But she won't let herself take any comfort in whatever he has to say about children's play and tells him that soon they must be moving again, reminds him of their need to find money and help before they have to return once more. She knows he would be content to sit in the warming sun and watch everything the park has to offer, to devour it voraciously and find in it some sustaining sustenance not open to her because already she can hear the low rumble of her stomach and feel the sharp stirring of a headache. There is no sunlight or reverie that can banish their insistent clamouring for her attention. Carefully she takes the cloth-wrapped portion of bread and the hardening wedge of cheese from her pocket then spreads a white handkerchief on her knees like a tablecloth and places the only food they have left on it. With a stub of a knife she slowly divides the bread and cheese into two portions and hands him his half. They have nothing to drink but perhaps the park will have a drinking fountain they can find when they have finished. She is instantaneously pleased but then irritated again by the look of gratitude and joy on his face. 'A feast fit for a king,' he says and there is no sarcasm in his voice. She hears herself reply, 'A feast only fit for a king in penurious exile.' Then they eat in silence, concentrating on prolonging the meagre meal, carefully retrieving every crumb that falls, trying perhaps to conjure some greater sense of pleasure than the stale ingredients afford.

'We must go soon,' she tells him when they have finished, suddenly conscious of how often she speaks as if a mother to her child. 'There are places we need to try. Time is getting on.'

He nods but makes no effort to move. Out in the pond the boy has retrieved the boat, pulling it towards him with a long hooked stick. Its sails are bedraggled.

'They'll dry soon in the sun,' he says loudly and she isn't sure if the words are for her or for the boys but she feels a flurry of anger at his capacity to be positive about so many things and tells herself it is a delusion, a dangerous delusion. On some whim that she doesn't fully understand his life has been momentarily allowed to him but he stands at the very edge of the abyss, exposed, vulnerable, and when the wind changes it will topple him into the pit as surely as night follows day. So what right has he to sit there and let the sun warm his face and believe that it will dry the sails? But she understands that there is another reason why he doesn't want to leave and for a second she too almost believes that if they sit still and quiet then time and the future might simply pass over them leaving them eternally in this moment, preserved like insects in aspic.

'You're right,' he says after a few minutes, 'we must go on, rattle our begging bowls, throw ourselves on the kindness of others,' and he brushes his coat as if there might exist the possibility of spilled crumbs. She folds the handkerchief away and arm in arm like some elderly couple they make their way out of the park and she is conscious of his breathing that sometimes brushes her cheek when he turns his head towards her. She is grateful that the intensity of the sun has slipped a little and welcoming of the breeze that is sneaking its way between buildings and stirring the awnings of shops, wakening the furled and sleeping flags. She tries to think her headache away but it feels as if the noise and grit of the city streets have taken lodgings in her brain and she wants to be in the park again watching the boat's sails drying in the sun. She also tries to tell herself that there is dignity in struggle, in not simply giving up, but at two houses where they had hoped they might find help they are turned away, one with nothing more than a shrug of the shoulders through a partially opened door, and one with a welter of platitudes and excuses that embarrassed the deliverer even more than them.

So they have no other choice and as much as they don't want to impose their need once more, desperation is always stronger than their sense of shame, and they make their way to the Shklovskis' where they know they will not be refused. Victor and Vasilisa are out and so it falls to their two children to offer them hospitality and act as surrogates for their parents and they provide them with food and drink in the kitchen. Little Varia, taking obvious pleasure in assuming the adult role, plies them also with chatter and laughter while her older brother Nikita keeps a quiet eye on her to ensure she's doing everything the way it should be done. It is a kindness they have experienced before but never take for granted and it is one of the few places, however briefly, they feel their life come closest to what they once knew. Osip jokes with

Varia, tells her increasingly fantastic stories that make her laugh, and tries to provoke the taciturn Nikita into some similar response but the most he allows himself is a shy smile. She looks at the two children and wonders if he resents their absence then tries to balance out whatever pleasures they might have brought with the unspeakable difficulties that would also have come, not least the crushing worry about their fate in the event of their parents being taken in the night. She thinks of Voronezh where there is a feral gang of seemingly abandoned children who scavenge the streets before disappearing at night into some secret refuge. Soon the authorities will round these up too and they will disappear so suddenly that some citizens will question if they ever existed at all or whether they were merely a trick of the memory.

'Nikita collects birds,' Varia says. 'He catches them – isn't that cruel?'

The boy blushes and pushes his tongue against the inside of his cheek before he says, 'I treat them well, it isn't cruel, and after a while I release them,' and he glares at his sister, looking directly at her as he adds, 'It's a hobby – lots of people do it.'

'And what type of birds do you catch?' Osip asks.

'Sometimes songbirds, but not always. There are collectors who have large collections and some even train their birds to do tricks or sing.'

'Just like the Union of Writers,' Osip says and he laughs so hard at his own joke that they laugh at his laughter as he slaps the table with the palm of his hand and makes the cups dance.

Varia challenges him to a game of chess and when Nikita tells her that she isn't a good enough player to challenge people she rolls her eyes and rattles on about how it's the only way to learn. It's been so long since Osip's played chess and she watches him handle the pieces with curiosity, turning them over in his hands as if trying to conjure their names and roles through the touch of his fingers. He puts the king and queen on the wrong squares and Varia reaches across the board and rights them and he shakes his head in an exaggerated frustration at his own stupidity.

They sit at the kitchen table and play and she doesn't know if he's deliberately letting her win or whether what has happened has damaged his memory of even this. Each time Varia takes a piece she lifts it with a flourish of her wrist and a wide smile and he shakes his head again from side to side.

'She's too good for me,' he says ruefully as Nikita gives a little snorting noise.

If she can only exist in the moment she could almost feel happy but as soon as she thinks this, the knowledge of where they must return and what ultimately awaits them prevents her. She touches the solidity of the table then searches for some residue of warmth in her cup but none of it is enough and frightened that it will show in her face she rises and walks into the hallway. Then on impulse she turns and pushes open the door to Nikita's bedroom.

There are four wooden cages hanging from the wall. In each a bird, she guesses, but they are only vaguely glimpsed. She doesn't know if they are songbirds are not. They are barely visible through the bars and her appearance evokes only their silence. The bars are not uniform but misshapen spindles of wood that look as if they might shatter under any determined burst for freedom. The fading afternoon light has dulled the room and as she stands in the doorway she struggles to see the birds but doesn't want to intrude. Then one hops from its perch and the whole rickety cage moves slightly on its hook. Some small ends of straw or husks of seed filter through the bars and pirouette silently to the floor.

From the outer hallway comes the sound of the lift. As always it fills her with dread and she remembers the suspicious, screwed-up face of the doorwoman who scrutinised them from top to bottom. Perhaps she has informed on them, perhaps they have been followed, and now the Shklovskis will be exposed to danger because of them. One of the birds shuffles again in its cage. All sounds from the kitchen have stopped – they too have heard. There are footsteps in the hall approaching the door of the apartment. Nikita appears at her shoulder, glances briefly towards his birds then walks past her towards the door. He is already taller than her but the awkwardness of his gangly, spindle-thin limbs is suddenly subsumed into a gliding elegance that almost makes him look as if he is silently skating. She watches him press his ear to it and then there is the sound of a key turning in the lock and he's helping his parents, Victor and Vasilisa, hurry through.

She has almost forgotten what it is to be greeted by the unguarded openness of a friend's smile and in its warmth she feels resurrected from the tomb, called momentarily back into the land of the living by an embrace and simple expressions of kindness.

'Have they looked after you properly?' Victor asks, looking at Nikita who is carefully locking the door again.

'Perfectly,' she says and then Vasilisa threads her arm and takes her through to the kitchen where Osip and Varia sit, their game suspended, and then Osip leaps up and in his desire to embrace his old friend upsets some of the chess pieces. Varia squeals at the prospect of her imminent victory being thwarted and starts to replace them.

'Later, Varia, later,' her father urges and she slumps back on her chair and folds her arms in sullen exaggeration.

'She's too good for me,' Osip says in an attempt to mollify her and with a melodramatic gesture topples his king and slowly bows his head.

Vasilisa requests a detailed list of what her children have provided and then despite their protests cooks something more. She runs baths for them, finds fresh underwear and insists they rest while she gets the meal ready. When she calls them to the table they are embarrassed by the trouble she's gone to and unsure whether to eat a little of the family's hard-won provisions or to store up for the hungry days they know are coming. At times they can hardly eat for the conversation that flows – the discussion of their predicament, possible sources of money and information and as much as anything a welter of news and gossip – the latest symphony by Shostakovich, whose writing fortunes have risen, whose have fallen. After the meal Victor presents Osip with a coat and he models it with good humour.

While the men sit smoking in the kitchen, quoting poetry to each other, she drinks yet another cup of tea sweetened with sugar and finds herself glancing at the clock, wishing she could slow its hands. There is only one kindness they can give their hosts and that is to decline their invitation to stay the night. She knows the invitation is genuine and there have been times when they have slept on a rug-covered mattress but she cannot bear the possibility that accepting such kindness might result in consequences too terrible for her to contemplate. Nikita is filling a little glass dish with water and she assumes it is for the birds. She hopes he will release them soon. She tries to catch Osip's eye but he is too deeply engaged in the pleasures of his conversation to notice. When Vasilisa offers to refill her cup she declines and tells her they must be going soon. It is as if her husband hasn't heard her words and she understands that he has found a heady excitement, even a momentary fulfilment, in his dialogue about books and writing that he hasn't been able to reach with her. So why should that be a surprise when they are locked together every minute of the day, their lives so tightly knotted that she no longer has any concept of one independent of his? She didn't have to go into exile with him and she tries to remember whether there was ever a moment when she made the conscious decision to accompany him into the wilderness, but it was a question that simply never arose and so needed no answer.

As she looks about the kitchen – Osip and Victor debating some point about poetry as if their lives depended on it, Vasilisa busying herself with pots and pans, Varia sorting through her schoolbooks – she wonders if they will ever be able to allow themselves to come there again. They are infected like carriers of smallpox and the welfare of others demands they hold themselves in isolation. Does he realise this as he declaims some lines of poetry as if they are a sweet wine on his lips? And she feels a slow surge of bitterness that it was words on his lips that have brought them to this reckoning. A couple of minutes' words slipping from his lips and the lives they knew taken from them. A particular set of words, the secret thoughts that swirl undetected in the mind suddenly made real and put in the world without thought for consequence. Was their release worth it, those words that now imprison their existence? And she wonders again how words can change a life so utterly. But of course they weren't just words – 'an act of terrorism' was how the interrogator had described them. And now the terror is visited on them as she sits conscious of every time the lift approaches their floor in the apartment and wonders whether it will stop or pass by, remembers the glance given to them by the doorwoman, the constant feeling that they are being watched. It is surely one of their greatest skills that they let you, their victim, create and slowly imbibe your own terror.

As Osip and Victor sing in creaking harmony some old sentimental ballad they share from their childhood she wonders why he has set his mind so firmly against taking their own lives. Is there part of him that secretly believes this thing will pass over them, that they will simply be forgotten, or that some powerful influence affected by a warm memory of his past work will intervene on their behalf, allowing them to return to Moscow and resume their old life? Osip's eyes are closed as if in some private place he's seeing the memories the song evokes. She wants to tell him if he believes any of these things then his eyes are closed to the truth.

It is getting late. They must leave soon but she knows a spell has settled on him and it's the happiest she has seen him in a long time, so whatever she does or says now will serve to break it. Getting up from the table she goes and sits in a corner, lets him drain the last pleasure from his song. Close by, Varia is humming her attempt at an accompaniment to a song that she doesn't really know so she follows a few notes behind the adults. She is sorting schoolbooks in a satchel, ostentatiously holding them up for her guest's perusal. Then as the song sidles into a melodramatic, drawn-out conclusion the child hands her an open textbook to look at. She takes it in both hands and tries not to let them tremble. There are pages of photographs and names pasted over with thick paper. More and more of them as she turns the pages. Party leaders, old revolutionaries, she guesses, erased by directive and from history itself as one by one they get swept into the pit. So this is how it ends. Removed from existence, excised from public memory. She looks at the faces still uncovered and wonders how many of them will be sent into the dark-ness – a bullet in the head in some cellar or prison courtyard, worked to death in the tundra – and then disappeared into unmarked graves. She looks at Osip. He has tears in his eyes – the sentiment of the song has proved too much. He rubs them dry with the back of his hand. What remains for those eyes still to see? He catches her looking at him, their eyes hold each other for a second, then without words she tells him what he already knows, that the time has come for them to go.

1947

A COUPLE ARE ROWING in the adjoining apartment, the thinness of the walls and the passionate anger of their voices playing out their marital failures to an audience who have no option but to listen. She shrugs her shoulders and lights the kerosene stove in the corridor. Reconstruction after the war promises them gas but she has little faith in promises any more. She measures out the leaves in the careful, miserly way that is ingrained in her and heats a pan of water. Then sitting on a little stool she rests her back against the shiver of wall that separates her from the warring pair. She warms her fingers on the flame and silently tells the couple on the other side of the wall that they should be grateful they have each other to fight with.

Despite knowing it no longer has any useful purpose and is a waste of precious energy she continues to ponder who betrayed them, even though she understands that its only result is to visit the guilt of one on all those in the apartment who heard him read the poem – some of them counted as dearest friends. All now tainted with suspicion. Perhaps if she had the guilty to hate it would be a comfort. She tries to remember those assembled, to compose the exact scene with the frozen clarity of a photograph, tries to match a face with an expression that might reveal the Judas as they listened to Osip declaiming those words that history will say have changed their lives. Sometimes she too likes to believe the poem did change their lives because it makes everything simpler, but if she's honest with herself she knows his fate was already sealed – it was there in the whisperings that grew too loud to be safely ignored, the veiled condemnation of previous works, the way he found himself pushed to the very margins.

There were always spies, of course, just as there still are. In every apartment block, in every single tributary of human engagement, a secret empire of listeners relay to their masters whatever it is they want to hear. But the night he delivered the poem about Stalin they both believed only the true and the faithful were his listeners. Would it have made any difference if he had known otherwise? Part of her suspects that this was the path he had chosen for himself and that it seemed to him that he had no other road to take. He never spoke to her about it, before or after. But when he uttered those words about 'the murderer and peasant-slayer' she sensed that he had freed himself in some way, so that the feeling he was left with was not fear of the consequences but in that moment a powerful release. In the poem's uncharacteristic and unsubtle directness everything that he had seen in the previous years and everything he felt about the inviolability of poetry's commitment to truth seemed to be released.

Part of her is proud of it but some part of her angry that he allowed their future to be determined by his own needs. As she sits alone in the tiny space that serves as a communal kitchen and heats tea on the stove she remembers the visit he had made to the Crimea, the journey through the Ukraine and the Kuban. She pushes her back against the wall as if its thin solidity might prevent her own images returning. But it's as if the voices next door pierce the seal of memory to reveal once more the spectres of starving peasants, moving like ghosts through a familiar landscape suddenly ripped from them and rendered remote and hostile. The swollen stomachs, the spindle-limbed children with hollowed sockets for eyes, almost too exhausted to hold out their begging hands. Heaped piles of corpses like broken, tangled bird nests fallen at the sides of roads waiting to be shovelled into the back of a cart. The black halos of buzzing flies. People clutching on to existence by eating grass and roots, the bark of trees.

'If you'd seen the half of what I've seen,' the man's voice next door asserts, 'you wouldn't go on like this.'

He's come back from the war but theirs has been no happy reunion. They have made her an unwilling participant in their lives. She tries to shut her ears to their clamour. But it wasn't just about what Osip had seen those years ago – it was what he saw in the future and how he felt it was poetry's responsibility always to tell the truth. He used to joke that this was a country that had the highest respect for poetry because there was no other place where more people were killed for it.

She makes the tea and wishes she had a little sugar or even a lemon. The shouting momentarily dies down. Part of her is glad and another part hopes that it won't result later in equally noisy lovemaking. The night in Moscow when they first came for him it was about one in the morning. She knew right away – they all knew. That moment and the moments after it constantly play out in her mind, the memory unwilling to be dimmed. There was the suddenness and the insistent loudness of the knock – just the way it had always sounded in her imagination – and yet when she opened the door for a second the absence of uniforms almost lulled her into a moment of hope. But it lasted no longer than the time it took for them to brush past her into the apartment, to demand their papers and then search them for weapons. Did they count a poem a weapon?

The couple in the next room are talking loudly now. Sometimes just before sleep, or in the early-morning drift into consciousness, when she hears a voice she imagines Osip has returned to her. He comes in and acts as if he's been out for a walk or running an errand and he chats to her about the weather as he takes off his coat and hangs it behind the door. But then when she goes to speak he vanishes. She calls silently out to him but her words return to her unanswered.

There were five of them – three police and two witnesses. They seemed to fill all the available space in the apartment and she sees for the first time the uniforms under the overcoats. Osip is given the warrant to read and he seems calm and then they start the search. They are looking for a copy of the poem even though it does not exist in written form, or at least recent work that can prove him guilty under Article 58 of the Criminal Code by which all political prisoners are charged. She almost admires their practised professionalism as they work as a team, searching out every potential hiding place while their leader concentrates on the contents of the chest where they store the manuscripts, carefully setting the papers that he will take away with him on a chair while throwing others on the floor so she has to sit and watch them trampled and foot-printed. It goes on for hours almost to daybreak. The youngest of the searchers lightly rebukes her for smoking so much. Does he think this reveals his compassionate concern for her wellbeing? And of course there is the inevitable joking response when they see her preparing things for him to take with him. 'Why so much? He'll be back. A few questions, that's all.' They must learn it in their training so that it's like a script they perform again and again because the words flow easily and naturally from their mouths. Akhmatova who had been visiting had insisted that Osip eat something and she gave him a hard-boiled egg which he salted and ate sitting at the kitchen table. Eventually when they have finished their search and they have taken him away it is not the scattered papers she remembers or the sound of the door closing so finally behind them, but the little pile of egg shell and its white speckle of salt.

Afterwards with Akhmatova she sits waiting for the new day to begin so that they can do all the things that are needed.

Some of the manuscripts are removed in shopping baskets, a few taken by trusted relatives who have come to help, and then there is the scurrying around the city, speaking to Bukharin and anyone she thinks whose influence could be brought to bear, and she is grateful when Pasternak comes and asks what might be done. But there is only the distant rattle of typewriters and a heavy-layered silence in the corridors in which she sits waiting for hour on hour and an unalterable sense seeping out from behind the shut doors that they have been cast off. How could she have thought that she would find anything different? The crime was committed against the Leader himself and soon it became obvious that no one would dare lend their voice to her and the one who made a phone call to try to ascertain the situation soon put the phone down with an ashen face, the warning printed on it.

Akhmatova tells her not to touch the discarded manuscripts that still litter the apartment floor and as she predicts they come back but this time there's only one of them – the senior man – and it's soon apparent that he's been sent for another rummage through their papers. They mustn't be satisfied with the evidence gathered in the first search. She can't decide if this is good or bad but what does it matter because she can remember the proud boast of a former official of the Cheka they had encountered in Yalta in 1928 – 'Give us a man, and we'll make a case.' If they so choose they can find a man guilty of whatever crime they wish so why waste this time in a search for their evidence? Perhaps because Osip and what still exists of his reputation represent a challenge and so requires more attention to detail than might normally be expected of them. But the second search reveals nothing more useful than the first. And so there is no more for her to do but wait.

She misses the taste of sugar in her tea but it's good and strong and warms her even now as the voices behind the wall suddenly flare up again. He's calling her lazy and a slut, accusing her of unfaithfulness in the years when he was fighting for Mother Russia. Her denials are angry, pressing themselves deep in the silence that suddenly smoulders in the hallways and the other rooms. Perhaps the whole block is listening and she imagines that for some at least this will count as entertainment in the dull listlessness of their days. She has seen them both several times on the stairs but they have barely acknowledged each other. It's always easier like this and no one ever wants to be drawn into the complications of someone else's life. So despite all the intimacies they have unwillingly shared on a daily basis they acted like strangers. Separated by the war years she thinks they should be grateful for their reunion, the restoration of the love they must surely have known.

What did her own separation feel like? She knows the shock of it made it sharper and more persistent than the dull pain she carries permanently with her now. And it was made worse too in all her imaginings of what might be happening to him and the constant nightmare that he might simply have vanished from her for ever. Never to see him again, for their earthly relationship to be terminated by a knock on a door – it didn't seem possible. So it felt in those first few days that she was sleepwalking, shut out from the normal realities and preoccupations of life. It was Akhmatova who made her eat and she is grateful every day for the strength that loyal friendship has given her.

After the initial flurry of their activity had faded into a despairing silence the phone call came. Osip's interrogator was summoning her to the Lubyanka and almost immediately she was issued with a pass. The name of the prison alone still makes her shiver. How many unshared nightmares about this place have rendered the city's citizens' sleep broken and fearful? At first rumours of what went on inside its high walls had been common currency but even these had died away, as if even mentioning the name might expose the speaker to its terror. The prison had assumed a reality and power beyond its physical existence so that it festered in the mind as an idea, divorced from location or boundaries. It lurked in the consciousness like some permanent inescapable anxiety that shadowed the very pavements they walked each day. She wanted to see her husband, to know what was happening to him, but she was frightened too about what might become of her in this place. She told herself that if they wanted her arrested they would have come already but she knew people who had entered through the prison gates and were never seen again. The voice on the phone had brooked no discussion, answered no questions, and left her only with a shocked silence.

When she stands in front of the building she is forced into a new awareness of the weakness of the flesh in the face of the state's walls of stone, in the unchallenged power of those who now rule over them. Her mouth is dry and she has to draw on all her reserves of strength and pride not to buckle and slink away. She shows her pass, undergoes a perfunctory search by a guard who seems disinterested as if counting the hours until his shift ends. A clerk administers a few details and gives her instructions. It is not what she expected. Her childish imaginings of dungeons and chains bear no connection to the offices, corridors, the large staircase she has been told to climb. It feels like another bureaucracy and if what is being processed is not paper but human beings then there are no outward signs of the work being undertaken. As she starts to mount the stairs she wonders if all those years they have been deceived, encouraged to create their own terror like children cautioned into good behaviour by tales of ogres. There are no screams rending the air but only the sharp clack of heels on wooden floors and doors being opened and in the seconds before they close again the clatter of typewriters escapes. A man in civilian clothes clutching a folder of paper approaches her and she thinks of showing her pass and asking if she is headed in the right direction but he looks right through her. She turns the corner in search of the office to which she has been directed when she sees them coming. A tall man holding his trousers to stop them falling and on either side two men she assumes are his interrogators. His head is shaven but blue-pitted, a swollen moon, and his skin wears the pallor of the confined. His cheekbones are dark-smudged and look as if they're trying to press themselves free from the bruised stretch of his skin. She sees them before they see her and immediately they bundle the man through the nearest door.

But it is enough. Enough to stay with her the rest of her life as one of the many things she wants to forget but cannot. Now as she leans against the wall and cups her tea the moment returns to her again and not even the heat she nurses between both hands can warm it away. It is the look in the man's eyes she can never forget. She has never seen fear this close before. Never fully understood what it looks like in the human face. It's in the eyes – their frantic, skittering movement, the way the pupils slowly dilate into the darkness of infinite space, the way he stares at her in silent appeal so desperate that he wants to believe even someone as helpless as her might be able to save him.

She has seen terrible things before. During the Civil War in Kiev she has seen bodies of those hostages shot by the Bolsheviks just before they gave up the city to the Whites, their own Red Army dead and wounded heaped on carts as they left with shouts that they would be back and the terrible fate of some women denounced as Cheka at the hands of the mob after their departure. All this shocked and sickened her but in this corridor with its numbered rooms and its walls painted a shade of green she has never seen in nature, the wild terror of the man's eyes touches her to the quick. If this is what they can do to you then what hope remains? She knows they take away the means of self-harm – the belt of your trousers and the laces of your shoes – and all the windows are bolted or barred. The moment and the means of your departure from this world are jealously guarded.

They will not let you usurp their power. She has to pause for a second and although she doesn't want to touch the wall with its slime-coloured paint she needs to find support and so she reaches out her hand and steadies herself trying to breathe deeply. Somewhere far off there is the sound of a door slamming and muffled voices. She has reached the appointed room. Part of her wants to turn quietly and return the way she came. But she likes to tell herself even now that it was never courage she lacked and so she knocks on the door with an attempted show of resolution and waits.

He sits behind a desk bare except for a neat sheaf of papers squared precisely in its middle and does not look up when she enters. She soon realises that it's just the first of his practised mannerisms and when she does so it drains away a little of her fear. He is probably in his early thirties, his face plumped with the benefits of his rank but bagged and blue-blotched below his eyes, the product no doubt of his frequent night work. His thick and oiled hair suggests he has spent significant time in its grooming. There is a faint scar on his left temple that looks as if it's been there since some childhood accident. It helps her a little to imagine him as a child once. Finally he acknowledges her and points to a seat but still doesn't speak, continuing to read through his papers as if he can't be interrupted. The room has two chairs besides his own and little else. There are two internal doors and she wonders why a room that size requires them both. But already she understands that in this building there are worlds within each other and she tries not to think of the one that is hidden to her. The walls are painted the same colour as the corridor and the small window behind his head affords only a square of colourless sky but she guesses that it is what those who are brought here from the cells must turn their eyes towards.

The interrogator is so obviously conscious of his performance that it leads him into artificialities of speech and theatrical gestures. And when he addresses her his words are delivered in what is meant to be a weighty and authoritarian tone, talking to her as if she is no more than a foolish wayward child, or a piece of dust that must be shaken from his clothing. It pleases her that she is able to despise him and part of her suspects that the anger he purports to display towards her husband's 'hideous crime' has to be stoked from a weary fire. Some years later she learns, but without pleasure, that their interrogator, this man who sat in judgement on them, was shot in 1938. The sow always eats her farrow. Over and over.

But now it is Osip he threatens with shooting. Osip and all his accomplices. Her husband has stumbled into the room with his guards, the front of his trousers bunched in his fist. She looks at him and sees immediately that he has travelled far from himself. And just as she is shocked by his appearance, he is shocked to see her – he is staring at the coat she's wearing – and then she realises that they have told him she too was arrested and held in the prison. He sits beside her but they do not dare touch and she notices for the first time that his wrists are bandaged before all their attention is demanded by their questioner whose job it soon transpires has been rendered largely meaningless because Osip has openly confessed to writing the poem about Stalin – there is a text of it in the interrogator's hand and he holds it away from him while reading it as if he's in danger of being contaminated by its obscene content.

There is a barrage of questions about the motivation behind the poem, and whether Osip chooses to answer vaguely or honestly his responses evoke a tirade of scorn and invective couched in familiar language. So he calls the poem 'a document' and rages about its counter-revolutionary criminality that is 'without precedent'. It's as if he wants to beat them into the dust with the righteousness of his words and he pauses only to take the opportunity to sneer at 'spineless intellectuals'. She catches Osip's eye and they know that in this time to be called an intellectual is to be despised and understand that there is something in this volley of accusation and reproach that seeks to sweep away all their pathetic ideas and books, even poetry itself, and smash them into splinters with the greater triumph of historical inevitability. He is in full flow now and has reached a part of his script where he turns to her and fires a series of rhetorical questions.

'What should a true Soviet citizen have done in the face of such outrageous and unprecedented criminality?'

'How could any Soviet citizen sit quietly and without protest in the presence of such vile slanders?'

She knows that he requires and expects no answers so she stares over his shoulder at the little sliver of light and wonders if it will be her last view of the outside world. They say the executions take place at night. She wonders if they blindfold those about to die somewhere in the hidden bowels of this place. A tiny bird moves across the sky. What must it be like to be free? What must it be like to live in freedom without the everlasting press of fear?

It's fear he's talking about now, teasing Osip by telling him that it can be a good stimulus for poetry. She glances again at the blood-stained bandages on her husband's wrists and when the interrogator momentarily runs out of threats and condemnations she asks about them and is told her husband has committed another criminal offence by smuggling forbidden items into his cell. With a razor blade hidden in his shoes he has tried to cut his wrists. This is a crime that clearly angers him almost as much as the poem itself. He must have hidden the blade there sometime before his arrest but never told her. If he had listened to her they could have done this thing together, spent their final precious moments as close as they have been in life. How they would have chosen to do it is unclear to her but it had to be better than this botched attempt in some darkened cell and far from the comfort of love. Then as the interrogator stands and momentarily turns his back on them she remembers what she saw in the eyes of the prisoner in the corridor and tells herself that she has no right to judge.

In the absence of their captor's gaze they glance at each other and the smile that passes between them contains more than words might say and she silently tells him to be strong, that she's all right. He tells her with his eyes that he loves her and she is glad that nothing that has happened has been able to weaken the certainty of that.

When their interrogator turns she realises that this is the moment when they will learn their fate and she senses by looking at his awkward, slouching stance and momentary hesitation that the script is about to deviate in some way from what he is used to. She cannot believe that the uncertain pause arises from any instinctive reluctance to announce their fate or any secret longing for mercy. Then he stands more formally and straightens his shoulders, dredges up again his authoritarian formality of voice. She is not to be charged and then he speaks almost affectionately about a labour camp on the White Sea Canal and with a lingering trace of regret tells them however that it is not to be Osip's destination. He hesitates again before seeking to impress on them that as a result of some magnanimous generosity of mercy 'from the highest level' the appropriate sentence has been commuted to exile in Cherdyn. For the first time she hears the words 'isolate but preserve' – it is the directive that will allow them the possibility of life. She will be allowed to accompany him if she wishes and then there is a sense of embarrassment evident in his face, almost as if he has been thwarted in his obligation to pursue revolutionary justice, and she is ushered quickly from the room. As she leaves she brushes her husband's shoulder lightly with her hand. It is the first time they have touched in weeks. She sees the final sneer of the interrogator's contempt and then she is in the corridor again and hurrying down the staircase.

What she remembers now as she drains the cup and presses her head back against the wall is how big the sky seemed when she stepped outside those doors, unfurling above her, stretching into some future that for the moment at least seemed released from darker certainties. There was no time yet to consider consequences or where their banishment might lead them because nothing seemed more important than that they would be allowed to be together and when that was true what did it matter if they lived in Moscow or somewhere else? As she hurried back to the apartment to start making the necessary preparations she tried to tell herself that it was no bad thing. They would disappear into some provincial backwater, far away from the whispering and the listeners, lead a quiet existence and slowly fade from the memory of the state. In her first flush of optimism she painted a picture of a small town in some idyllic pastoral setting where they would not be prisoners of their disease, where their minds would be free to exist without the suffocating weight of fear crushing the life out of them.

So as the voices next door start up again as if the lull was merely derived from exhaustion, rather than reconciliation, she momentarily thinks of knocking the wall and shouting that they should be grateful for what they have, however imperfect, that the fragile ties of love are easily sundered in the days in which they live. She remembers again that brush of her hand on his shoulder in a room in the Lubyanka. Had that room ever been witness to such a touch in all its history? She wonders if somehow the fleeting moment is stored still in its memory, a tiny exorcism of fear. It is his touch she misses most now and as an attempt to compensate she hugs herself briefly but it brings nothing except the self-pity she has always sought to avoid. Now there is a child crying next door in a high-pitched accompaniment to her parents' shouts. All the warmth has gone out of the cup. On the other side of the wall everything falls suddenly silent.

1952

So what is the true nature of love and how could it ever hope to endure in the world in which they found themselves? There was no great ceremony in their marriage, all of that dismissed as a bourgeois decadence from the past. Later a certificate on cheap paper. Cheap as the two blue rings they bought for a kopeck each near the Mikhailov monastery even though it was still a secret and so he carried his in a pocket while she wore hers hidden on a neck chain. He was older than her and they had no extended courtship with all the flowers and rituals that go with wooing. It simply happened and felt right that it had happened, so she gave herself to it despite the warnings of her friends who seemed to think that it would never work.

He lost his ring. She broke hers within a year. When she's tempted into sentimentality she thinks she would have liked him to have had it with him at the end but tells herself that what they carried of each other was more real and more lasting than any ring. Yet early on it sometimes felt as if her friends would be proved right and she couldn't be sure that what they had embarked on would endure. She was feisty, independent and found it difficult to submit in the ways he expected. He for all his liberalism and free-spirit thinking was surprisingly traditional in what he conceived as the role of a wife. So he wanted her to be at home and at hand when she felt herself young and wanting to experience all the social possibilities that existed, the cafés and the gossip, the music and the dancing. Often they fought like cat and dog and more than once she thought they wouldn't see the next year out.

She stands at the window at the end of the corridor where it meets the stairs. Outside the summer has almost slipped away once more and the clusters of trees that encircle the dormitories have nearly shed their leaves. A few hang on, too stubborn or too weary to give themselves to the fall. She shivers against the realisation that winter is coming and tries again to warm herself with memories of love. There is the sound of someone crying below. It's one of the students in the teacher training college where she has found a temporary post teaching English. She hesitates on the landing uncertain about what she should do. It is always dangerous to get involved in the personal affairs of others when it can never be gauged where such involvement will lead. And the college itself is a hotbed of intrigue where the staff spend their spare time writing anonymous letters denouncing each other and sitting in committees adjudicating on various issues of discipline – everything from student dress and sexual morality to ideological purity. And of course in the classes themselves there are informers, ever vigilant for deviance from the official line even if it involves how to teach grammar. So it is imperative that she continues to keep a low profile, doesn't stir the waters. The young woman's face is hidden from her, veiled by the thick fall of her dark hair, and the preoccupation with her sorrows leaves her unaware of another's presence. She is about to turn away, quietly climb the stairs, when she hears the girl sob deeply, her attempts to stifle the sound spilling into stuttering gasps.

She tells herself that it is a sentimental foolishness, but instead of returning to her room she slowly descends. The girl sitting on the step shuffles closer to the wall as if to let her pass and turns her face away. Able to see now that she isn't a student in one of her classes for a second she thinks that this might perhaps absolve her of whatever responsibility she instinctively feels. The reason she stops and sits on the step beside her is not just the memory of those who chose to help them despite the dangers, it's because she knows that to walk on will admit victory to those who have made people suspicious of each other, who despite all their talk about the collective have driven them into separate, silent entities. So each time she finds a connection with another, however fleeting or superficial, it feels like a small, silent act of resistance.

She says nothing to the young woman at first but simply sits on the step beside her. Perhaps that will be enough and already in her presence the sobbing has faded into almost silence. The student wipes her eyes with the heel of her hand but won't look at her.

'What is your name?' she asks.

'Frida,' she answers in what is barely more than a whisper.

'So what is it that makes you so upset, Frida?'

But the girl only shakes her head leaving her to consider the possibilities. An affair of the heart? Disappointing marks in her examinations? Some petty fall-out amongst friends? These are the usual student dramas. She looks for clues in the student's appearance and demeanour but nothing yields itself. And if truth be told she doesn't think she can muster much sympathy for a heart broken by juvenile love. She pats the girl silently on her shoulder and stands up.

'Can I trust you?' the girl asks, suddenly looking up at her.

'No you can't,' she says immediately. 'Because you must never trust anyone you don't know. And if there are important things that you need to say you must find someone you trust with your life.'

'There is no one.'

'Then you must keep everything to yourself until you find that person.'

'I think I can trust you,' she says.

'But you don't know anything about me other than I am a teacher.'

A door slams shut somewhere and they both fall into a momentary silence. She is already regretting having spoken to the girl; it was an indulgence that she can't afford. Since finding work in the college she has kept her head down, adopted a persona that offers no glimpse of the person she is. So she has offered no opinions, bitten her tongue in the presence of idiots and time-servers, bowed her head to the inane ramblings of the Director. She needs to survive, to feed and clothe herself so she can endure in the hope that she will preserve the poems beyond the existing world. This young girl's problems might be nothing that a bit of common sense won't fix but there is the possibility that if she becomes privy to them then they will draw her into a spotlight she has sought so hard to avoid.

'I know your husband was arrested.'

The words are frozen motionless, so suddenly real that she can almost touch their coldness, but she lets her face register nothing and does not answer.

'It's what they say,' the girl adds, as if trying to justify what she has said.

'You shouldn't listen to gossip,' she tells her but when she turns to leave, she feels a hand clutch her arm.

'Please. I meant no harm. I understand.'

She wants to slap her, to tell her that she can't understand, but instead she pauses because now she needs to know what if anything is the consequence of this knowledge. The young woman takes her pause as an indication that she is willing to listen but instead of speaking points to the little store that is in the corner of the stairwell. She opens the door with a clearly practised stealth and beckons her in. She hesitates. Nothing feels right any more but she enters. There are bundles of shovels for clearing the winter snow, their blades rusted but white-speckled; brooms and buckets and an untidy pile of heaped logs lolling at an angle. Open pipework lattices the walls and some of them are lagged with old sacking. The girl closes the door behind them, holding it open just long enough to put her eye to the narrowed seam of outer light. A small high window allows a shadowy smear of daylight to define the cluttered basement space. It suddenly feels like a game that she doesn't want to be playing, a game where the forfeit for losing is not yet fully known.

'We come here sometimes,' she says as she sits on a broken remnant of a classroom desk, its wood stained with blots of black ink and carved with initials.

She doesn't want to know this, she doesn't want to know who it is that comes or what they do. Doesn't like the way this student feels able to include her in her secrets. All her focus is now on how she will extricate herself from this situation. And there is a sudden fear that somehow her own fate is in danger of being bound to the emotionally fragile state of this young woman whose cheekbones still glitter with the traces of her tears.

'Tell me now,' she says to the young woman and she inflects her voice deliberately with a teacher's impatience.

She sees the girl's hesitation, her stalling for time in the way she pushes her hand through the untidiness of her hair. So she nods at her, signalling her to start. Leaves fritter and whisper against the thick glass of the window then blow elsewhere. Already she knows that what she is about to be told is of consequence but she can find little in her that cares about the girl, thinking only now of how it will affect herself and what danger it might bring. The girl hesitates again and then the words tumble out and she cries again when she has finished.

So she has a boyfriend whom she loves dearly and who treats her better than anyone has ever done. He is the son of someone important in the local Party. She has met both his parents and they have also treated her well. Her own parents have perished bravely in the war. Except they haven't. Instead, at the start of collectivisation, her father was exiled as a kulak to Arkhangelsk and her mother had fled with her to distant relations who had conspired to keep their origins hidden. As a teenager Frida has simply invented a new identity for herself and thrown herself into it with all the vigour she could muster, joining the Pioneers and then gaining admission to the Komsomol. But now she has received an anonymous letter that threatens her with exposure if she doesn't break off her relationship. She thinks it's from someone jealous of her newfound love, even someone who sees him as quite a catch and wants him for herself. She doesn't know how this person has found out about her background – she has never told anyone, not a single soul.

The type of story she's just listened to is not unknown to her in its essential form. All over the country people reinvent themselves constantly. Some earnestly try to erase all the details of their previous life, seek especially to banish any present trace of affiliations to those who have proved themselves enemies of the people. Some will blissfully contradict what they publicly earlier declared was their passionate belief; disown even their wives or husbands. The individual concept of self is now built on shifting sands, destined to move in parallel with wherever prevailing winds might blow. So what now must she say to this young woman who faces the loss of her love? She looks up at the small window and remembers the one above the interrogator's head, the glimpse it briefly afforded of far-off sky.

But already she knows she has no answer to give. There are spent matches on the floor. The room has been used as a smoking den.

'I'm sorry,' she says, then turns to go.

'What must I do?' the young woman demands as she stands and holds out a hand towards her in a gesture of entreaty.

'Do you love him? Truly love him?'

'With all my heart.'

'Then there's nothing can be done except to hope that he loves you equally,' she says and she shakes her head to try and stop the futility of further questions. 'I hope he does. And if he doesn't then you're better off without him.'

And then she opens the door and climbs the stairs and walks quickly along the corridor to the small room that has been provided for her in return for the duties she carries out in supervising the dormitories. She has no more thoughts for the young woman except that if it comes to her drowning she hopes she does so without pulling anyone else under with her. Her position has been too hard won and she is not yet ready to search out another bolthole.

She kicks off her shoes and curls herself under the blanket that she persists with for the little warmth it provides despite its coarseness that scratches the skin. She makes herself small in the bed trying to generate as much heat as she can muster before slowly stretching her limbs into the colder spaces. She tries to remember what it is like to sleep with someone close whose warmth and words could shut out the outer world. Her hand moves to her face and she remembers how when she'd return after they'd been apart, even for a few short hours, he'd touch it, tracing its contours as if he was restoring her to his memory.

Did he carry her face bright and sharp to the very end? Did it linger, a print on the tips of his fingers? Or did all the things he had to see blur her image into a shadowed vagueness? She tries to remember his touch in hers as she lets her fingers linger on her skin. Never the most beautiful face in the world. Not like Olga's, not even for a second. She sees her now in all her youthful beauty, the dark wave of her hair – dark like the young woman on the stairs – and the shiny jet of her eyes. It was when she nearly lost him, the closest they ever came to separation, and there are times when she wonders about the course her life would have taken if she had. He treated her badly during that period and there is part of her that still smarts at the humiliations she had to endure. Only her packed suitcase sitting on the kitchen table brought him to his senses, shocked him into a realisation of what she was prepared to do.

Perhaps it is anger that makes her feel a gradual warmth creep into the bed as she remembers the simpering Olga swanning around the apartment without a trace of embarrassment or shame, staking her claim in the most vulgar manner and without a single word of rebuke from him. She should have packed the case sooner, forced him to make his choice instead of standing by while they blatantly conducted an affair. But he was besotted and although he never said it, there was somehow an unspoken sense that he was entitled to this relationship. Did he think the title of poet gave him permission to sleep with another woman in such a brazen way? He wouldn't even deign to talk about it, with Olga continuing to appear at the apartment at all hours of the day and night as if she had established formal rights to residency.

As she remembers her own misery during this time she thinks of the young student on the stairwell and regrets that her words have sounded harsh. She thinks of going back but rejects the idea. Perhaps there comes a time when all love requires a sacrifice which no one else can help with. Whether or not to accompany Osip into exile was not a question she even had to consider – she would have gone to the ends of the earth for him because she knew the possibility of no other life except in their love. She thinks again of his expression of utter shock when he came back unexpectedly and saw her packed case. How strange is fate – if he hadn't returned so soon after going out because he had forgotten something, she would have gone. She imagines him calling her name in the empty apartment and it returning to him unanswered. Would he have tried to find her or simply fallen forever into the willing arms of Olga? She will never know but what she does have is the memory of his words pleading with her to stay, the welter of words that expresses his need of her, the promise to throw Olga over for good. She would have liked it more if there had been some recognition of the hurt he had caused her and there is a part of her that wonders even now as she pushes the scratch of the blanket away from the bare skin of her arm whether what he needed most at that moment was the care she gave him, her understanding of the poetry and the work that needed to be done. He insisted she listen while he broke it off on the phone so that even in his rejection of his lover she was made subservient to his will.

If the doubt still lingers there is no trace of it when she thinks of what their life became, what bond between them was established and strengthened. But her pleasure at the memory of it also edges into bitterness at the knowledge it has been taken from her, that the path which stretches ahead is a solitary one. So now there is only the coarseness of a blanket in a tiny bed in a tiny room in a remote provincial town to protect her from the loneliness of the night that she thinks of as starless and over-arching. They knew the reality of love even before he was cast out and then arrested so it was much more than just a case of the danger in which they found themselves forcing them together. And they didn't cling together in fear even in the final years – he wasn't capable of existing like that, never living his life like some withered leaf waiting for winter's final blast. Despite it all he went on finding limitless pleasure in the simplest of things – sunlight on water, frost on a snowed tree, the early-morning song of a bird. And his deep enjoyment of people who lived uncomplicated lives and who could contribute a folk song or a verse of some old poem they had learned as a child never left him.

And slowly, steadily, she becomes close to the poetry itself until it almost feels as if it's being breathed through her. He composes in his head and generally there is a surge of restlessness as he frames into words the poem that somehow already exists. She watches him walk – sometimes outside in the winter street, sometimes around the space in which they live – sees the relentless flow of his concentrated energy, his lips moving, and readies herself. She must do nothing now that will be a distraction, so she holds herself still or lies motionless on the bed. And then he speaks the poem and she transcribes it, trying to keep up, trying not to have to query a word, or a spelling, trying not to mishear even when he's rushing or whispering. So the poems come on to the page through her hand and her eyes are the first to see them born. And she comes to believe that she is more than just a scribe but somehow part of the moment and it feels sometimes as if the poem is water entrusted into her hand to carry and she must not spill even a drop. Only when it is finished does he come and look, standing at her side and resting a hand lightly on her shoulder, and she feels and shares his sense of intense curiosity at what has been formed there in black ink.

Only the love poems, the ones written for Olga, are not written in her hand but they exist on paper with the other manuscripts. She wishes it were not so but their existence can't be denied or disowned so when the time comes and they are forced to organise the original copies of all the poems and think how best to preserve them, they splay out on the table between them. They stare silently at the pages and then he reaches out his hand and gathers them to him and tells her he will destroy them. She grabs him by the wrist and tells him these too must be preserved. She ignores the flush of embarrassment flooding his face and insistently prises the pages from his hand, smooths away some of their bruises. He gets up from the table while she carefully places them in sequence and stands with his back to her as if he won't allow himself to look at them any more, then lights a cigarette and the smoke is a blue gauze of unwanted memory garlanding his head.

So these too are preserved and stored in the memory. And to ensure they haven't slipped away they must be silently repeated – over and over – in the lonely moments before sleep or when walking in the streets where the cleared snow decays into blackness like rotting teeth. And yes sometimes they feel like a scourge and she is tempted to let them go, to see them gently slip away, but something stronger prevents her. There is only one poem she has destroyed and expunged from her memory, and she has done that out of love for him and not herself, a poem he wrote in a moment of fear because he hoped to save his life, even though it was already too late, and which would bring hurt to him if future generations were to read it. It worries her that perhaps there are other copies of it that some day will emerge and be used by those who seek to destroy his name. Everything else must be preserved, even these love poems that are hooked on the bitterest barb of memory.

It is the memory of the pain that love can bring that makes her push the blanket away from her and get out of the bed. She looks at her face in the small mirror with the cracked lacquer frame. She isn't ageing into beauty in the way that is the late blessing of some women. She never had the looks of Akhmatova or even Olga so perhaps she should be glad that at least there won't be time's cruel fading, the journey that renders the mirror's unwelcome truth sharper with each passing day. If he were to touch her face now would it feel different to the one he knew? He will never come back to her – she will never know where his body is buried or be able to visit it. So life decrees that he walks through a door, there is the sound of a lorry's engine and then she is never to see him again. Perhaps, she tells herself, some good thought can be found in that there was no breach in love, that they were separated at the time when it was at its most intense.

She thinks again of the young woman on the stairs and wonders what will happen to her. She leaves her room and walks along the empty corridor. At the end window she stops and watches what must be a rising wind shiver and fret the trees. It will surely pluck the few remaining leaves. The sun is dropping low in the sky. The days are shortening. She feels the inescapable weariness of facing another winter. On the stairs the only sound is that of her own feet. The door of the store is slightly open. She hesitates then opens it and steps inside. There is no sign of the young woman. Sudden debris blowing against the slit of window startles her. It sounds as if a storm is coming. She stands by the same broken desk where earlier the young woman had sat and touches the wood with her fingers. What will happen to her? She would like to be wrong but she doesn't think it likely that a young man whose family is important in the Party will be strong or brave enough to throw over everything for love. Perhaps the young woman will not make him choose but think that the forces ranged against her are too powerful and so will try to preserve her own secret by being the one who makes the break. She doesn't want to ponder the possibilities because she knows that most of them hold only the likelihood of regret.

Why does regret linger so long? When they were taking Osip that final time she had already played out the scene in her head and rehearsed what she would say and yet in that very moment no words could be uttered. So she had spoken them every day until the news of his death in the desperate need to believe that somehow they would reach him however far away he was being held. She looks at the spades piled in the corner. Soon they will be needed again to clear the snow.

There is a hollow thumping and moan of complaint from the fretwork of pipes. Did he need those words to take with him in the back of the lorry or were they already written on his heart because there were many times in those last years of exile when he seemed to know what she was thinking without her speaking? She wants to speak to him now and so she starts to tell him what she had prepared for the final moment but the words falter and then fade into nothing. She looks in desperation at the narrow window and tries again but in their place comes only the consciousness that winter is coming when the white-barked birch trees shorn of their leaves will slowly make shivering ghosts of themselves.

1934

THERE ARE ONLY TWO beds and one chair in the room that serves as their hospital ward in Cherdyn. Even in hospital they are isolated in case their supposed infection is passed to others. Osip lies on the bed beside her and stares at the large clock that hangs on the opposite wall. Its face is moon white with thick black hands and numerals. He's stared at it for a long time but speaks little.

Staff check on them at regular intervals. She carries their curses in her memory at her failure to look after him. After so many nights without sleep she had drifted off and when she awoke he had already clambered out of the second-floor window, and even though she had desperately tried to hold on to him by his arms, he had slipped out of the sleeves of his jacket and fallen to the ground outside. It's his second attempt to kill himself and no more successful than the first, resulting only in the pain of a dislocated shoulder which amidst the curses and shouts a woman doctor had set back in place. The staff are frightened and angry that their negligence in allowing this thing to happen might incur the wrath of those whose orders were that he should be preserved. They blame her and as she is not to be trusted they are inspected regularly.

Sometimes the open door briefly reveals the presence of peasants come for treatment, their beards and dress making them look like remnants from a different century.

Long journeys on trains, a river steamer and in the back of a truck have brought them here to this their first place of banishment with the three guards constantly at their side, keeping them separated from other travellers. Always vigilant but not unkind when out of the public gaze. It's on the train journey that she first realises things aren't right with Osip as he sits looking at the thickly wooded mountains of the Urals. He seems to stare somewhere far beyond the landscape and his talk is all of imminent death. Again and again he asks her if she can hear it, hear the voices, but for her there is only the rattle of the train, the snores of a passenger she can't see and the squeak of the soldiers' leather boots when they stretch their limbs or adjust their stance as they maintain the required separation from other passengers.

'Can't you hear them?' he asks again.

'What is it you hear?' she asks, trying to calm him by taking his hand.

'All the voices. Voices calling and whispering,' he says, pressing her hand against his ear as if to stop the sounds.

'There are no voices.'

He looks at her and she sees the disbelief fixed there. She believes they have done something to his mind in the prison and despite her thinking that they have given back her husband, the person who sits opposite her is changed in some ways she can't understand.

'What do the voices say?' she asks.

'I can't make them out. They're calling and shouting but their words aren't clear. Are you telling me the truth when you say you hear nothing?'

She nods and reaching across gently prises their hands from his ear and tries to calm him once again by talking about anything that comes into her head so she remembers things from their past, places they've been, their old circle of friends, tells him quietly about the women who came to the apartment with money when they heard that they'd been exiled. But none of her words seem to penetrate beyond his fear. She remembers how going through the forest in the back of the truck he had seen a peasant standing with an axe and he had said that they were going to behead him. Nor does it seem to be death he now fears but the ever-present reality of its imminent and sudden violence – the bullet to the back of the head, the firing squad. He sits hunched and tense as if expectant that he will be taken to such an end at any moment, even there on the train as it cuts a path through steep-banked swathes of trees whose branches seem to reach out like hands towards the glass.

Much later when he starts to recover and they have been allowed to reside in Voronezh he will try to tell her some of what happened in the Lubyanka – the sleepless nights under the lights; the night-time interrogations with their threats and insults and the constant repetition of questions he's already answered; the stool pigeon who shares his cell and whose purpose is to pile more stress on him with his talk of darkest consequences; being taken from the cell by the guards and being made to wait for hours for more sessions, or something worse, that never happens. Being put in a straitjacket after the first suicide attempt. There were voices there too, the voices of a crying woman he thought was her but again whose words he couldn't make out. They had led him to believe that they were holding her. He tries to tell her about what happened to him but for all his skill with language she can see his frustration as he struggles to convey what is so far beyond the reach of human words. However she comes to understand that whatever the details of his experience in those weeks, the truth is that his mind has been battered and bruised and he has been forced asunder from who he is. As she looks at his fear-flecked eyes that seem to see menace in every fleeting glimpse of the landscape she too is frightened and unsure whether the man she knows will ever come back to her.

Later on she will be told by those who have also experienced the terror that it is what happens to everyone who goes through the hands of their oppressors. But she also believes how much worse it must have been for a man whose every sense is sharpened and who sees the world and everything around him with the clear-eyed vision of the poet. So now every brick and every smell, every silence and every scream are branded in his consciousness and for the moment at least their memory threatens to unbalance him and leave him frightened by each shadow that falls across his path.

He lies on the bed and stares at the clock. Its ticking seems to grow ever louder in the silence. His arm in a sling prevents him turning on his side away from her and so he either rests on his back or lies facing her but it is as if he isn't able to find all his old comfort in her presence. Sometimes she's not sure he even knows who she is and then she tries to use her voice to reach him and to pull him back to her and to himself. But he has only eyes and ears for the ticking clock. Although she tries to block it out she remembers the eyes of the prisoner in the corridor and she wonders if there is a moment that comes to all when fear tips the mind out of its normal buoyant hope and sends it sinking into darker depths. She needs to sleep but is frightened to leave him even though he seems momentarily calmer and has displayed no further signs of wanting to harm himself. But the journey's sleepless nights and the burden of worry have left her exhausted so although at first she tries to resist, gradually she feels herself slipping into sleep and knows she is powerless to prevent it.

Now it is her own voices she can hear – during the Civil War the screams of the trapped women thought to be Cheka who had fallen into the hands of the mob; the sound of Osip's exultant voice pouring out his poem about Stalin; the late night, instantly recognisable knock on the apartment door. But there are silences too – the world outside the train's window; the endless sitting in empty corridors when she tries to find people who will help. Sometimes she dreams of childhood and then everything is briefly different and the life that stretches ahead seems nothing so much as an adventure where she will play the leading role. But then everything changes again and it's like some old story told in a different childhood where in the shadows lurks unseen evil that waits its chance to snatch the unsuspecting. And then she's straying too close to the woods, ignoring all the warnings her parents have given, and she's not paying any attention to anything other than the moment when it bursts from the darkness of the trees and is carrying her away. When she tries to scream no sounds come and she can see everyone in the village going about their business but she can't find a voice to summon their help.

As she drifts into consciousness she thinks of songbirds in cages, small and huddled, half-hidden by the bars. She too is conscious of the clock's ticking. Then her eyes are slowly opening and she feels no benefit of sleep but only an increased heaviness in her head that sinks through her whole body and leaves her limbs leaden. The back of her throat is sore and she tells herself to ignore it because it would be an unspeakable nightmare if she were to become ill. Then she blinks her eyes wide and sees that he's not there, for a second starts to believe they have come for him, the images that so plagued him transformed into a physical reality. She whimpers then tries to calm herself by repeating 'isolate but preserve' – that was their sentence, but who is to know whether they were meaningless words that can be transmuted at the changing whim of someone in the chain of power? Perhaps now after this second attempted suicide they think they need to exercise their authority over his life before he is able to challenge it again, this time finally and fully.

She hurries from the bed and her legs feel shaky. She has to find him. But when she stumbles into the corridor and calls his name there is no sign of him. At first the nurses ignore her, walking by her as if she doesn't exist, and for a moment she feels she is still in her dream and has no voice. Only the curious stare of a peasant woman sitting on a narrow wooden bench cradling a baby confirms her existence and she hurries on desperate to find him or where he's been taken, until a nurse grabs her roughly by the arm and wordlessly points her to a kind of open courtyard. She sees him almost at once sitting at the end of what looks like a stone water trough and he's staring up at the branches of a rowan tree. She stands beside him and at first she's relieved to have found him, then she's angry that he has caused her such worry, but he looks at her as if he's just seen her for the first time and he's point-ing at the clusters of red berries with which the tree is laden. She glances up and the sun slanting through the branches makes her shade her eyes. The berries are intensely red and he's pointing as if he's never seen anything like them before. She sits beside him on the edge of the empty trough that holds the sun's heat deep inside itself.

'When there's a good crop of berries they say the winter will be short and the snows less deep,' he tells her, 'and if the berries are few and lose their colour then the winter will bring illness and hardship.'

'There's plenty of berries,' she answers. 'The whole tree is covered in them.'

'But the birds are beginning to eat them.'

'We can't begrudge them.'

'No, no, they must survive but if they strip the tree then the winter will be hard, the sorrows deep.'

He is a man with no superstitions who now sees signs and portends in everything.

'Perhaps you could write something about the tree,' she suggests.

'No, no,' he says, shivering. 'Hasn't poetry brought us enough trouble?'

'They can't find fault with a poem about rowan berries,' she tells him, thinking about the member of the Writers' Union who suggested that if only he had kept on writing poems about flowers and bees then he would never have found himself in this position.

'But the berries are red,' he says as he looks at her and suddenly smiles, 'and they will surely say they stand for blood or something else that is counter-revolutionary.'

She smiles in return but it is false. Bringing the trouble on themselves was how many others liked to see it, so if only they had been good citizens and kept their heads down then supposedly everything would have been all right. That is what they tell themselves just as they publicly insist that no one is ever arrested without due cause no matter how incredible the charges might seem. So there are saboteurs and plotters hiding in every nook and cranny of the state whose only aim is to sow the seeds of its destruction. Look at how they confess their crimes, they say, when the guilty realise they have been found out. But she doesn't believe any of it and knows that right from the start he too was marked out, even before he had written what they didn't like. There's something in this new breed of creatures that is able to recognise both their own sort and those who can never be. So whether it was his independence of spirit, his deep affinity for the poor and suffering, or just his stubborn and seemingly wilful reluctance to conform to anything other than his own vision of himself, he was never destined to survive. She knows that if he hadn't written the poem they would have found some other reason to arrest him.

She looks at the brightness of the berries and thinks of those who with such avidity grasped the prizes that were on offer to the compliant and the state servers. So now they have their apartments, their country dachas and are given access to what is denied to the masses. But as the sun makes her squint again she remembers Nikita's songbirds silent in their cages. A bird flutters around the berries, its beak pecking rapidly, before flying off again to the hospital roof. They will never sing now that they have given up their souls. They have chosen their own cages. She puts her arm on Osip's shoulder and wonders whether he will ever write again. They would see it as their greatest achievement and yet even abstaining is not permissible because it is taken to signify the malcontent, the skulking subversive with counter-revolutionary tendencies. The bird wants to come back for the fruit but is mindful of their presence. There is a hospital attendant who watches them from a window above and another who indulges in regular journeys back and forward across the courtyard makes little effort to disguise his surveillance.

For the moment at least he appears calmer and when it starts to get a little colder she leads him back to the ward. He walks slowly, is less straight-backed than is his normal posture and looks as though the winter of old age is already settling deep in his bones. So how would Olga feel if she could see him now? Would she have followed him into exile? She knows the answers and takes pride in them. Of all the women she is the only one to stand at his side, a side that only death will make her leave.

The ward seems bigger and emptier than before – she guesses the building was once a grand house and in places there are still traces of decorative plasterwork and marble. From time to time she hears the whispering scurry of mice behind the wainscot. Perhaps once this very room was a place of music and dancing. She strains to hear some distant echo that surely lingers deep in the room's memory but it resists the reach of her imagination. As she tries to get him comfortable on his bed she sees how his eyes have started to rove randomly about the ward as if its strangeness is being seen for the first time but as always they return to the clock. He is still staring at it when some hours later a doctor comes to check on him. It is not the doctor who dealt with him after his attempted suicide but one who is younger and gives the impression of wanting to be faithful to her job as she examines his arm and adjusts the sling, even though her white coat is stained in places and there is a wide tear in the hem of a sleeve. Perhaps she preserves the tear as a counter to potential charges of bourgeois elitism. Perhaps she merely has no needle and thread. Then she stands at a little distance from the foot of his bed.

'If you try to harm yourself again they will strip you and put you in a cell. Do you want that?' she asks and she sounds as if she's speaking to a child.

He shakes his head in reply and stares at her empty-eyed. She turns away and asks, 'How long has he been in this state?'

'It started on the journey here. After he had been released from the Lubyanka. What is wrong with him?'

The doctor blinks and says nothing for a second before she answers, 'They all arrive like this. If you're lucky and you take close care of him it will pass.'

Then she is gone, her white coat melting silently through the dark seam of the opened door. The night is coming on but no one has brought them anything to eat and she is too frightened of leaving him to go in search of food. There is a kerosene lamp in the corner but no fuel or matches so what light there is comes from the barred windows that are spaced above their beds. He slips into a fitful sleep disturbed by sudden jerks and quivers. She wants to try and calm him with the press of her hand but doesn't touch him in case he thinks it is the touch of a guard or executioner. She lies on her bed and watches him, helpless to give anything that will still his mind's turmoil. A brooding intensity of loneliness settles on her and she can't shake it off. Together she felt she could bear most things but now it's as if he's journeyed to some distant place where she is unable to follow.

She needs to find food for them and tries to convince herself that if she can get him to eat something then it might help restore him. In the corridor she realises that there is nothing to be found in the hospital – everywhere is shut. And even if it wasn't so, no one is willing any more to make even the simplest decision until it has been approved by someone higher. She must go out of the hospital and try to find someone willing to sell her what she needs. A dread of him waking and finding her gone makes her hurry in the direction that seems to have the most people and activity. There is a bakery on a corner but its door is barred. She enters a narrow warren of streets but every step takes her further away from him. And then there is a voice in her head that she refuses to recognise as her own, telling her that she is not exiled, that she can make her way to the station and take a train to some place beyond the misery of this moment. She has the money the women gave her before they left Moscow. And then the voice tells her that he is drowning and in his desperation he will pull her under the water so why not cut herself loose and who would blame her if she saved herself? In a back street she stops at some type of inn and suddenly feels dizzy with the voice swirling its insistent thoughts.

Inside there is raucous laughing and arguing. What sounds like a violin is starting up in a high-pitched screech. She remembers the cheap blue rings they bought and how he lost his and how she broke hers and asks herself if this was an omen and whether love itself can be so easily severed and sent spinning into some hidden corners from where it can never be retrieved. Already, however, she knows the answer because it is only in their love that she finds herself complete and only in his life is hers lived fully. The voice that was in her head sounds now like the voice of the interrogator, asking the same type of questions, insidiously trying to make her abandon all the things she is sure of in exchange for admission to some supposedly better life. There can be no better place, she tells him, than with Osip, sharing the way he sees the world, feeling the freedom that exists in their private words and the words she commits to paper. Even now in this place of interrogation and fear she knows she has the strength to turn her eyes towards the sky above her questioner's head.

She pushes open the door of the inn and inhales the smell of smoke and male sweat and understands at once that this is a place where people come to forget their troubles not to offer help to a stranger. The fire in the corner and the kerosene lamps flick shadows over the huddled groups who sit on narrow benches around roughly-hewn tables and as she stands in the still open doorway she sees how the light reflects in someone's pince-nez, on a raised glass.

'Close the door, woman!' a voice shouts. 'Either come in or get out.'

She hesitates and another voice invites her to come and warm herself at his fire with the promise that he'll 'put some colour in her pale cheeks'. She asks herself what it is she wouldn't do if it helped them and she doesn't know the answer any more. A burly barrel of a man she assumes is the owner approaches her, looks her up and down in a demeaning way then asks her what she wants. Over his shoulder a thin-faced woman, possibly his wife, looks at her with suspicious eyes. Her hair is covered by a headscarf in peasant style but it has slipped back on her head and black locks push out from under it.

'I need food. I have money to pay for it.'

'Are you a working girl?' he asks with a sneer. 'You don't look the sort.'

'I'm Nadezhda Mandelstam,' she wants to say as she draws herself proudly straight but instead merely shakes her head and tells him again that she has money, then as she turns and looks at the curious faces staring at her regrets what she has just said.

'You'll find no food here, but if you want a drink we'll sell you that,' he says as if he's just lost all interest in her.

'This isn't the place for you,' the woman she takes to be his wife says to her. In her hand she's holding a jug of some indeterminate liquid. But her voice isn't harsh and so fired by her need she quietly says again, 'I have money.'

In reply the woman takes her by the arm as if ushering her impatiently outside but whispers, 'Go round to the back in five minutes,' and then with a theatrical flourish slams the door shut after her.

The alley is dark. She passes a man urinating and he makes a crude joke. And then it dawns on her that she has been a fool and in the shadowy narrowness of the alley what she is most likely to encounter is robbery and not help and she has delivered herself into their grasping hands. But just as she turns to go a door opens and in the narrow seam of yellow light stands only the thin-faced woman. She hesitates then walks towards it, her fingers tightening their grip on the money nestled deep in her pocket. The door opens wider and she is beckoned into a small room that has bottles and chairs stacked in it. On the table under a cloth sits what she assumes to be food of some sort. The cloth is removed in the style of a magician doing a trick and then she pays wildly over the odds for some stale bread, cheese and a few thin slices of dried meat. The woman inspects the money with greater scrutiny than her customer inspects her purchase and when she's satisfied pockets it somewhere inside her apron.

'You're not from around here,' she says and her face is unable to disguise its curiosity.

'We're passing through.'

'So where are you staying?'

'The hotel near the station,' she says but the initial hesitation makes the answer unconvincing even in her own ears and so she gathers up the miserable bundle that has cost too much and turns to go.

'If you wanted to work, I can arrange it,' the woman says. 'You're not going to turn many heads but there's something about you an educated man might like. We get all sorts.'

She stops herself from thanking her then hurries the length of the entry towards the brighter lights that mark her way home to the hospital. She has already been gone too long and prays that Osip has been sleeping soundly in her absence. When she returns an orderly insists on searching the bundle but seems content to establish that it contains nothing of danger or of potential use in a suicide attempt. But the search and the questions delay her yet more so it is a great relief when she enters the ward to see that he is still in the bed where she left him. The relief however is short-lived because he refuses all her attempts to feed him and continues to fall in and out of shallow and disturbed sleep. As the hours pass he grows more agitated, calling out until he wakens himself, jerking upright in the bed, and he's pointing at the clock and declaring that they are coming for him at nine o'clock. At nine o'clock they'll come and drag him away to some secret place and there they'll take his life without another moment's hesitation. She tries to calm him, cradling his head, but nothing she says or does makes any difference and each tiny movement of the clock's hands serves to tighten his paranoia.

He insists they'll come for him at that very hour. It's the appointed time and all the necessary documents have been signed. There can be no pardon, no commutation of the sentence. Then for a short while he calms and his eyes turn from the clock to look with curiosity at the patterned shadows cast on the opposite wall. They form a trembling frieze and it seems to lull him but when eventually they fade he falls into a renewed fervour. He begs her to go to the window to see if the rowan tree still has its berries. He shouts out random answers to unknown questions and sometimes he presses a protective hand to his face as if blows are raining on his head.

She thinks of calling for the doctor but knows it would be useless and that if they were to see him in this extreme state there would be a chance that they would lock him up in some asylum with those who are mad.

She has to believe that if she cares for him and watches over him then she can bring him through this fit, that her love can help him find his way back from wherever he has journeyed. So she recites his poems, trying to give her voice the echo of his own inflections, but even these words seem powerless to reach him.

'Has the tree lost its berries?' he asks again.

Once more she has to go to the window to see if the tree has shed its berries but even when she tells him that they're still there in heavy clusters he shakes his head in disbelief and tells her that the snows are coming, snows deeper than anyone has ever seen. It is the most terrible thing she has ever experienced in their life together. When she touches his forehead it feels feverish and as he points to the clock again she tries to calm him by whispering whatever words come into her mind, whispering as to the child she never had.

Why should she think of children now when she has already decided that never being a mother was life's blessing because it took away the pain of what would have been an inevitable separation? She thinks too of Varia's schoolbook with its blanked-out faces. But what of the fate of the children of those faces? Were they supposed to suppress all memories of the mothers and fathers taken from them, to never speak of them again or even possess a photograph where the face they knew, and presumably loved, looked out at them untrammelled by condemnation or guilt? Perhaps Osip is to be her child now. She watches him drift once more into an uneasy sleep, hears but can't make sense of the jumble of words that he utters. She looks at the clock whose hands move slowly but inexorably towards nine. She kisses his brow and taking the chair places it against the wall, then standing on it reaches up to the glass face of the clock that for the briefest of seconds bears an image of her own, opens it and carefully moves the hands beyond his appointed time.

1950

BECAUSE THERE ARE SPIES everywhere it is no longer possible to remember what it feels like to be unwatched or to have a voice that can say what it thinks. It is only in her deepest most secret parts that she holds the print of the person life has slowly formed. It is seen by no one, except perhaps Akhmatova, and even then despite their deep trust there are moments when they feel the need to be circumspect. So even when they are sure that their conversation goes unheard by the informers in the apartments they are afflicted by the fear that in some unknown way the powers have access to what they say. And sometimes too she suffers the fleeting belief that they can see the most secret thoughts so even the mind is not totally free.

No one trusts the phones, they have become a people speaking in whispers and it is the system's greatest strength that it has bred suspicion and paranoia everywhere, so everyone stays protective of their own singularity and never shares with others except what they believe is ideologically correct. And most, despite everything, still believe, and look to the Leader to preserve them from those outside who would seek to invade and enslave, and those counter-revolutionaries inside the gates who conspire to sow the seeds of chaos. She knows that the greatest source of their power, a power that seems destined to endure, is that they have silenced the voices. And not just the voices of political dissent but also the voices of the artists – writers, composers, painters, playwrights. All of them bound to a lifetime of artistic servitude. She believes that Osip was right when he declared that in this their country poetry was held in such high esteem that a poem could cost you your life. They had come to know the bitter truth of that.

As she prepares for her morning class in yet one more small-town college she wonders why they are so fearful of writers then, as she flicks the pages of the textbook she will be referencing, decides it must be to do with how they see the imagination. Individualistic, unpredictable, able to touch the heart and stir emotions – what could inspire their greater mistrust? As she packs the book carefully into her satchel she is struck once again by the irony that Osip's first collection of poems was called *Stone* and in the transit camp she's heard they made him work at breaking rocks. Such knowledge threatens to make her own heart turn to stone. Sometimes she thinks it foolish to try and resist because it must surely make her stronger and it is strength she needs if she is to survive. So let her heart be like stone that no axe can break.

She sets off for the short walk to the college taking the river path. It is her favourite part of the day when the morning sun has not yet baked the streets into dust and rendered everything dry and brittle to the eyes. The river is already skimmed with light that makes the surface quiver into a luminous life. If her heart were stone, she tells herself, then she wouldn't know this pleasure but nor would she feel the relentless pull of loneliness that lingers at the edge of every waking thought. There are men fishing on the far bank whipping their lines across the fret and dance of light. He wouldn't want her to live her life under the shadow of his loss but these things aren't inside her control no matter how often she seeks to exercise her will over such feelings. With him was the part of her life which gave her most pleasure and now there is only a sense of emptiness and a road to be followed and a responsibility that has to be borne.

A man and a boy pass her carrying two fish wrapped in an old newspaper from whose end open mouths peep out. She hurries on – she always likes to be in the classroom early with all her notes organised and everything in place for the delivery of the lesson. There are spies amongst the class of course – their identity is well-known and while some may show a sense of creeping shame in their demeanour, others display an open pride and an enjoyment of whatever importance they think it gives themselves. The system is skilled at seeking out the vulnerable and pressuring them into service or recognising the ambitious who can be easily recruited. She has tried to give nothing to them or anyone else in the college that would merit a report or raise even the slightest concern. There is a price to be paid for this and so she carries a sense of having a permanent limit placed on who she is and sometimes this curtailment feels as if it is stifling and choking the life out of her. It doesn't come easy to bend her will to those she hates, or suppress the fire of her anger, but the knowledge that she still carries a voice inside her head, a voice that frightened them so much that they deemed it necessary to try and silence it, sustains her through all but the lowest moments.

She takes one last look at the river that courses to some distant sea without restraint then lowers her head and climbs the short flight of steps to the front door of the college. As always the elderly woman who seems permanently to monitor the front door responds to her polite good morning with an almost imperceptible nod and stares at her with ill-disguised suspicion. She appears to be there at all hours of the day and night, so much that Nadezhda has started to believe that she must live somewhere in the building. Her grey hair that is pinned up in a bun always seems to be on the edge of sliding into chaos. Usually a cat slinks around her ankles or sits sleeping in her lap. She has never heard her voice but this morning she speaks.

'The assistant director wants to see you before classes,' she says, her eyes narrowed and unblinking, one hand stroking the cat nestling on the broad cradle of her skirt.

So what can he want and yet she already knows. A woman always knows when a man looks at her in that way, even though she never thought it was a look she would ever experience again. She isn't beautiful – time's press has engraved its mark on her. But it's signalled in his eyes that linger just too long no matter how they try to disguise it with politeness or conversation. She finds herself smoothing her hair like some foolish young woman and straightening her blouse as she makes her way to his office on the ground floor. So it would be better now if her heart had indeed turned to stone because then she wouldn't be thinking about how she looks or feeling the slight quickening of her pulse. But the awareness makes her experience a flare of shame. Let her heart be dead to her. Let her memories of love quicken her strength and consume the full need of her loneliness. She tells herself there is no other man's words she wishes to hear or which can ever replace what was once hers.

She knows, however, that kindness is dangerously seductive and she has been starved of that since the day her husband left her side. But the shame doesn't stop her catching at her reflection in the glass of Anatoli Lebedev's office door. And when she knocks she is glad to feel the calming hard coldness of the glass against the slight quiver of her hand. He calls her in and standing behind his desk beckons her to a seat.

'Good morning,' he says. 'Thank you for coming. I wanted to speak to you before class started,' and he is smiling slightly longer than even good manners requires.

He's still standing behind his desk as if he's waiting for her to tell him to sit. She has sat before desks in the past and she's almost grateful for the memories because they warn her now to be cautious and so she doesn't return his smile but with both hands holds her satchel in front of her like a shield. But she looks at him all the same and as always is struck by how young he appears despite his middle age and how untainted by whatever it is deadens the faces of so many of those who have climbed their way up into positions of power. Even the war years where he lost his wife and who knew what else, while gaining a chest full of medals, have left no obvious scars. His sprightliness is also accentuated by the stooped and weary old age that holds his college boss in its tightening grip. The gossip is that soon the younger man will replace the older and it is a belief that seems universally popular with staff and students alike.

'So how are you?' he asks. 'Fully recovered from your cold, I hope.'

'It was nothing really. Just one of those coughs that come calling and then don't want to leave.'

'And you're comfortable in your lodgings?'

'Yes, thanks.'

She knows now it was a mistake to have accepted his offer to help her with a place to live but at the time of her arrival it seemed a welcome way to circumvent the usual trudging round in search of rooms and the inevitable trawling through a series of hovels, each more squalid than the last, before eventually finding one that passed muster. So when he told her that his widowed aunt had a room that could be made available she had availed herself of the opportunity and while it is true that now she has a clean bed in a perfectly adequately sized room and access to a small garden where she can sit when the weather is good, it has not come without its complications. Not the least of these is her landlady's curiosity about her and the seemingly innocuous questions with which she attempts to solicit information. It appears nothing more than the product of the old woman's boredom but means she always has to be on guard when all she wants to do is rest and try to find at least one space in her day when she can feel able to be her undisguised self.

'And my aunt tells me that you're getting on well together. I think the company is good for her. Her spirits have been low since she lost her husband.'

She nods and thinks what a terribly conscientious nephew he must be to visit his elderly aunt so frequently and wonders how often he came before the new lodger arrived at the beginning of term. But he can't have summoned her to his office just on the pretext of enquiring about her wellbeing, or merely to look at her, and she deliberately shuffles on the seat so that her restlessness is obvious even to him whose eyes have never left her.

'Was there something else? I need to get a few things ready for my first class.'

'Of course, of course. It was just to tell you that your position will be available to you next term if you wish to continue. We've just learned that your predecessor won't be returning.'

The mysterious Nikoli Surkov in whose classroom she now teaches and whose departure from the college has never been fully explained. It's obvious he left in a hurry because everywhere she discovers little parts of who he was and in moments of boredom she tries to piece them together and form them into his identity. So there is the sketchbook of landscape drawings and portraits done in pencil and charcoal; his library of personal books – some of which she approves of and some not; a little envelope of photographs inside a book of possibly family members but all of which he is absent from. A sudden departure usually means only one thing – a summons in the middle of the night. But none of the staff or students ever make mention of him, not even to express shock at his designated crime. Despite her curiosity it would be unhelpful to make enquiries.

'Yes, I would like to stay,' she says, giving him the briefest of smiles. 'And I can continue to lodge with your aunt?'

'That would be most satisfactory to all parties,' he says, smiling and standing again before stretching his arm out in a vague but expansive gesture. When he smiles his face takes on a boyish quality that makes her think of how everything that happened to Osip accelerated his journey into old age. She remembers him on her arm on their expedition to Moscow in search of money and help, hears again the laboured wheeze of his chest that accompanied the tired shuffle of his steps.

She is no longer a young woman and that makes it harder to live a life that is constantly moving from place to place. As she walks to her class she is more confused than she normally allows herself to be and the self-indulgence feels dangerous and with the potential to cause her to veer off her chosen course. Is it possible she could find herself a more permanent nest in this town that sits on a river and which seems content to let much of modern life flow quietly by? She is no longer a young woman and there will be few more offers. So what is it he sees in her? She can't believe he is enamoured by her beauty – perhaps he seeks a companion in his old age, a replacement for the wife he lost in the war. And what is it she wants? She has never even considered taking up with someone else, knowing that they would fall short of the man she loved. But if love can be set aside is the possibility of coming to an agreement with someone who is kind to her, and whose career would preserve her ability to teach and live in some unfamiliar comfort, something to be dismissed lightly?

As always she works the students hard – she isn't interested in being their best friend or making their life easy. And there are sharp words for the indolent or those who fail to understand that in language important meanings can be damaged by slovenliness. In the middle of the day she eats on her own in the grounds of the college and doesn't feel the need to share the time with her colleagues. When she has finished and before afternoon classes begin she goes to the library and returns the books she has borrowed and searches for something new. There is little in English except a few copies of Dickens and she has read all of the available titles so she contents herself with borrowing a copy of Turgenev's *A Nest of the Gentry*. She never reads poetry because she's frightened of what she's read seeping in amongst the lines that she needs to preserve like tares amongst the wheat.

The memory of what she carries inside her keeps her focused through the afternoon and stops it dragging. At the end of classes she packs her satchel and the dictations the students have handed in for marking. If the day still retains enough heat after her evening meal she will sit in the garden and mark them. She smiles at the realisation that in her present life this represents a small pleasure. When she walks back to her lodgings she takes the path along by the river once more and so avoids the crowded town streets and their layering of dust that waits as always for some breeze to stir it into mischief. She misses Moscow and the life she once had there, misses the concerts and theatre, the endless evenings given to readings and debates about books. The river seems to flow more slowly than in the morning but there are still men fishing on the far bank. Some giant logs, escaped she imagines from the timber mills upstream, float lazily by, a temporary resting place for small birds.

After her meal that she takes at the kitchen table with her landlady who babbles on with the indefatigable enthusiasm of someone who has had no one to talk to all day, she decides it's warm enough to sit outside with her marking but is still able to hear the arrival of Anatoli Lebedev. She isn't surprised but doesn't know if what she feels is pleasure or irritation. She keeps her head in her papers even when she senses that he has come to the back door of the house to watch her. It feels already that he is approaching the time when he will say something to her and when that moment comes she must know how she will answer. It would be easier if only he tried to exert pressure on her, exploit the leverage of his position, because then she would know him unworthy but instead all he has done so far is wait patiently and when the opportunity arose show her a polite kindness that appeared not to require any form of return. It is true that in some ways, such as now, he likes quietly to observe her but it feels like it shares nothing with all those other creatures who have spied on her. So to whom does he report each night except his heart and despite everything else that rattles round her head she is conscious of being flattered.

'So I see you are still working hard,' he says as he steps into the garden.

She stands up as if she is aware of him for the first time and because it shows appropriate respect but he tells her to sit and apologises for disturbing her.

'And are they producing good work?' he asks, peering at the papers.

'Some do, some are a little slower to grasp what they need to know.'

She is suddenly conscious of the absurdity of being with someone to whom she has shown nothing of her real self. She feels like an impostor but because she has acted as this new person for so long wonders if the old one still exists except in her memory.

'It's a lovely night,' he says and then gets embarrassed and flounders into silence.

She takes pity on him by simply agreeing and then as he shuffles a little she realises that he's working up to saying something and as she stares at the papers she's still to mark doesn't know whether she wants him to or not.

'Would you like to take a walk along the river?' he asks, pulling himself up straight and finding the courage that she presumes he has in abundance.

It will be better if she goes with him and saves him the pain of failure under the prying eyes of his aunt who is already peering through the glass.

'Give me a minute to put these papers away and get my shawl,' she says as she slips quickly past him into the house where she almost collides with his aunt who is too slow to retreat from her vantage point. In her room she places the papers in her satchel then sits at the end of the bed. She tries to calm the pulse of her breathing then puts on the shawl and before she goes back to the garden allows herself the briefest of glances in the small mirror that hangs behind her door.

They walk against the river's flow along a beaten path that seems to crumble to dust under their feet. Their shoulders brush from time to time but he doesn't give her his arm or try to touch her in any way and instead channels his concentration on pointing out the different types of water fowl and birds that skim the surface. Little clouds of insects spiral up from the water and scavenging birds dive in amongst them. Then they talk about inconsequential things and she feels the urge to stop him and say, 'I am Nadezhda Mandelstam, the wife of the poet,' and stare at his face to see how quickly he registers the full significance of those words. If he were to shrug and say it didn't matter then he would deserve another medal pinned to his chest. She knows she can't risk telling him but can't go on either being someone other than the person he thinks.

There is a small boat with a discoloured and ragged sail that looks like a crumpled page torn from some old book and from its bow boys dive into the water, their entry marked by shouts and sudden splashes of white and the boat left rocking behind them. They pause under the light-blotched canopy of some overhanging trees and she knows that he is going to speak to her. In front of them is a thick cluster of rushes, their furred heads heavy with the fecund weight of the season. She has to stop him because she is confused and there are voices in her head that she doesn't recognise and because she feels all the conviction that exists at her core and which makes her who she is in danger of slipping away with the steady flow of the river.

'What happened to Surkov?' she asks.

The question throws him and as he looks across the river she sees immediately that he is uncertain of what he should say.

'Why do you ask about Surkov?'

'I'm curious, that's all. Sometimes I come across things that obviously belonged to him.'

'That should all have been cleared,' he says and his voice is edged with an irritation she hasn't heard before. 'What did you find?'

'Some books, a sketchpad, a few photographs. Not much.' Already she is regretting mentioning it.

'Shall we walk a little further while we still have the light?' he asks and as if answering his own question sets off. 'I'll have someone clear the things in the morning if you show them where to find them.'

She follows a step behind and knows not to ask any further questions. It is a few minutes before he speaks again but some of the tension lingers in his voice.

'Surkov was guilty of anti-revolutionary activity. He wrote some foolish, dangerous articles and circulated them to a secret cabal of students he had organised, taking advantage of their impressionable minds.'

'He was discovered?'

'One of the group reported him. We informed the authorities immediately. It was quite a shock to discover that such a thing had happened in the college. It had to be stamped out right away.'

When he looks at her she nods in what he must take to be her agreement but which is instead a silent affirmation of her own understanding. So she tells him it is getting a little cold and that she wants to finish her marking before tomorrow so that she can return the papers and go over common mistakes while it is still fresh in the students' minds. She has been a fool momentarily borne off course by vanity and the unaccustomed and almost forgotten pleasure of kindness.

'Although we discovered Surkov's activities in time there is a view from above that the Director has grown lax, relaxed his vigilance, and that a younger man is now needed to fill the post.'

He doesn't need to say any more. So exposing Surkov as a traitor, as well as the resulting discrediting of his boss, has enhanced his career and is now being laid out in front of her like a dowry. She wants to tell him more than ever but for a different reason than before that he is out walking with the wife of a so-called traitor. He stops briefly to point out a heron nesting in the rushes and then they walk on towards her lodgings. At the door he shakes her hand formally. The moment has slipped away from him but as he bows and takes his leave she knows that he will make other moments. She watches him walk away, his broad shoulders a little stooped with failure. When she enters the house his aunt is waiting for her and looks at her in a way that suggests she has been anticipating an outcome so she too is to be disappointed.

In her room she sits once more on the bed and glances around, one of the better places she has known. But it was a foolishness and while she is embarrassed by that sharpening consciousness she is also aware of a lingering sadness. The road stretching ahead of her is solitary and she must accept that now and live within both the freedom and confines of herself. There is no other way and she finds a new resolution in that knowledge. And all that is left is the work that she has to do so she finishes marking the remaining dictations, each mistake she finds underlining her own.

* * *

On an almost empty night train that rattles through an invisible landscape she sits with her head angled to the glass. Out there in the blackness stretch new uncertainties of place and sustenance. Her case is safely ensconced in the luggage rack and the compartment is empty except for an elderly couple and a young sailor whose canvas bag has an accordion attached to it. She looks at the dozing couple whose white-haired heads rest against each other and she feels a little envy at what has endured for them. She will never know if love changes over time, never know if it's strengthened or rendered weaker by the passing years. Everything sifts through her – the flow of the river, the drawings in the sketchbook, the garden she sat in during the evening sun. She moves her face closer to the glass but sees nothing except the reflection of the inside of the carriage. Her hand touches her hair – slowly greying now, coarser to the touch – but hers will be the only hand to know its feel. She tries to summon the memory of his touch again, the feel of his fingers tracing the contours of her face, but struggles to realise it, almost as if it hides from her somewhere in the unknown expanse of darkness.

The old man snores a little and his mouth falls open but their angled and balanced heads remain undisturbed. Osip made no demands on her future life, extracted no foolish promise of faithfulness, and although they talked about it only briefly, she knows he wanted nothing more from her than that she should go on living and find what happiness she could. Nor did he ever obligate her with the preservation of the poems – this was her resolution alone and the vocation that now gives her life purpose.

The train hurries through the night slowing but not stopping as it passes through stations. Another name on a map, another new start. She grows too old for it but has no other choice. Always moving, never stopping long enough for her to come to the attention of the authorities. Trying to find teaching posts but willing, as she has done already, to turn her hand to anything, whether it meant working in a factory or labouring at some job that if nothing else served to numb the mind. She rubs the window in the vain hope of clearing even a fleeting glimpse of the world outside but it leaves nothing other than the squeak of the glass and the momentary smear of her fingers. Perhaps the darkness will never be cleared. Perhaps outside the window there is only the night's unrelenting emptiness. The young sailor looks at her briefly then turns his eyes away again as if he hasn't registered her. She finds a pleasure in that. So let her be invisible, a small stone hidden at the side of the road while history passes her by on its reckless rush to wherever destiny beckons. Perhaps Osip was right and they should leave the clamour of the great cities and take refuge with the peasants who endure as they have done over the centuries.

The train speeds its way on a journey that seems endless and without prospect of a concluding destination. She looks at her reflection in the glass and for a moment seems so strange to herself that she has to turn away. The old man's snores are louder now. Surely he will disturb his wife but she continues sleeping, seemingly oblivious. Perhaps before the journey ends the sailor will play his accordion and sing some sad song of home. She tries to think of where home is but there is only the furled darkness of the world outside the window and then she thinks of the room she slept in a night ago where hangs a mirror that shows no reflection and, on the end of the bed waiting to be returned, a neat pile of students' work and a library book she never had time to read.

1939

S HE SAYS HIS NAME and hands her small parcel through
the tiny window on the Sophia Embankment. His ink-
stained fingers brush it to one side as an inconvenience when
he starts to flick the pages of the ledger. She is afforded a
glimpse of the lists of names – they seem never-ending. All
disappeared into the night. How many, if any, will ever come
back? Some of those who are released find themselves re-
arrested while others return only to find their wife has been
taken. Soon surely they will come for her. She watches the
clerk's fingers quickly turning the pages. He has come too far
and has to work backwards again. He glances up at her while
he does so as if he has forgotten why he's doing the search.
Their eyes meet for a second, long enough for her to look for
something she recognises as human and to wonder if he has
a wife and children, some life beyond this little square of
window and this seemingly endless queue. There must be
times when he too feels fear, the fear that comes to all with
too much knowledge because in a world devoid of trust
knowledge is a dangerous burden that must eventually be
removed. So she wonders as he flicks the final pages and runs
his finger down the column if he imagines a different finger

searching for his name, written in the same black ink that makes his fingers look as if they are wearing dark gloves.

His finger stops. He double-checks, his eyes squinting behind his glasses. His thin lips momentarily pull back in concentration to reveal uneven and yellowing lower teeth. Then without looking at her he pushes the parcel back through the window before raising his head to say, 'The addressee is dead.' That is all he says and as she stares at him she knows that nothing will prise further words out of him. Almost immediately he is looking over her shoulder to beckon silently the next woman forward and angling his head to catch the new name. But she can't step aside from the window that now feels like the only possible portal through which she might catch one last glimpse of the man she loves. As her fingers press against the paper and her nails start to tear into it the parcel feels like the most terrible thing she's ever had to hold. No words come out of her mouth. Already the woman behind her – the one who smells of cheap scent and onions – is brushing impatiently against her shoulder. She's desperately trying to force herself into thought but there will be no how or when, there never is, and she knows it's futile to try for answers, not even likely that such things are known to this man who is already turning his good ear to hear the next name for which he must search. The guard at the side of the window is looking at her and there is impatience in his movements as he starts to unfold himself from the stiffness of his slumber.

She finds the strength to move, stepping slowly to one side. This is not where she wants her grief to be known. She will not give them her tears. She will not share it with anyone but herself. So clutching the parcel under her arm that immediately marks her with the badge of widowhood, then almost tucking it out of sight, she walks back down the length of the queue with her head high, her eyes almost clear. But the news follows her in a whisper passed from head to head until it begins to sound like a wave rolling in behind her. It is the most difficult walk she has ever had to make but she tries to channel everything into the resolution of her steps even though all of her wants to fall apart. And then as the whisper's wave seems to splash over her she feels as if she's being swept to some place far beyond herself.

On the walk from the last of the queuing women the first tear comes but she shrugs it away angrily. It is a mercy, she tells herself, a blessed release from the horrors and suffering that awaited him in Kolyma so her tears are a selfishness. His weakening heart has proved his truest friend. He will not have to suffer another winter. She should not begrudge his escape or indulge in self-pity but something more powerful runs counter to these unfolding thoughts until it sweeps them aside and she is left only with the overwhelming shudder of grief. And what or who is there now to comfort her except the knowledge of the life they had. She tries to staunch the grief, protect herself with these thoughts, but as she's pummelled and pushed by the crowd getting on the same tram it feels as if every touch serves to breach what seem now like thin-walled defences. They're packed in tightly and suddenly she feels like she might faint but she presses her face to the coldness of the glass and makes herself breathe steadily. There are slivers of ice in the corners of the window and outside the snow has started again, if only drifting in half-heartedly on the breeze. She wants to get out of the tram where people push themselves into every available space and are indifferent to any need except their own. They're choking the life out of her and unable to stand it any longer she elbows her way aggressively towards the door at the first stop despite the distance it means she will have to walk, ignoring the complaints of her fellow passengers.

When she steps down her feet almost slip from below her. She hasn't been able to harvest enough suitable winter clothing and the shoes she's wearing will never last the coming months. Then finding the entrance to a derelict building she is sick, retching long after her stomach has given up its contents. When she's finished she kicks fresh snow over the traces. She's been on her own since they took him from the rest home but now as she straightens and tries to spit away the lingering taste of sickness she understands the full meaning of loneliness. Before it was as if their lives existed in parallel but were still connected through love; now there is only an overwhelming sense of isolation, of a road that must be followed alone until death.

She hesitates before she steps back into the thoroughfare, scanning the faces that pass, suddenly frightened that she's being followed. They'll come for her now – she knows it. They've already come once when she was in Kalinin only to find her gone. They don't like loose ends and that's what she is and she also knows that again and again they sweep up the closest relatives of those who've been taken. It's to protect themselves from the embittered offspring, the loved-one who will suffer in silence and patiently wait the moment to take revenge. His death will bring her back to their mind and they have plenty of reasons to believe that she is infected, a carrier, because she is belligerent with them, unwilling to be cowed in their presence, so now more than ever she feels at risk. But as she hesitates no heads turn to give her a second look and after crossing her mouth with the back of a gloved hand she steps out into the throng.

The falling snow forces everyone's heads into submission and as she trudges onwards she tries to tell herself that she must find comfort in the knowledge that he has escaped the full horrors of what awaited him. In the one short letter received from the transit camp near Vladivostok he told her he had been given five years for his 'counter-revolutionary activity'. The high-ranking Special Tribunal that sentenced him meted out Soviet justice to 'socially dangerous persons'. He might just have been pleased by that description. But he had also spoken of the cold, his ill-health, and the hope that she might be able to send some clothes. It hurts her to the core to think of him shivering in some frost-bitten wooden barracks through which a sharp-toothed wind relentlessly gnawed at the bones. She carries the parcel under her arm and knows its meagre offerings would have done little to preserve him. Only the letter it contains in which she affirms her love might have helped his mind, if not his body, bear whatever each day brought. His own letter expressed love and concern for her – as she recites the words to herself and keeps her head angled to avoid the snow hitting her eyes she guesses the fear that she had been arrested was an additional torment to the already heavy burden he carried.

There is a team of supervised men clearing snow – she wonders if they are petty criminals conscripted into public service – their long-handled shovels scooping and flinging it in an unbroken rhythm. Sometimes when shovels hit the pavement there are sparks and dull clacks that sound like horse's hooves. A tram goes past, its roof temporarily painted white. For a second she regrets alighting so soon before her stop. At intervals she glances over her shoulder to convince herself she isn't being followed. If they believe she holds hidden manuscripts they will seek her out and if that happens then the poems that exist now only in her memory will also tumble with her into the pit. The determination to avoid this fate for both the poems and herself spurs her on. As long as the poems are preserved then they have not succeeded in killing him. She must get out of Moscow, this time exile herself in some far-off town where her file will struggle to find her. She must keep running, try to outrun the slow turning of the bureaucratic wheels that seeks to determine her destiny. So she ignores the cold seeping into her toes and the tips of her fingers and hurries on to pack whatever pathetic amount of possessions life has left her with.

The snow is heavier now, pelting in with greater fury as if its earlier languid fall was merely a rehearsal for this, its real performance. It plasters and sticks against her coat, plashing on her cheekbones and eyebrows, but she welcomes it, trying to convince herself that its coldness might deaden some of the pain of grief that burns inside her. For a fleeting second she regrets the absence of a child – a daughter – to whom she might have given her love and received it in return, a child who might if favoured by fortune outlive her and survive long enough to reach a world where truth once more is honoured.

It will take her half an hour to reach the apartment and once more she berates her impetuosity in getting off the tram but she felt as she was being suffocated in the tight press and she will not risk subjecting herself to that again. Two black horses with glistening flanks and harnesses lined with white plod along beside her as they pull a cartload of barrels. Flurries of flakes vanish in the stream of their nostrils. The driver is hunched and caped, his shoulders braided with snow. She imagines the bodies of the dead in the camps thrown in the back of such a cart and then dumped naked into some pit. He will have no headstone, no place where she can visit, and she understands as she watches the cart's wheels leave the briefest tracks that his memorial is carried deep inside herself and so even now in the midst of her grief and with the snow trying to freeze her face into a death mask her lips begin to move.

She speaks silent lines in a requiem to him, words that speak of mystery and beauty, and as the snow continues to fall, the city, even now, even in this moment, seems slowly to assume a new image of itself, dressing itself in fresh raiment of white. The voice she hears is not her own but the cadences and rhythms of his and it's as if he is speaking to her once more and she tells herself so long as she has these words layered inside her then she will always have him as part of her life. And despite the dark recurring impulses that have fastened to her since his being taken, she knows that she must go on living and has to go on walking now despite the cold and the distance.

Part of her wants to go to the Writers' Union and confront them with the news of his death, shout their shame in their faces, but to do so will sign her own death warrant and death is a luxury, a welcome fate, that must be denied to her. So she must try to outrun the wolves that search for the trail of her scent. She must cover her traces and hope such a snowfall as this will obliterate her tracks. As she crosses the bridge a squad of soldiers push their truck that has skidded to an angled halt. Competing instructions are shouted to the driver and as it rights itself there is much backslapping and laughter. Down below in the river great ice floes choke the black throat of the water.

Her feet are worryingly cold now and she needs to find a temporary refuge from the snowfall that shows no sign of relenting and which has slowly drained the day of all vestiges of light. There is a teahouse on the corner of the next street and although she begrudges the cost she sets her sights on its yellow windows that offer an invitation which is difficult to refuse. So shaking off some of the snow that coats her she pushes open the heavy door and searches for a corner table. The wooden floor is black with damp and printed with the customers' footsteps but there is heat and, despite the smell that reminds her of the sodden queue she has just left, there is the welcome respite of a seat and a chance to stiffen herself for what remains of her journey. She is glad when no one comes to serve her as it increases the time she can justify spending there but when her tea arrives she drinks it greedily as if its heat might rush to her fingers and toes. She looks with alarm at her shoes that now appear on the edge of collapse. A decent pair of shoes in Moscow is as rare as so many other things. She will have to try and make some repairs or find that other scarcity, a cobbler who won't charge her a king's ransom for his services.

Already she is making herself think of practical things in the futile hope that it will fill the emptiness that is opening inside her. So she tries to concentrate on trains and locations, contacts and possible employments, but all of this is replaced by anger, anger that she is not even to be allowed the natural expression of grief. She looks around her and sees a group of students laughing and flirting with each other, the excited chimes of their voices ringing in her consciousness. A mother instructs her child to sit up properly and a group of men, whose overcoats remind her of those worn by the agents who carried out Osip's first arrest, huddle their heads together across the table under a stale coil of cigarette smoke.

She finds it hard to accept the reality that life goes on seemingly unaltered since the clerk returned her parcel and spoke those few words. Surely somehow notice must be taken and for a second she feels the crazed impulse to stand and shout at them until she holds their attention and tell them that they have killed a great poet who wanted nothing more than to be able to find words that were true to the world. But she slumps back on the chair already defeated by the fact that she knows they now live in a time that has no need for truth unless it is the one publicly given to them, and where the death of some unknown individual has less significance than a grain of sand washed away by the tide. So she sits in silence and stares at them as if they exist in some different universe and for a second she isn't sure if it's she or they who are the outsiders to what she conceives of as reality. So that now even if she were to stand and shout it feels as if there would be some invisible barrier between them and whatever words she chose to use would simply fall back rebuffed by this thing that separates them. So her anger blunted once more by the supremacy of loneliness grows slowly cold as the tea she holds.

When she ventures outside again the snow has temporarily stopped with only a few wind-drifted eddies falling from roofs and the ledges of buildings. She is suddenly frightened of going back to the apartment. What if they are waiting there for her, and the apartment is a sprung trap? She hesitates, uncertain of what she must do or where she must go, and then she thinks of the Shklovskis and although part of her doesn't want to ask more of them than they have already given so generously, she has nowhere else and they would want to know of her loss so she heads towards their apartment, what's left of her shoes squeaking as they press fresh imprints on the newly fallen snow.

The elderly woman janitor at the Shklovskis' greets her with her usual suspicious scowl and looks at her white-blistered coat with ill-concealed disdain as if she has no right to bring snow into the building. She herself is wearing galoshes and a stained green apron that reaches to her ankles. From a leather belt hang keys that rattle when she walks. Her hair is pinned high on her head like a turban. Their eyes meet silently for a second and she thinks that in the afterlife these women will find employment as the gatekeepers of the Underworld.

'So where's that husband of yours?' she suddenly hears the old woman say – she's not sure she's ever had anything from her except an inspectorial stare.

'He's dead,' she says and although she doesn't want this to be the first person to hear of her loss, there is a release as she speaks the words, almost as if it frees a little of what is whelming up inside her.

They stand facing each other silently for a second. The old woman replaces a straying strand of grey hair.

'He was arrested?'

'Yes. He got five years but he died.'

The woman nods but at first says nothing, then turns her eyes to the doorway.

'Heavy snows,' she says after a moment's hesitation. Then she turns away.

The lift seems slower than ever as it takes her towards the place that has never barred its door and which now more than anything else is where she will be able to share her grief because it suddenly feels too big for her to bear on her own. So when Vasilisa opens the door, her friend's smile of greeting is almost immediately replaced by an instinctive awareness of what has happened without words being spoken. She takes her by the hand and says, 'Nadia, Nadia,' over and over, leading her to the kitchen table and helping her into a seat, then as if awakening from a trance says, 'Get your wet clothes off, Nadia, you'll catch your death.'

Victor, Nikita and Varia are standing in the doorway and Victor is holding his hand up to silence his daughter's questions. Suddenly she is aware of the sodden weight of her coat which Vasilisa slowly and awkwardly prises from her, skimming off snow patches as she does it. 'Your shoes,' she says, 'look at your shoes.' And as she glances down she sees that they have almost disintegrated into what seems like a papery pulp. Under her friend's motherly ministration she feels like a child and she doesn't resist it – she has given so much of herself to looking after Osip that it feels an unfamiliar but welcome lightness to receive another's care. Varia is summoned from the other room to help and given a rush of instructions – the wet clothing to the stove, shoes from the cupboard, soup heated.

She sinks into the kitchen chair while Vasilisa towels her hair and then Victor comes and holds her hand and says with a breaking voice, 'A great loss to you and a great loss to Russia.' He's wiping tears from his eyes and stands shaking his head until his wife nods him away and they're momentarily left on their own again.

'It's very hard, Nadia, very, very hard, but he will not suffer now.'

'His suffering is over,' she says, nodding in agreement while the cloth continues to dry her hair. 'What about my suffering?' she wants to add but instead starts to cry quietly holding back as much as she can.

Vasilisa cradles her head and whispers consolations until she forces herself to stop crying and when Varia comes with the bowl of soup she gives the child the best semblance of a smile that she can find. Her hair is bedraggled and hangs about her face as she takes the soup glad of its warmth and then she feels Varia slipping a pair of her mother's shoes on her feet under the table. Victor, with Nikita hovering behind the shelter of his father's shoulder, comes back into the doorway and she lifts her head from the soup and thanks them all. Then the children are ushered away and their parents sit at the table and talk about their memories of Osip, about the poems, about better days in the past and ones which might come again in the future. She is grateful for all of it.

'It's better he died before he was transported on to Kolyma,' she says, forcing her voice into a new resolve and speaking as much to herself as to them. 'His heart probably just gave out. He will not have to endure the winter now.'

They nod their silent agreement. She looks at their faces and wonders why such people can't rule the world.

'What will you do now?' Victor asks before adding, 'You can stay here as long as you need.'

'I can't stay,' she tells him, touching the back of his hand. 'I think they will come for me when word of his death becomes public. They won't want witnesses to their crime, particularly one who sometimes doesn't know when to keep her mouth shut.'

'Where will you go?' Vasilisa asks, trying to get her to take more soup.

'I don't know but somewhere far from Moscow, some-where in the country. In the shadows as much as possible.'

'You must stay here tonight whatever you decide,' Victor insists and she is pleased to accept because already she feels a greater weariness than she has ever known, as if all her life's energy has been drained out of her.

'I'm frightened to go back to the apartment to get my things,' she says, 'in case they are waiting for me, or come in the night.'

'Victor and Nikita will go for you, bring what you need here.'

She reluctantly agrees and hands them her key once a list has been made of what she wants and after they have gone, with her ringing admonition to be careful and to return immediately if they suspect anything is wrong, she allows herself to be shepherded to where she will sleep for the night. It is where she has slept with Osip in the past and so her final wakening moments are laced with that consciousness but which is somehow comforting and sooner than she could hope everything falls away into the respite of a dreamless sleep.

When she wakes in the morning she struggles for a few seconds to grasp where she is and then she hears what sounds like a bird and thinks of the goldfinch described by Osip in one of his last poems in Voronezh. She wants it to sing but there is nothing except the voice of Varia piping loudly and her mother entreating her to be quiet so that she doesn't wake their guest. She stirs slowly and everything comes rushing through her again making her turn her face to the wall and tightly close her eyes to block the morning light. She has no idea of the hour but it feels as if she has slept a long time. Then she knows that she must be gone but as always it is only concern for the safety of her friends that makes her stir. Vasilisa appears with a cup of strong tea laced with sugar and sitting beside her strokes her head.

'We thought you were never going to wake,' she says. 'You must have been exhausted.'

'My things from the apartment?'

'All here waiting for you.'

'And did Victor and Nikita see anyone?'

'No, they said everything seemed normal and because it was late when they went they don't believe anyone saw them leaving with your case.'

She tries to stand and wants to begin getting herself ready but Vasilisa stops her and makes her wait until she has drained the tea and eaten some of the bread Varia has brought. Then they help her dress in a mixture of her own dried clothes and new garments belonging to Vasilisa. She feels as if she's dressed in love and takes strength from that and tries not to think of the uncertainties that stretch out ahead of her. Once more she has gently to refuse their entreaty to stay longer but despite her protests is forced to submit to their insistence that they will accompany her to the station. Her new shoes pinch a little but the leather feels strong and promises to do its best to keep her feet dry. There is no sign of the ones she discarded the previous night and she assumes they have been thrown out with the rubbish. She wishes there was something she could give to them to show her gratitude but in its absence she simply kisses both her friends and makes a joke about Odysseus setting out on his adventures. Varia comes and hugs her and she makes another joke about not forgetting her and expresses the hope that she will not block out her memory like the faces in her schoolbook. As she kisses Nikita on both cheeks she whispers so that only he can hear, 'Let them fly free,' but he merely smiles and blushes a little.

Then as both parents refuse Varia's plea to be allowed to come with them and with Victor carrying her case they take the lift. Close to the ground floor she has a sudden fear that when the doors open they will be faced by the secret police but when they walk out it is the keeper of the door they meet. She nods neutrally at Victor and Vasilisa, stares at the case and then inspects her from head to toe, and she is suddenly struck by their vulnerability and how a single phone call about 'suspicious activity' might send them tumbling into disaster.

But, 'So you have new shoes,' is all the old woman says and after watching them struggling with the door she turns away again.

As soon as they step into the street the cold crimps their faces tight and they struggle for a few minutes before establishing a purposeful rhythm. They pass the Epiphany Monastery that now houses a factory and living quarters for those working on the underground construction, past more teams of men clearing snow. Already the fresh fall of the previous night is trampled and soiled and as they make their way towards the station she is fearful that she is dragging her friends into a morass from which they will not escape, so when eventually they come in sight of it with its fluttering flags and guarded entrance she compels Victor to give her the suitcase and forbids them to journey any further with her. They reluctantly agree and then despite her attempts to strike a light note they part with solemnity that they all know is edged with finality.

She only turns round once to wave as she walks away and sees them standing as if frozen by the cold, their hands slow to rise in response. There is nothing now to be gained from looking back. She understands that she is about to turn Osip's description of her as 'the beggar-friend' into a reality and the thought almost makes her smile.

In the station she refuses the offers from porters. She will need all the little money she has. Need all her wits and good fortune. Soldiers are checking the papers of someone they have stopped. Averting her face, she hurries past. She has a train to catch. Already she can hear its impatient whistle and the hiss of steam.

1956

S HE IS FALLING HEAD over heels into old age, her body
shrinking into itself, and with it comes a new danger,
except it's not the brittleness of her bones or the weariness of
the flesh that torment her now but the slow weakening of
memory. So between the lines she silently recites stray all the
scattered images of her life, each half glimpsed before it slips
back again into the deeply grooved rhythm of the words.
Endless journeys on trains, an uncertain future unfolding in
countless framed windows of ravenous forests seemingly
gorging on the body of the land; windswept steppes and
nameless villages looking back at her with faces scarred from
the years of forced collectivisation and starvation. The journeys by boat and huddled in the back of carts. And the litany
of all the backwater towns in which she has sought refuge
and sustenance keeps insisting that she also speaks their
names and when she tries to stifle them they assert their right
to be included because they too are part of everything.

Mostly small towns with nothing to offer beyond a
temporary refuge and the brief hope of living below the
surface, of never casting a shadow, and then at the first sign
of attention, or suspicious questions, abandoning the little

that has been built and moving on. During the war, when she found herself fleeing the new terror of Hitler, Akhmatova managed to get her evacuated to Tashkent. Other times she has hidden in places she couldn't with any certainty locate on a map. Terrible to have lived such a nomadic life, never sure whether at any moment they would come for her. All through the different terrors, the temporary respites as its leaders were themselves eventually consumed, only to be replaced by worse, all the times that quotas had to be met, the sweeps driven by some new paranoia. Sleeping in dormitories, back rooms, corridors, spaces that were not much more than cupboards, and never having the capacity or the need to own anything other than the basic necessities for existence.

Sometimes too she thinks of her childhood with the semblance of a smile, about all its comforts, the elegant, cultured home, the prim little English governesses straight out of *Jane Eyre* to whom she is grateful for her knowledge of English. It's often been as a teacher of languages that she has found temporary employment. Perhaps there was a greater safety in a language not her own. And she tries not to think of Anatoli Lebedev because it is an embarrassment now to remember what she almost felt and what she would have had to give up. There's no longer a consciousness of what might have been gained so much as what would have been lost and it frightens her to think that she nearly put it at risk.

She tries to insist on the purity of her memory, tries to tongue-lash it into faithful servitude with insults and curses and to banish all those names and images that aren't part of what has to be remembered. But almost imperceptibly her memory is weakening – perhaps losing a single word here or there, or the sequence of a line. To try and help she attempts to recall the very moment she wrote the poems for the first time when the words still hung on his lips, tries to hear his voice ringing true. Sometimes it comes but at others it crumbles away like a cliff being slowly eroded by the sea. And that frightens her, even more than the sound of a stopping car or the lift halting on her floor in the middle of the night.

She does not live her life, as he did not, held in the tight fist of fear, but it's always a penumbral presence whose shadowy reality can never be fully escaped. What would it be like to live a life unencumbered by that deadening weight? She can't even begin to imagine it. She lights a cigarette and sits in the room's one chair. She knows it a foolish thought but wonders if the smoke might clear her mind, the way it would some nest of bees under the eaves. So far, she tells herself, time has been on her side. The great father is finally gone, his patricide committed behind the closed doors of the Twentieth Congress and all his crimes supposedly denounced. But how much of what is whispered on the streets is truth and how much rumour? Time has aided her to this moment but now it twists and slithers things into new shapes and so she trusts nothing any longer except her anger and the strength that gives her.

She has slipped through the tightening clutch of her country's history – she remembers how in the poem about Stalin he referred to his thick worm-like fingers – and despite everything somehow she has survived. There are those who will call it a miracle but she doesn't believe in such things. She sits in a tiny room in a communal apartment surrounded by the little that she owns and smokes her cigarette. She glances around the room, austere as a monk's cell. There are few books – it is still what Akhmatova likes to call the pre-Gutenberg era and what books that come into her possession are read and passed to others. Ideas and a smattering of new literature have still survived, if only in samizdat – precious scraps and manuscripts passed from trusted hand to hand. And she thinks she has the most precious of them all inside her if only someone will come for it. Surely someone will come soon, relieve her of this responsibility that she has carried for so long and before time succeeds in blunting the sharpness of her memory.

The smoke doesn't clear any of the confusions she harbours. These are still dangerous times. Returnees come back every day, most barely recognisable as the men and women who entered the camps. They try to sift back silently into their lives and mostly never talk about what they have seen, in part because they fear that the telling will be held against them and lay themselves open to some new charge, but also because they cannot bring the terror and suffering back through words in case it finally destroys what's left of them. And there are always those who whisper that there was no smoke without fire, that they're not necessarily innocent of the crimes with which they were charged. But already she has heard of some people and some writers being rehabilitated so whatever her apprehensions she believes this is the road she must take.

When the day comes for her to go to the Writers' Union she makes a special effort with her appearance, putting on what passes for her best clothes. It's spring but she thinks herself too wise to allow herself to think of that as a portend, nor is there any great sense of change about to blossom – life feels as if it continues as it always has, although some of the hardships of the war years have ebbed away. But she takes some consolation at least from the birch trees beginning to swell towards leaf and the knowledge that she has survived what the worst of another winter could offer. It is a journey that she has made many times, often with him, but on this new day she is resolved not to go like a little mouse, not cap in hand for the doling out of meagre charity but with her head held high and looking them in the eye.

So it is her anger and her disdain for the parasites and lick-spittles that weren't worthy to be given the name of writers which fire her steps and stop her shaking inside as she enters the building that looks unchanged from before the war. But a man steps into the lift she must take just before the doors close. He looks at her, immediately recognises her and then glances away. It is Fadeyev. They are alone in the lift. She is used to being shunned by those who knew her and stares straight ahead. Fadeyev who cried when Osip read some of his poems to him in 1937 and on hearing of his death supposedly said, 'We have done away with a great poet.' But she carries other thoughts about him in her head and remembers his reaction when they had told him excitedly about being offered a temporary place in the Writers' Union rest home in Samatikha – the place that was laid out as a trap for them and from where Osip could be quietly taken. It is obvious to her now that he knew the fate that would await them but was unwilling or powerless to warn them. She remembers his farewell embrace, his Judas kiss in response to Osip's declaration that they would visit him on their return.

She stands in the lift with this man and the silent space between them seems stretched so tight and thin that it feels like it will break at any moment. The doors close, the lift begins to move. Only then does he shuffle closer and whisper in her ear, 'It was Andreyev who handled the case.' His breath smells of alcohol. Nothing more is said and when the doors open at the first floor he hurries out. So this is how it is to be now. What happened was always someone else's doing. Perhaps they think it true because they need that self-justifying belief to survive, to go on living in the world and sleep soundly in their beds. She thinks of the newsreel films that showed German citizens forced to look at the horrors of the concentration camps and knows it will never happen here. And who can ever know the truth about whose name was on the bottom of the sentence during the terrors and if it hadn't been this signature it would always have been some willing other. But one thing of which she is sure is that they will have no absolution from her, none of them.

She steps out into the corridor in which she has often been left to sit for hours on end and treated with scorn. She remembers one of the first times she came here with Osip, summoned by the censor who had taken objection to some early poem and the vitriolic treatment he had received and how as they walked away they heard him address a colleague loudly and obviously for their benefit, declaring that Osip was someone 'who would have to be watched closely' and whose views were 'suspect'. She wonders again if it might not have been possible to carve out a different future from that moment but understands that it would have demanded a price that could never have been paid.

The secretary recognises her immediately and although there is no need to identify herself she straightens and says in as clear and steady a voice as she can muster, 'I am Nadezhda Mandelstam, wife of Osip Emilievich Mandelstam.' She watches her scurry to inform Surkov of her presence and wonders how many hours she will have to wait but almost immediately he bounds out of his office and greets her with great politeness.

'Terrible things have happened,' he says as his greeting, wringing his hands as if the memory might be expunged. 'What is your situation? Tell me your situation.'

She tells him about her desire to return to Moscow and the need for a teaching job. She listens to him burble on and in her head it sounds as if he's talking about the past as a period of bad weather, a harsh winter, some almost natural playing out of the seasons.

'Do you have the poems?' he eventually asks and is almost disbelieving when she tells him she has them all.

'They are preserved,' is what she says proudly and if she could she would have the words echo through every room and corridor in the building that represented nothing more than a straitjacket for everything she holds dear.

She is almost tempted to believe that things have changed as she listens to him and there are hints of rehabilitation and a Moscow apartment to compensate for the one that was taken from them. What she does eventually get is a small widow's pension and the securing of a teaching job in

Cheboksary almost five hundred miles east of Moscow that had been previously denied to her. In the weeks that follow it slowly becomes obvious that the powers above him have poured cold water on his promises and she knows she will be forced to leave Moscow again. When she speaks to him on the phone or tries face to face she hears him increasingly use the meaningless, tightly circumspect language of the earlier years. The genie is back in the bottle. As a sop she is sent two hundred roubles and she satisfies her pride by using it to buy a copy of Osip's *Stone*.

It feels like everything has supposedly changed but everything remains the same. She wants to believe that they are sincere when they speak of publishing him again but nothing occurs to make it a reality and she begins to doubt that it will happen in her lifetime. She receives a letter from the Prosecutor telling her that Osip has been cleared of the charges brought against him in 1938 but an application to have him exonerated relating to the poem about Stalin is rejected.

There is one more thing she must do before she has to leave the city, something important that fills her with equal uncertainty but to whose lingering questions she wants answers even though she knows they may tell her more than she is able to bear. Already she has heard stories about Osip's last months in the camp from returnees, sometimes contradictory, sometimes hopelessly second or third hand, and others although fragmented carrying more semblance of truth. She feels it part of the act of preserving that whatever truth exists should be known and so she gives herself to its pursuit.

Then on a prearranged day she journeys across the city to see a man who wants her to call him only by the name of Lev who has reluctantly, and only after patient weeks of reassurance, agreed to see her. He is a survivor, a returnee, whose name has come to her through a convoluted route. She finds the apartment block in the south of the city; it looks almost identical to the one in which she has taken temporary lodging but the lift is broken and she has to climb the stairs to the fifth floor. So when she knocks on the door she is a little breathless and when he opens it and while she is still introducing herself he is more interested in peering over her shoulder.

'Were you followed here? Are you running from someone?'

She guesses he is in his late thirties, hollow-eyed and sunken-chested, withered to the bone, and already because she has seen it so often in the past she knows he has tuberculosis. Only a shock of black hair retains the vigour of his youth.

'The lift is broken,' she tells him and when she sees more reassurance is needed, 'no one has followed me.'

Still he stares over her shoulder and then to confirm her words he walks to the stairwell and peers over. Even in that short distance she can hear the wheeze in his lungs, the insistent complaint of his breathing. A woman she assumes to be his wife comes to the door. She could pass for his daughter.

'It's all right,' she says to them all. 'I bring you no trouble. No trouble, I promise.'

In a gesture that contains no sign of conviction he invites her inside while he still checks the stairs and she enters a tidy room that compensates for its basic furnishing with a neatness and sense of order. A glass jar containing bluebells sits in the middle of the table. There is a small picture of Lenin on one wall but none of Stalin. She is invited to sit at the table but when she brings out a notebook and a pencil he tells her that he doesn't want anything written down. Willing to agree with any condition he might impose she slips them away again and accepts the tea his wife offers her. She tries to break the ice by complimenting them on their apartment but it evokes little response and they continue to look at her with ill-concealed suspicion.

'Osip has been cleared of the charges that sent him to the camps,' she tells him and shows him the letter from the

Prosecutor's office. 'And the source of whatever you tell me now will never be revealed.'

He stares at the letter and looks at her and she understands that the word of a stranger must count for little to a man who has endured and survived the worst the camps could offer and she can tell that despite his condition he is a true survivor. It's something in the undiminished blue of his eyes, the way he sits straight-backed on the chair. And his hands that hold the letter are strong, strong and impeccably clean. She already knows that he's not a talker and is glad of it because too often she's had to meet with those whose versions of their encounter with Osip were garbled mishmashes of dates and places, spun out on endless tales of what they half-remembered and what they possibly imagined. And who is she to blame them when the camps destroyed any accurate concept of time and so many other human faculties? But from this survivor she already expects more and she reminds herself that he was a physicist in his former life and lets herself hope that she is talking to a man who still maintains some of the disciplines required by that profession.

'So when did you first meet Osip?' she asks but he holds his hand up to silence her, then wordlessly signals to his wife and she responds by getting a coat and with a simple bow of her head to their visitor leaves the apartment. He raises himself to his feet and for a second she thinks he too is about to go but he presses down on the splay of his fingers and then goes to a dresser and turns on the radio. It's a mixture of folk songs and martial music. Then he sits opposite her again.

'Things might be better now,' he says, 'but who can tell when the former things might return? I want to live my life for as long as possible. My wife's never heard the truth about the camps although she asks often enough. What good would it do? Better in this world to know as little as possible. And are you sure you want to hear?' He stares at her with unblinking eyes and she simply nods in reply and hopes that he can see that she too is strong.

'I met your husband, the man they called "The Poet", in September 1938 on the transport train. I had been brought from Taganka, Osip and others I think from Butyrki. We travelled east to Vladivostok. The journey was bad but stepping into the transit camp for the first time was like stepping into hell. None of us could have imagined it even in our nightmares. It was badly overcrowded, conditions you wouldn't keep animals in, lice everywhere, but because the weather hadn't turned people hadn't yet started fighting for places in the barracks. Even then there were people dying – some from disease, some because they simply gave up and chose not to live another day. And there were fights, I never saw such fights as I saw in the transit camp – a man could get his throat cut for a few crumbs of bread. The politicals weren't supposed to be in with the criminals but they hadn't sorted that yet. The most physically able were moved on to Kolyma to work on construction. Osip wasn't ever going to be one of those.'

He pauses and looks at his hands before saying, 'Right from the start he wasn't well.' Then he pauses again, this time for longer.

'He had a weak heart,' she offers.

'He wasn't well in the head,' he tells her.

She nods to show she understands and that it's all right for him to go on.

'He had a problem with food – he thought they were trying to poison him and often he ended up giving food away. He had,' he hesitates again, 'a simple nature. People could take advantage of him. And already he looked like an old man. We all ended up looking like old men but he was old from the start. But he interested me and I talked with him, got to know him, and understood he had something that others didn't. But he also wandered about too much and drew too much attention to himself just by being different. To survive in the camps firstly you need to want to more than anything else and despite everything you have to endure, to be single-minded about what it takes to survive and never draw attention to yourself. Be as close to invisible as possible – that's what's required. You understand?'

He stops, raises himself from the table again and goes into another room where she hears him spitting. Even the strident music coming from the radio can't block out the wheeze of his chest as he returns.

'I've never spoken to anyone about these things. It feels strange.'

She knows he still wants to cloak himself in invisibility, that it is only this in which he feels safe. She wants to tell him that they need voices who will be witnesses to what was done but she says nothing that will discourage him from telling her everything he knows.

His words are chosen carefully and he has no need for elaboration or stories whose purpose is to aggrandise himself or present himself as a saint. And there are times he calmly tells her of things he saw and had to do because his survival depended on it and he recounts them without either shame or pride. And she knows he's telling her both about Osip and himself, the words released for the first time. When he pauses she pours him a glass of water and his hand shakes a little as he drinks. She looks at the little bunch of bluebells and thinks of all the unmarked graves, a whole generation swallowed up by the tundra. She is suddenly struck by the intense beauty of these most simple of flowers, the deep richness of the blue, even the green stems in the water. Her eyes hold them, for a moment oblivious to everything else until he continues speaking.

'They wanted workers to go outside the camp to clear ground. I volunteered and took Osip with me. Strange to volunteer for work but it was worth it to get out of the camp that every day grew more crowded and into air and space that wasn't polluted with every conceivable disease and human weakness. We moved a few stones about and he made a joke about his book of poems being called *Stone*. Was that really what it was called? I remember thinking it was a strange name for poems.'

'Yes, that's what it was called,' she says, her voice shaking a little because in that moment it feels as if she is standing once again beside her husband, so close that she can almost reach her arms out through the years. And with those hands she wants to strip him of the tattered rags he wears, dress him in love just as she was by Vasilisa Shklovski. Wants to take him from the bareness of that wooden bunk in some forsaken barracks full of disease and suffering and bear him away in the arms of her love, carry him high so there is no wire can stop him escaping to a world that exists forever beyond their reach. And let him see these bluebells, find the words to tell their story to the world and she will write the words on her heart. Let him breathe the air. Let him see these flowers. Let him live.

'Later the weather changed, the rains came and then with them an outbreak of typhus. Prisoners got locked in their barracks and then those who were ill were placed in quarantine. Some used to believe that no one ever came back from quarantine. I got it but bluffed it out at first and then was taken first to quarantine and then to the infirmary. When I recovered I heard Osip was dead. I don't think it was typhus but no one knew for sure. Perhaps his heart just gave out.'

He shrugs his shoulders as if to say that's all he knows before he adds, 'It's not easy for you to hear but it was best for him. It meant he didn't have to suffer any more, didn't have to know what was waiting for him in Kolyma.'

She makes herself sit as straight-backed as he is then thanks him for everything he has told her and for the kindness he showed Osip. She asks a few simple questions and then understands as he grows restless that it's time for her to go – she has no wish to inflict memories on this man for any longer than is necessary. She takes a deep breath and then stands. There is nothing she can give him except her thanks and he has that already so she shakes his hand, holding it for a few seconds longer than is normal.

Then as she releases it he signals her to sit and says, 'There is one more thing. You might wish to hear it.' He hesitates until she nods her permission for him to continue. 'There was a group of criminals in one of the barracks who had marked out their own territory as was the custom but they weren't a bad bunch as criminals went. They'd barter and exchange news and although they stuck together they weren't violent – I think they were just as frightened as the rest of us. I got to know some of them. One night I was invited to join them and because I hadn't a single thing worth stealing I went to where they'd holed up and when I went in Osip was there. There was an upturned barrel and on it a candle and some white bread, bread like no other I'd seen in the camp, and Osip was reciting his poems to the sitting circle of men. They listened in silence and sometimes when he'd finished a poem they'd call for him to deliver it again. And when he spoke I never before, or after, heard such a silent listening in the camps. It stays with me. He was a great poet, wasn't he?'

'Yes, he was, he was a great poet.'

They sit in silence for a few moments then as she rises he also levers himself up from the chair and going to the dresser opens a drawer and lifts out a sheet of newspaper. She doesn't understand what he's doing and then decides he's going to show her some story but instead he lifts the bluebells out of the glass jar and wraps them in the paper.

'For the grave you don't have,' he says as he hands them to her.

Then she thanks him again and she is gone, taking the stairs and making herself think, not of death and an unmarked grave, but the light of a candle in the darkness, a loaf of white bread and the sound of poetry. It gives her something to hold on to even now when she knows all the rest. And when she steps out into the street she tilts her face up to the light and lets the strengthening sun touch it the way he used to touch it when they'd been apart.

Soon her residency permit will expire and she will have to leave Moscow again. There won't be much for her to pack, she thinks as she sits in the apartment and inspects its contents once more. Her eyes linger on the bluebells that she's placed on the small table beside her bed and which give the room its only brightness of colour. There are still things to be done, phone calls to be made. Surely they must come for the poems soon and give them back to the world. She will phone Surkov yet again and see what progress has been made by his committee that is supposed to be reviewing the situation. Not much, she guesses, and believes that there are those who are still determined to block any publication. Perhaps Osip is still too great a reminder of what was done and will always prove so. But she will not let it go, not let the poems sift and spill like sand through her hands. She has carried them this far, she will carry them further if she needs to. And of course they will be happy for her to disappear once more out of Moscow – the further the better as far as they are concerned. No one wants a constant witness to past failures haranguing them at every opportunity – some of the things she has said to the apparatchiks in the past few months would have sent her hurtling to the camps in previous years.

She lights another cigarette. She has started to smoke too much but allows herself this one indulgence. As always there is the low murmur of life from beyond the thin walls of the apartment block. Indistinct and fragmented it exists as a permanent hum in the ears, peaking into consciousness only when a baby cries or voices are raised in one of the constant disputes over the communal areas. She must find a new place to live and be settled before the winter comes. Already her body is complaining of its weariness, telling her of its reluctance to set out once more towards an uncertain destination. Has it been life's cruel joke that her name means hope? It's a question to which she never knows the answer.

But it is hope and her memory that must not fail her now, not after coming this far. She sits on the only seat and watches the evening light drifting gently through the window. Is it part of the plan for a great new world that insists they must live high in the sky like birds in little nest boxes? She stands and goes to the glass. Soon she will need to start the preparations for her journey but not just yet. They truly believed they had silenced everyone, cut or bought their tongues. One more thing about which they were mistaken and how it must fill them with the very fear in which they dealt. For now there are living tongues in the skulls of the dead and they will speak for all the nameless, voiceless ones who were swept into the abyss. There is nothing they can do to stop them. She understands this at last because whatever happens, whatever they do, there will always be those who will not hide in silence. And she has resolved in the days since hearing the circumstances of Osip's end that she is going to be her own voice, as well as the preserver of his, and write her story that is also his but also hers alone, write it for those who are still to come and who must know the truth of what was done.

Outside, soft-edged striations of clouds sift their way through a blue sky like the cigarette smoke that slowly spirals about her. She thinks of a candle, white bread and the spoken words. A sacrament, holy and true, even there, even in that place. She goes closer to the glass so that her face is almost touching its coldness. Some day the cage doors will be thrown open, bluebells planted on the grave she will never see. Her lips begin to move. A voice for the dead, the words engraved eternally on the hidden chambers of the heart.

Lydia

THE FRUIT IN THE bowl had either withered into a shrivelled blackness or else blotched itself luridly with decay. On the kitchen table a loaf of bread was white-furred and blue-measled. In the vase on the window sill the heads of flowers wilted wearily, a brown wreath of fallen petals circling its base. No one had entered the cottage after her husband's body was taken away and John Gibson's phone call had been at pains to assure her that everything remained untouched, as if he imagined that because of her absence from his final moments, she would think it important to see the scene in its final state. In the subsequent weeks, however, he had gone on cutting the grass, just as for the past twenty years. It looked as if it had been done in the previous few days and she tried to rekindle the fresh scent that had greeted her arrival in the hope of dispelling the damp mustiness now seemingly infecting every corner of the cottage.

In the grate the thick bed of ashes remained uncleared while on the black, salt-spotted hearth hunkered the final small pile of bleached driftwood that her husband had gathered. Propped open on the arm of the fireside chair was a copy of Virgil's *Aeneid* with his reading glasses resting on top – the ones he still refused to wear in public. She lifted them and from habit polished the perpetually smeared lens with the hem of her blouse, then folded the arms and set them on the mantelpiece. Closing the book she placed it beside the glasses.

The crimped seat of the leather chair still retained his creased print. Of course she should have come sooner to tidy up but something had prevented her and so when she had been summoned too late to do anything, and his body already removed to the morgue, she had simply asked John to lock and secure the place. There was the funeral organisation to preoccupy her, made both easier and more complicated by the detailed list of instructions. Even a sudden and unexpected death had not caught him unprepared for his claim on posterity and she had followed his wishes as directed with the minister firmly locked out of the service, bar a few and speedy necessities of ritual. He would have enjoyed the orations of his fellow poets, all white-haired men but with steady voices as they read the chosen poems and gave their eulogies. One chose to read a poem Don had written in the first week after they had taken ownership of the cottage located on the North Coast and renovated it as much as money had allowed. They always referred to it as the cottage even though in reality it was a rather ugly bungalow built between the wars by the local stationmaster. The poem described the expectant breakers spending themselves and then drawing slowly back into the emptiness of the starless night. A cold poem, she had always found it, but in the richness of the voice delivering it at the funeral it had momentarily assumed unfamiliar warmth.

She could hear the low thrum of the sea now and it was enough to remind her of the dampness of the cottage that seemed to clam and veil her face. It wasn't enough simply to switch on the central heating – she knew she needed to see the fire lit to disperse the coldness that lingered insistently over everything and which she wanted to dispel before her two daughters arrived in the morning. She stared at the chair again, then moved it slightly away from its place at the fire. It was where John had found him. Saw him through the window when he didn't answer the door. Dead from a heart attack at sixty-seven years of age, an attack that gave him no warning of its imminent arrival and twisted his face into a shape that made it angry and strange to her fleeting glance before the mortuary drawer had been closed again. As she had driven home she guessed his anger arose from having been given no prior sign and so had been deprived of the creative blessing of a tumour, or slow spread of cancerous cells, that would have allowed him to chart his demise, bleed every aspect of his mortality into metre.

She looked again at the leather chair in which he had died and saw its mottled and bruised patina, the whitened circle on the arm where a cup had once balanced, the fine tributary of creases where his head lolled in his daily doze. Everywhere she looked was infused with his being – the chair itself; the books and papers splayed across the desk under the window where he chose to write; the CDs out of their cases; the half-finished crossword on the side table. The force of him was always, and continued to be, so real that she found it difficult to accept that he was dead, almost expected at any moment to hear his voice. Forty years of marriage had ensured that parts of them were grafted to the other so that it wasn't possible any more to know where she ended and he began. But already she had begun to feel different and she thought that what she felt was lighter, freer and at the same time a little frightened of feeling these things when it was still as if he was the ever-present observer and attempted scribe of even her hidden parts. She looked at the glasses on the mantelpiece watching her and, seeing their case on the table acting as a paperweight, placed them inside and snapped the lid.

What she knew she had to do now was complete her last duties before she could be absolved and finally released. She turned again to the fire and taking off her coat knelt to light it but as she did so remembered the urn was still in the car, wedged in the back between her case and the Tesco bags of groceries she had stopped for on the way to the coast. She knew the girls were not staying any longer than was needed before they scurried back to their lives in London and in truth neither of them had displayed much enthusiasm for returning so soon after the funeral, even when she had relayed their father's wishes for his final leave-taking. So the fact that they had eventually agreed to come after conferring with each other at some length was due, she guessed, to her need and what she hoped had been the subtle calling in of past favours. She didn't want to do it on her own, didn't want even to be there alone in the cottage if truth be told because it didn't fully feel as if she was on her own and his insistent presence was unsettling and edged with too many things she didn't want to think about.

She had to empty the overflowing ash pan from the grate, silently criticising him for his lack of diligence, and taking it out through the back door deposited its contents in the ash pile at the corner of the low hedge that separated the small garden from the ploughed field beyond. Then going back inside she lit the fire, using the last of the firelighters and the dried-out bits of driftwood before adding coal from the plastic bucket. He always insisted he couldn't feel warm unless he could see flames. A lifetime earlier during their courtship he had once asked her what she could see in the fire and she hadn't understood and so said something about flames and coal and he had laughed and called her a literalist, teased her about an absence of imagination. As the wood caught it hissed and crackled in protest. It was the last of his gathering in and now she saw many different things in the flames. He often liked to describe himself as nothing more than a beachcomber. But she knew enough to know that little in words was ever simply itself and that everything was loaded with some reverberating meaning.

Warming her palms against the gradually growing flames she pressed them together as if in momentary prayer. But she didn't pray any more – that was something he had taken away from her right at the start with his bitter mockery of what he saw only as superstition and backwardness. There was only ever room for one God in their marriage and it wasn't one who watched over them from some heavenly paradise, and without him ever expressing it in words she knew that what she was supposed to worship was poetry, which he habitually declared was the highest form of art. Everything else – her, the children, their lost son, the daily realities of living – all were subservient to that deity. And as she levered a little air into the base of the fire she wondered how the poet and his art had become so indistinguishable in his mind. When had he first assumed this divinity?

She couldn't remember but took some pleasure from knowing that it wasn't imagination had paid for the refurbishment and extension of the cottage – the putting on of a new roof, installing central heating and an updated kitchen and bathroom – and it wasn't imagination that had put food on the family table and paid the bills down all the years. The cottage itself had been left to them by her mother and although almost immediately he had annexed it as a place for writing, the actual house was part of her childhood summers when all the family had come up from the city and spent most of each July and August there, in what was now only a blurred haze of roaming through days that seemed to stretch slowly to remote and gentle dusks. He had smothered her memories with the press of his own which insisted on their primacy through the reality of his printed words. So she struggled to recall much beyond the fishing trips in the bay in Gibson's boat, catching crabs in buckets or the occasional dance up in the church hall.

Mostly now when she thought of the past it was his memories that loomed large and subsumed hers. His early poems had often proved his most popular, worming their way regularly into anthologies about childhood and the new collection to be used in Northern schools. There was 'Home Calling', describing their childish games 'in streets shadowed by dusk and the silhouettes of cranes' where they played until the shout of his father summoned him home. She thought it strange that no one had ever queried how his home in the Edwardian suburbs had been shadowed by shipyard cranes but, if they had, he would no doubt have explained it as poetic licence.

Poetic licence. Yes, that was what he based his life on, a licence to be selfish, eternally happy taking the comforts of her labours in a frequently dull nine to five job while contributing little himself to the budget beyond a few meagre bursaries that were a spit in the ocean of the cost of raising a family and keeping a roof over their heads. If poetry was such a rich and beneficent god why did it pay so much less to its followers than just about any other profession? No one bought poetry, no publishers had doled out huge advances for any of his five slim volumes and if he could muster an audience at festivals or readings and sustained a decent reputation, it never translated into financial security. For that he was reliant on her and her former life of managing in the public health service where there were never enough beds, never enough staff and never enough money to make her job seem anything other than a constant exercise in trying to cut a shrinking cloth to match an expanding coat. She could have accepted it because she knew her children benefited from her career if he hadn't always affected an indifference to money while expecting what it provided. And she had never fully lost her irritation at the memory of how the children in their late teens had taken in conversation to ignoring her daily job that supplied everything they had, and instead enjoyed luxuriating in the attention generated when people realised their father was a poet. His dying was the most financially generous thing he had ever done and the life insurance policy she had taken out coupled with her modest pension ensured that she would survive. It was possible that she would have to sell the cottage, particularly as her daughters seemed intent on taking their holidays in more sophisticated locations and showed little desire to revisit the scene of so many of their childhood summers. But that was a decision for the future.

She went into the kitchen, put the kettle on and then started to clear out the fridge, almost retching at the curdled sourness of the milk. At first she looked at sell-by dates but then simply swept everything into a plastic bag and knotted it for the bin then sprayed the inside of the fridge quickly and wiped it with a clean cloth. After she had finished she went to the car to bring in the bags of groceries. Out in the bay a light was winking green and she paused to let the smell of the sea spread through her senses. The vestiges of summer light were still strong enough to let her look across to the headland of Donegal. Closer by there were lights on in the clubhouse of the links golf course and on the beach an elderly man was walking his dog, its scurrying scampering speed in sharp contrast to the slow pace of its owner.

'It's good to see you, Lydia,' John said and his unseen approach made her jump. 'I saw your smoke. I came up to see if you need anything.'

'Thanks, John. I was going to call down later after I get everything unpacked. And thanks for cutting the grass. If you're happy, we'll continue with the normal arrangement.' She was conscious of the urn and transferring a bag from her right hand gently closed the boot.

'Sure it's no trouble. Can I help you with those bags?'

Knowing it would be easier to accept his offer than decline she handed him the two bags and when he had started towards the door of the cottage she opened the boot again and draped her waterproof coat over the urn. There were only a few more bags and she gathered them up quickly.

'Go on in, John,' she called as she saw him hesitate at the door. 'I'm just locking the car.'

A gentle man imbued with diffidence and manners. Someone who never left the village and who worked for the local council in their parks and cemeteries department until he too retired. It was his father's boat they used to go fishing in all those years ago. At the funeral in Belfast she had hardly recognised him in a suit whose wide lapels suggested it had been bought in the eighties. Afterwards he and his wife Gillian had almost apologised to her for coming and she thought the occasion had been an intimidating one for them but she had appreciated their presence as much as any dignitary's. She would give them something when it was all over – one of Don's books signed to them perhaps and a small cheque if she came eventually to sell up.

'Strange without him,' John said as he placed the bags on the kitchen table. 'I was used to going by the house and seeing him sitting working at his desk in front of the window. Worked all hours, he did. Looking for the words, I suppose.' He wiped the back of his hand slowly across his mouth as if his own words had surprised him and some embarrassing residue still lingered on his lips.

'Looking for the words. That's right, John. Will you stay for a cup of tea? – the kettle's on.' But she knew him well enough to guess that he wouldn't and when he thanked her but declined she followed him back to the door. 'Say hello to Gillian for me. I appreciate you both coming to the funeral. The girls are coming up tomorrow for a day or so. Call in and we'll speak soon.'

In reply he simply nodded and took his familiar slow walk back down the path. There was a light breeze drifting in laden with the scent of the night sea as thin curlicues of white fretted the shifting blackness of the surface that stretched immeasurably into the distance.

She took her cup of tea and sat down on a footstool close to the fire. Some of the driftwood crackled and a little shower of sparks sprayed to the hearth. She looked at the small black burn marks stippling the carpet in front of the grate and smoothed her foot across them as if this might rub them away. He was always one for burning wood. Sometimes she thought he would set the chimney on fire. Once he burned a review he didn't like – cremated the whole newspaper, stuffing it into the grate then pushing it in with a stick as the flames made it fan open. Of course it was the drama of it he liked best. Not that he had many bad reviews – it was all too incestuous for that, too much of a boys' club and in a world that was based on a tight network of connections, no one was going to rock the boat or venture into dissent, even if she suspected his work was increasingly seen by some as old-fashioned. And yet always below his surface simmered the bitter awareness that his talents, and thus his recognition, fell short of the truly great Northern poets who throughout his career had taken all the prizes that were on offer.

It always pleased him to appear magnanimous. If only everyone had known what resentments, what paranoid jeal-ousies, what acute divination he possessed for any possible slight, lingered just below the surface of his engaging embrace of newly-fledged poets, they wouldn't have been so quick to flush with the pleasure of his commendation. And no one got more encouragement than those young women whose talents, however meagre, combined with prettiness. She tried not to think of the women but the more she tried the more the fire seemed to spark the memories until their faces and names flared lambent in its spreading flame. The ones she knew about. And she was glad not to know about the others. By now she should have been simply weary of it all but some-thing insisted on tipping her into new anger and both her trembling hands clasped the cup as if holding a bitter chalice, frightened that at any moment it might overflow and spill each of the old hurts into fresh life.

There was Lorna the university librarian – she was probably the first – a raven-haired stick of a woman with plucked eyebrows and tight skirts who looked as if she had been pressed thin between the pages of the legal tomes she so zealously guarded. Publishers' editors – at least two of those. Did they see it as an additional accomplishment on their CVs? Always convenient on his trips to London and no doubt available to him like room service. Their faces and names existed now only vaguely in her memory but she saw them as wide-eyed public school girls with plummy voices shimmering out of red-lipsticked mouths who no doubt thought it would be an opportunity missed if they had passed on such an intimate literary connection. Then in later years there were the research students, Americans mostly, chasing some ludicrously titled dissertation that was invariably rooted in a misty-eyed vision of Romantic Ireland and who inevitably claimed some distant lineage to the land. These were also the most persistent, insensitive in the frequency of their contacts and simpering requests for just one more answer. All of them used and discarded – he probably wouldn't even have remembered their names after a few years had passed and eventually she presumed they tired of sending him unanswered emails, or ignored invitations to read their finished opuses. Except for Antonia of course. That memory at least made her smile just as the fire released a sudden corroborating cackle.

Outside the wind was rising and it sneaked in under the roof tiles, momentarily stretching and lifting them into a shudder of protest. A little spume of smoke blew into the room and she tried to fan it away with her hand. 'A bunny boiler' he had called her and perhaps the reference to a film she knew he had never seen was apt enough. A stalking bunny boiler who was clearly unbalanced by whatever intimacy had passed between them, and who had foolishly mistaken it for a future promise of a relationship that instead ended as soon as it had begun. He had come whining to her like a little boy, unnerved by the intensity of the harpy who seemed to have shed all other aspects of her life in pursuit of this one true faith and whose lurking presence suddenly shadowed every waking part of his daily round. She was in his in-box, on the end of his phone late at night murmuring her incantatory affirmations like a demented Molly Bloom or perched in the front row of his every reading or appearance like a hooded crow with her black scapula of wiry hair. Once after supper they had glimpsed her hiding in the shrubbery of the garden. She had taken pleasure in the episode, asking repeatedly with feigned innocence what would have made this woman behave in such a way and amusing herself by nodding with apparent sincerity when he had attributed it to some kind of mental breakdown.

It was a matter of some teasing regret that Antonia's visa had proved to have long expired and allowed the university to pack her quickly back to America. She had enjoyed the momentary pulse of fear her crazed pursuit had injected into his ordered existence, the little shiver he had experienced of things spiralling out of his rigid control. But what was it with these women? It was true that right through to his death, he retained a rough-hewn, slender handsomeness, his tall straight back unstooped, his once red hair weathered into bronze and then aided and abetted into lingering colour by what came out of a bottle. For all his vanity his strong green eyes never became clouded or lost their piercing vigour. But as she stared at the fire's secret caverns she told herself that the physical alone couldn't explain the attachments he'd forged during his life. Did they think he'd immortalise them in sonnets? Did they think that when he spent himself he expelled his desire in iambic pentameters? Or was it the mystery that enthralled them – the connection they hoped to make with some primitive force of the imagination that would quicken them into their own richness of life? It was too easy for her now to say that she herself had never sought that quickening and too easy for her to lay all the blame for that at his feet. The sourness of that knowledge felt sharp in her mouth and for a second she thought of spitting it into the fire but even that angry impulse beached itself on pitiful hesitation.

The tea was cold now but she went on holding it. Perhaps she had never been brave enough, then gradually over the years when passion had settled to the mundane necessities of a marriage, she had let herself be worn down by the unspoken force of his will and bending her life to the ever-present, future possibility of what might flow from his pen had become a way of thinking, an unchallenged way of living. Once she had taken pleasure at each new arrival, counting it as a blessing, the bestowing of the gift that shed penumbral light on her, but even that had faded and it was her children who brought her what was needed to survive the gradual fraying and unravelling of daily life. She thought of her two daughters arriving in the morning. She thought of her lost son who would never come home. If she sat any longer she knew she would cry so getting up she took her cup to the kitchen and drained what little was left of its contents. The empty Tesco bags reminded her of the urn still in the car but she didn't want to bring it in, didn't want to share the night with him, because she knew that deep down he had resented their children. Loved them too of course but hiding somewhere deep inside his love, she believed, was the thought that they were interlopers who distracted her and at times him from what should have been their primary service.

She placed the last of the wood on the fire and tried not to see anything other than what was there and tried too not to think of Roseanne. But it was as if her name was whispered by the wind that snaked about the outside of the cottage trembling the thin-paned windows that they had never got round to replacing with double-glazing. Roseanne, not one to be so easily blanked out or relegated to the status of a passing ship in the night. But it wasn't bitterness that she felt about her now even though she was the one who had lasted the longest and the one for whom she guessed he had felt something that might have been as true and real as love. At the funeral she had been there and crying real tears, her eyes still wet as they brushed cheeks. Perhaps she would have been right for him. His intellectual equal and if only a little younger still holding on stubbornly to the fading flush of her beauty. A poet herself, a writer, a permanent player in the world of the arts, their relationship had endured over two decades. She had been in the cottage on a range of occasions, ostensibly for interviews or features she had been writing – probably had slept with him here too. If anyone should have been on the beach for the final farewell she knew it was Roseanne but thankfully he had thought better of including that prescription on his list and, even if he had, she couldn't have inflicted such embarrassment on their children.

Knowing she couldn't put it off any longer she went to the car and lifted out the urn. She hoped the wind would have died away before the early-morning ceremony that he had scripted. As if to find the answer she looked up at black-blotched clouds that looked raddled at their edges and heard the strangled cries of the gulls buffeted by the currents. Perhaps she had been foolish to listen to his voice beyond the grave and shouldn't have persuaded the girls to make the trip that they had already hinted was a significant and unexpected inconvenience. But she had done everything else in accordance with his wishes and so she felt she should see this last obligation met and it was also the case that she didn't want to do it on her own, didn't want to be with him on her own ever again. It was foolish but she had started to think any divergence from his written wishes would incur his displeasure, a displeasure that might somehow find its own assertive way of making itself known. She wanted it finished. So the girls after flying in from London would come from Belfast on the train and she'd meet them at the station, they'd do it the following morning and then later that same day she'd drive them both back to the airport.

She carried the urn into the house, placed it on the mantelpiece then lifted it down and looked for somewhere less conspicuous. She tried different places, setting it down carefully and observing it as if it were a decorative vase to be placed in the finishing touch to an interior design, but nowhere seemed right and so she placed it on the slate hearth where the driftwood for the fire had been, then going to the kitchen opened one of the two bottles of wine she had brought.

Of her two daughters Anna had taken the most persuasion. The first phone call had ended with the impression that she couldn't possibly come as she cited work commitments and the importance of the story she was working on for the paper about the exploitation of illegal immigrants and how it had a deadline that she was struggling to meet. Perhaps it was the absence of angry argument on her mother's behalf that had managed to win the day; perhaps it was because she had asked for her presence in a manner that made it seem like a personal kindness. Maybe it was simply the filial guilt of the child who has made her way in the world without ever feeling the need to look back. Whatever the reason, an hour later there had been a phone call reversing her initial decision. And she was glad Anna was coming because a ten-year career in journalism had made her, if not hard-nosed, then strongly self-confident and perhaps she could draw on some of her daughter's strength until the curtain had fallen on this, his final little public performance.

If equally unenthusiastic, Francesca had been more readily compliant to the request. She had been the daughter who was most upset at the funeral and she had held her mother's hand throughout the service, in what felt like not so much an attempt to offer comfort but a need to receive it. Strange to see such outpouring of emotion for a father who had so often withheld his blessing from her. 'Let him go, Francesca,' she had whispered to her. 'Let him go.' Let a father go who had teased her constantly and with what sometimes felt like barbs about a career and a small business she had started in London, designing and making wedding dresses and hats for the city's wealthy. Perhaps he deemed it an unworthy occupation for a daughter of his. 'Coating debutantes in icing sugar' was how he had described it, smirking at his own wit and giving no credit for all the hard slog and commitment she had invested in it over the years, building it up from nothing after she had finished her art college degree. Now she was trying like everyone else to ride out the recession and never once had she asked for, or had they been able to give her, any form of financial support.

At least with Anna, even though he espoused to despise the popular press – 'carrion crows pecking over the living and the dead' was how he liked to characterise it – there had been a begrudging respect for a profession involving words. The one thing that irritated Anna, however, was his occasional and completely erroneous hint that being his daughter must have advantaged her and advanced her career. Whereas Francesca was never fully able to protect her own vulnerability, Anna as she grew up welcomed the jousting and often gave as good as she got. As a teenager she had sussed out her father's shining lights and then enjoyed sniping at them and comparing them unfavourably to others she knew he looked down upon or resented. Sometimes in passing she would quote stanzas at him from inane pop songs and then proclaim, 'That's real poetry.'

So why was it that Anna had stood stony-faced while Francesca had cried like a child? She poured herself another glass of wine and the light from the fire suffused it as she turned it slowly in her hand. Was it that Francesca realised that now she would never receive the father's approval she had secretly longed for? They had never been a family that went in for ostentatious or revelatory expressions of emotion and if it was possible these had diminished even further after the death of Rory. She knew if she were to think now of Rory everything would fall apart more than it already had and she had to get over this final hurdle so she stood up and walked to the window but the glass gave her nothing except her own vague reflection. Behind her the fire sparked and in the still-unlit room a frantic flurry of shadow flames stuttered against the white walls. Suddenly she felt confined and wanted the freedom of the night so draining the last of the wine she rested the glass on his desk, set the fireguard in place and putting on her coat walked across the road and took the narrow path through the dunes.

The razor-edged grass fawned up round her legs but she knew better than to touch it having discovered as a child its power to cut. In the new holiday apartment block that nestled beside the golf course there was only one lit window. She had signed the petition objecting to its planning approval. He too had fumed at the proposal, even broken his lifelong resistance to signing petitions – he hadn't even signed the one about the war in Iraq, or the cuts to arts funding. Perhaps he had been swayed by the naïve belief of the organisers that his name on their petition would carry weight with the planners, perhaps even believed it himself, then fumed even more when it proved an illusion. She didn't mind the apartments that were generally only occupied at weekends or during the holiday periods, believing that they brought a renewed sense of life to the place with children wearing wetsuits in the summer sea and the smell of barbecues. The extra income helped the few local shops and everyone seemed able to rub along without any problems.

And the recession had occurred at the right time in the sense that it was unlikely that developers would now move in wholesale as they had done in other places on the coast and apartment it out of recognition.

As she stumbled a little on the downward path to the beach it was the breeze off the sea that was keen against her face as it tousled her hair and for a second she thought of returning to the heat of the fire but then remembered how confined she had felt and strode out briskly along the length of the beach. The tide was slowly going out and she walked where the reclaimed sand sheened and stretched cleanly ahead of her. It suddenly struck her that perhaps she should have checked the tides. Would it be incoming or outgoing when the moment came? And did it matter? She thought of *David Copperfield* and the death of Barkis and how Mr Peggotty tells David that people can't die along the coast 'except when the tide's pretty nigh out'. Would there be an early-morning tide to take his ashes out? She told herself that it didn't matter, that despite the time he spent in the cottage, despite his description of himself as a beachcomber, he was a city person. She looked again for the green light but it had disappeared and in the dropping light the horizon smeared into a blurred bevel of charcoal. Her daughters would come in the morning and she was glad because already she understood that there was a price to be paid for what she had earlier felt as lightness but which had now slowly edged into an awareness that she was alone. Whatever loneliness she had experienced in her forty-year marriage had been one that ebbed and flowed in her head and ulti-mately always faded away when faced with the requirements of daily living. Now there seemed no escape from its reality and although she told herself that being alone wasn't the same as loneliness she was unable to distinguish any differ-ence between the two states as her feet suddenly sank a little into softer sand.

Was it foolish nostalgia, a selective amnesia, that now made her think of their early days when what existed between them seemed like a force of nature, when he had blown into her life with all the strength of instinct and impulse that rendered every practical consideration inconsequential? He cared nothing for the things she had been told it was important to believe in, and because she hadn't ever known why exactly she too should believe in them, they had been swept away in the flood of what she could give no other name to than passion. Despite the cold that peppered her cheekbones and made her pull the collar of her coat higher she warmed with the heat of the memory. Five years younger than him and with only the thinnest knowledge of books or poetry, it seemed like an adventure that life had never given her and might not ever give again. And yes he did woo her with words, whispering them in her ear like the sea's soft lace that now frilled and lightly enticed the shore. He had taken all of her – no, that wasn't true – she had given all of herself with not so much as a glance backwards or forwards but desperate only to exist in the moment where it seemed that there resided everything that she could ever need. And yes she was there in some of the earliest poems, unnamed but woven in the weft and warp of the words. If there wasn't a single one dedicated formally to her she knew she was part of some, even if it was only because she had stood in the shadow of the described experience.

A long time ago. A lifetime away. A time when he knew how to be light and funny, skilled in impersonation and accents, a lover of a late-night drink and a well-told joke. What had blunted that? What had stopped the whispered words in those closest moments that spoke as often as not of the sun, the moon and the stars? Perhaps it was her fault. Perhaps in the end she could never be enough to satisfy whatever need it was that rendered him distant, making him drift slowly away into some other orbit that she could only barely glimpse and never explore. Even when he came back to her it was never the same, and never was there that sweet tumble of mysterious and only half-understood words that he had used to woo her. She thought of Desdemona and the greed with which she devoured Othello's tales then swept it aside with the knowledge that whatever emotions she had once stirred in her word-spinning lover, none had ever achieved the intensity of jealousy.

They never collided in anger; he never humiliated her in public or criticised her. Perhaps he didn't need to. Instead there was just a slow release like clasped hands gradually slipping the tightness of their grip and then both of them falling slowly backwards into the separate pathways of their lives.

A man was fishing on the rocks at the end of the pier, his casting arm flung out over the sea but the line invisible in the dusk. She would walk along the stone pier that was girdled on both sides by protective rocks and speak to him. Ask him if he had caught anything. She'd ask him if it was her fault for not being enough. If she should have built her own life and tried to find someone who would love her for what she was and only ever use words that were true and which would endure longer than it took a flurry of passion to spend itself. There had been someone else – just the one and lasting no more than a few months. Almost twenty years ago a work colleague looking for comfort on the back of his divorce and afterwards nothing but a daily embarrassment until he had applied for a transfer. If anything she was glad when he'd made his escape, knew she had done it merely as a sad little kickback against her husband's latest indiscretion but it had only made things worse, when despite her hints and willingness to avow confessional remorse, she had faltered into silence against the bulwark of his indifference.

There was a green light blinking again. She thought of Gatsby standing in supplication to the light at the end of Daisy's pier. That was one thing for which she should be grateful – her self-education, her diligent pursuit of books. And if that too had failed to make her worthy then at least it had bestowed a pleasure and a critical knowledge that she could use. So in time she was able to recognise the weaker of his poems, the ones that were space fillers, the ones she knew without being told were what he labelled as 'confetti' and those that deserved the praise. The poems that were truest worried her most because she couldn't bring herself to understand how such perfect truth could spring from someone who was so frequently false. These she found threatening in that they seemed able to rise up above her and shadow her, almost taunting her with their complete detachment from the life the world assumed they shared.

She looked back to the shore where the sea-facing houses had their uncurtained windows lit. No need to draw them perhaps when all that peered in was the sea. A bird teased and skimmed itself across the water, its wings almost touching the springing snare of the waves. Her feet crunched an unseen shell. Once she had tried to write her own poems, hiding them scrupulously from his gaze before her fear of his discovering them and imagining the scorn of his laughter made her destroy them, cutting each into the tiniest fragments as if they were love letters that if discovered might destroy her life. It made her hope that on the morning after next when she would gather with her daughters in this very place that the wind would have died away and the tide would be outgoing, taking the final remnants of his being far out to distant seas.

She wanted Rory to be there. Her only son, sweet as love in her memory. She wanted him somehow to come back to her through the years. Her feet stumbled in a wedge of soft sand and when she momentarily stretched out her hands it felt as if her body was reaching to pull him back from the grasp of death.

She could never forgive Don for Rory because he alone had been allowed to reclaim her son. Reclaimed him in the eight sonnets he had written about their lost child with his supposed heartbreak preserved forever in the eyes of the world. And so even in grief he had made her subservient and what she suffered in the most terrible pain she had ever known had found no voice or release, every last corrosive drop of it gnawing away at her over the years as again and again readers of the poems offered him their sympathy. A sympathy he had never shared, in the same way he had never sought to shoulder or try to salve any of what she had endured. And in not a single poem was the love with which she had brought her son into the world and given him every one of his twenty-seven years. So the loss and grief was all his father's, a father who through his son's life had never been anything but disinterested and remote, in later years even that being replaced by a growing sense of frustration at his supposed lack of career.

She reached out to her child now and pulled him from the shades into the fragmenting light of her memory so that for a second as she bowed her head lower against the wind, he was there with her because she made herself believe that love was always stronger than words, and it was the force of her love alone that caused him now to form silently about her. Her son who loved mountains and high places, whose restless adventurous spirit made him travel to worlds she could only dream of and who sent her postcards with his flowing excited writing that always told her not to worry. And he's there now as if made of grains of light with his eyes washed clean of death by the soft shuck of the sea's caress and he flows around her and when she asks him if he's all right he rests his arm on her shoulder the way he always did and he's telling her not to worry, that every-thing's all right and that he's coming home soon. He's coming home soon and the words repeat like a whisper to which she holds tightly. That's good, she says, and tells him she'll air his room and stock up the fridge because he's always a little thinner when he comes home. Once, after a longer climbing trip, he'd looked like a bag of bones and when he'd put on the fresh clothes from his drawer they'd hung so loosely on him that he looked like a man wearing someone else's things. She tries to see what he's wearing now but as the serried waves suddenly break white and the man fishing casts his arm towards the sea he's already slipping away again. She calls his name aloud but it's as if that too is borne away by the wind and the ceaseless ebb of the sea so all that flows around her now are the night's currents and she wants to shout that the borrowed clothes of death he wears belong to someone else. To someone else. To his father. She'll give them back to her husband, a man of whom the world thinks highly. She'll dress him in them freely and unconditionally but just let them have her son a little longer.

The cries of gulls blown ragged by the wind sliced through the stillness of the night before slipping into silence but their echoes lingered and she turned her eyes again to where the man fishing stood motionless at the end of the pier. Might even he not help save her son and stop him fading back below the waves? Catch him on the soft hook of her love. She strode out more quickly, reaching the end of the beach then tracing the line of rocks until she found a point where it was possible to step up on to the concrete pier. It always felt like a path that was taking you into the sea itself and there was a warning sign cautioning that it could be subject to strong waves. When they were children they had often fished for crabs off the end but she had always felt a little unsafe, frightened when the others had laughed if a sudden burst of spray showered over them.

The moon had appeared now but was soon smothered again into vagueness by clouds. The swell of the sea seemed to surge more strongly as it splashed white against the girdle of rocks on either side. She hoped that her footsteps would

announce her approach because she didn't want to material-
ise suddenly out of the gloom. Then she hesitated and thought
of going back as she turned and looked at the lights illumi-
nating the bar of the clubhouse. It was one of his haunts
although he never played and despised all sports. Sometimes
too he took an evening meal there. He did fish occasionally,
if mostly without much success, and had stood in the very
place that was occupied now by the solitary figure casting his
arm slowly and gracefully towards the dark shift of the sea.
She decided it was too late to turn back and that to do so
would suggest an unwillingness to make the human contact
on which the village put so much store. A few words to pass
herself would be enough and then she'd return to the cottage
and start to do all the things that needed to be done before
her daughters arrived.

But she hesitated as some of her old childhood apprehensions returned when the sudden surge of a wave splashed a
little spray around her feet. She glanced again at the figure
now standing motionless and in a sudden pulse of fear imagined that it was her husband. The same height and weight,
the same straight-backed stance that made it seem as if he
was braced against whatever the world might throw at him.
Slipping out from cloud the moon quivered the water with
thin shards of light. And if he looked at her now she knew
that his face would be frozen into that same anger that was
the last expression he had shown her. She stood perfectly still
unwilling to go another step but at that very moment the
figure turned and raised his arm slowly in greeting. She
couldn't go back; she had to go forward to the end. The path
seemed to have grown narrower, the press of the sea stronger.
The concrete underfoot was pitted and uneven. He was wearing a waterproof coat and a woollen hat and she was near
enough now to recognise his face although she didn't know
his name. As she came close he set the fishing rod at his feet
and faced her, almost as if he was waiting for her to arrive.

'Not a bad evening,' he said, pushing his hat off his forehead.

'Any luck?' she asked.

'It's giving nothing back tonight.' He pointed with his toe to the two tiny fish, ivory notes against the blackness of his boots. 'The most it's shared with me is a couple of hours of peace and quiet so I suppose I shouldn't complain.'

'Two small fish – all you need now are five barley loaves and you'd have a miracle.'

'A miracle indeed if you could feed five thousand with these.'

He lifted them up and dropped them into a white plastic bag then stretched it out towards her. 'Could you use these?'

She didn't want them, wanted nothing more that was dead about her, but it was a kindness that she knew she couldn't refuse so she thanked him and took the bag. Then he bent down and started to pack away his stuff. The moon slipped momentarily behind clouds once more and she stopped herself asking him if he had seen her son, if he could help her pull him back from the sea where he floundered alone and beyond her reach.

'I'm sorry for your loss,' he said as he stood up again, before scattering what looked like tiny boluses of bread on the surface of the water.

She thought of her son but said, 'You knew my husband?'

'He fished here a few times but I think he was better with words than he was at catching fish.'

'You've read his work?'

'Aye, I've read a couple. My son brought a book home from school. He'd a way of expressing things all right.'

There was silence for a few moments and then she thanked him again and headed back down the pier. Along the shore road there was a seam of yellow house lights, made brighter by the thickening darkness. The wind had fallen away as if exhausted by its earlier efforts and only the occasional ragged splinter of moonlight scratched the blackness of the sea. She didn't return to the cottage by the sand dunes for fear of tripping and falling but took the longer way through the main entrance then up to the road. The fish weighed almost nothing and if it hadn't been too late for them she would have given them back to the sea so when she reached the front door she paused for a second, unwilling to bring them inside, then took her key out of the lock and, going round to the rear garden, set the two small slivers of almost perfect white on the pyre of ash.

There was work to be done and in preparation she had brought black bin bags and some cardboard boxes. She started in the wardrobe, lifting out the clothes that hung there and folding them into the bags. There was a faint smell of must and one of the older pairs of trousers had white spots. There was too another sour smell that reminded her of tobacco although he had never smoked. The metal hangers trilled excitedly in the almost empty wardrobe. She would dump the bags at one of the local recycling points. It was a job she had already carried out at home and in truth there weren't that many clothes he kept in the cottage. She lifted his walking boots from the bottom of the wardrobe and realised the sour smell was from the soil trapped in the grooves and ridges of the soles. Why he had stored them uncleaned in the bottom of the wardrobe she didn't know. She held them at arm's length and thought of all the places that he had walked in them, the same times when they were most happy together, and then sitting down on the edge of the bed remembered that he had worn them in the Atlas Mountains in Morocco when they had brought Rory home. She let them fall and stared at the way the long laces spiralled on the floor.

The Atlas Mountains, white-capped in the distance despite the trembling waves of heat that separated them from the city and where she stood on the rooftop of the small riad in which he had chosen for them to stay overnight. The call to worship, a call that she would never heed now that God had taken her only son – about that at least Don had been right – rubbed raw at the edge of her senses and she wanted to salve it with an angry spew of words and a desperate insistence that it was all a terrible mistake and when they reached him he'd greet her with his arm outstretched, the gesture that always invited her to shelter under the shadow of his love. Staring at the white peaks of the distant mountains across the pink-walled houses with their satellite dishes and rooftop washing hanging to dry. Staring across the walls of the old palace where storks nested on woven beds of sticks. Crying in a strange country where the heat of the day pressed right to the edge of the settling darkness and gave no respite or mercy. Never had she felt so far away from home and yet needed to go even further, to travel in the morning with her husband and the official from the consul to identify their son and begin his return journey. From the nearby square drifted the babble of drums and voices while in the courtyard below he sat at a mosaic-topped table lit by candles and already writing in one of the black Moleskine notebooks that he always carried with him. Already writing his loss and his pain for the world to read. Who would read hers? Who would understand the slow pulling apart of her heart until it felt as if all that existed was an immeasurable abyss into which she was free-falling without knowing when she would ever reach its lowest point?

She sat motionless on the edge of the bed and for a moment felt as if all her energy had drained away then turning her face caught her reflection in the wardrobe mirror. Her hair was shapeless and pressed flat as if she had been wearing a hat, cut short and too severe, and at the age of sixty-two she had given up the trouble and expense of having it coloured. Let come what will. No man would ever desire her again but she wanted no desire except to live the rest of her life with as little pain as possible and to see her daughters happy. She wouldn't let herself go and resolved to keep making the effort if only for their sakes but she sensed a weariness spreading through her like she had never known before. The earlier sense of lightness now seemed an illusion, a mere carrying on a temporary current of air that had fallen away, so it was with an effort of will that she made herself get up again and place the boots in a separate smaller plastic bag then knot it tightly.

There was so much more to be done before the morning – it seemed important to her to have everything cleared and aired before her daughters arrived. She didn't want that sense of damp, of must and untidiness, lingering over what might be their last memory of the cottage. She sat on the bed as if tired again and wondered if her daughters had instinctively understood the slipping grasp of love that was their parents' marriage and in that realisation had absorbed a reluctance to follow a similar path. It upset her to think that this might be so and suddenly drained of will she curled herself on top of the bed and faced the almost empty wardrobe.

As a comfort she told herself that in those early years, when Don was still taken by the novelty of fatherhood and had enjoyed the children, they'd given them a secure and happy childhood. C. S. Lewis had once taken summer holidays in the village and she remembered how the children gathered avidly at the cottage fire and Don would read the Narnia stories, pleased when they wouldn't allow him to stop. A lifetime away. She looked at the black bin bags and the empty wardrobe that suddenly seemed cavernous and tried to remember how it felt when love first invited you to step inside and share its mystery but the welter of the intervening years made it impossible to recall that first flush of light, the sense of stepping where no other footsteps had ever smirched the snow. Then she got off the bed and grabbed the last item – his blue dressing gown – and knew if it had been a film she would have pressed it to her face and inhaled the vestiges of the loved-one but instead, already feeling angry at the foolish fancy of her earlier imagination, held its clogged and matted mustiness at arm's length, then quickly bundled it into a bag where it bulged outwards against a tear in the over-stretched plastic.

She carried the bags out to the car and threw them in the back – there'd be time to leave them off before her daughters' arrival. They smudged against each other like giant plums with their skin bruised and leaking. When she went inside again she sat down at the fire with another glass of wine. She would have liked to burn everything but it wasn't physically possible and would have taken too long, not to say risk setting the chimney on fire. It was when the children had grown older that he had lost interest in them, when they no longer needed him and slowly realised that after all he wasn't Aslan. He had become a kind of commentator on their lives rather than a participant, watching from an increasingly remote and critical position, forever prone to the same complaint that no one told him anything. She could never forgive him for the disappointment he had felt in them whatever they achieved and how at times he had deliberately let that disappointment, even when it was unspoken, leach into their consciousness.

He'd driven them away, driven her children away from her so that all of them had sought lives far from their home. She told herself that was why Rory had died in the Atlas Mountains, that it was his father who was to blame that he had died in such a place, so far away and beyond the reach of her love. A young man who had climbed Mont Blanc on his twentieth birthday, who had walked in high places and completed some of the less difficult climbs in the Himalayas, dead as a result of a fall from a path where every day middle-aged out-of-breath tourists safely followed their guide. Late at night and on his own: it was decided that he'd somehow lost his footing and hit his head on a rock as he slid down the steep scree. A child herding goats had found him in the morning, his body so unmarked the boy had thought him merely sleeping. A tragic accident, the authorities had called it, and quietly led them to believe that it had been a dangerous choice to go walking at night and that his purpose in doing so would always be unknown. Her son dead amongst the stars and the snow-caps of distant mountains. She knew she was going back. After everything was finally done and this last business settled she would return to that very place because she needed to go there without her husband, without his book in which he wrote over her grief with the public permanence of his own. Somehow if it was only her, and with all the love that her memory of her son burnished every day, she knew she would be able to evoke him into even momentary life again, finally bring him home.

She forced herself to stir, was clear-headed enough to know that self-pity would bring nothing but a paralysing loss of will. She promised herself that she wouldn't drink any more wine – there was too much work to be done – and she started by piling the shelves of books into cardboard boxes, occasionally separating some that belonged to her, or one that she wanted to keep. When she reached the collections of other writers' poetry she checked each one and if any was a signed copy or had a dedication she set it aside. She would take the rest to the second-hand bookshop in Belfast near the university and donate them. She'd organised them in the boxes carefully with their spines up so that the girls could peruse them and take anything that caught their fancy. But she didn't imagine they would – not even the yellowed and grubby Narnia paperbacks that somehow had managed to linger on despite the intervening years of neglect. Her daughters didn't seem to do nostalgia or looking back and she wasn't sure if this was a good or a bad thing.

She saw the copy of the *Aeneid* that she had earlier placed on the mantelpiece. The book still lolled partly open where it had been folded over the arm of the chair. Out of curiosity she glanced at the pages to find that he had been reading in Book 6 where Aeneas journeyed down into the Underworld. She thought it a wonder he needed to read it at all given the amount of time he had spent with it over the years. She let her eyes take in one of the many sections underlined in pencil where Aeneas tried three times to embrace his father but three times the phantom melted in his hands 'as weightless as the wind, as light as the flight of sleep'. She closed it and stuffed it in the box, didn't want to think about what meaning, if any, it might have. And it wasn't the Underworld that he'd instructed her to give him to but the eternal motion of the sea and the dawning brightness of a new day. It suddenly felt like she was required to facilitate this, his one last escape, the final avoidance of what weighted everyone else in death.

The desk at the window was covered in papers and documents. She didn't know where to start but realised it was important that she organise everything into some kind of order. Through his agent he had already negotiated a modest deal with the library of an American university to buy all his papers and had spent a great deal of time archiving the raft of material into arch lever files, dating them by the titles of each new collection. She knew the files contained early drafts of poems, literary correspondence, reviews and articles he had written for journals and newspapers. As far as she was aware there was nothing included that was personal to her or the family but she resolved to check before they were finally handed over. It was another way of his side-stepping death. There were the poems themselves and the library archive where in the future she assumed a handful of researchers would ponder over every line and score-out. Already she had been asked for an interview by the editor of one of those poetry magazines that proliferated around the world and which bristled with their own unique importance, bestowing or withholding publication like oligarchs dispensing judgement. He'd rattled on about his magazine's artistic credentials then ventured the real purpose of his contact which was to inveigle some unpublished final poem and in so doing scoop his no doubt hated rival publications. She'd declined on both requests. Passing on everything to the American college library would allow her to avoid all the other vultures circling to pick at the carcass of his work and life.

But there were new poems. She knew he had been actively working on a collection and after she shuffled papers and unanswered letters, set aside the reference books and the old newspapers with their half-finished crosswords, she found them inside a manila folder. Some were typed, so although not the finished product, she knew that they had moved on beyond a first tentative draft while others were still at the early handwritten stage. Some didn't have titles but each had a number that approximated to their potential order. It didn't look as if there was a full complement but close enough perhaps. There was a title page as well – he had called the collection *Sea Dreams* – a title that evoked no special insight for her but she felt suddenly nervous as she held the folder in her hands. She set the poems back on the desk and knew that if she were to read them now she would hear his voice again and wasn't sure if she wanted that. Despite her eyes turning instinctively to the urn still sitting on the hearth it was as if in everything he conspired to surpass death, that some part of him refused to be fettered, and then she thought of Rory, who never dressed anything other than casually, buried in one of his father's dark suits, her son who wanted all his life to venture into the bright air, buried under the cold soil, and she felt angry that it was his father who now sought to escape. Let him take back their son's clothes of death, let him weight himself with the knowledge that his life was already lived, his poems written.

Her hand was shaking a little as she hesitated. Already

what she held in her hand was asserting its primacy and the responsibility that was hers as their custodian. She knew that despite everything else she had to deliver them safely to his agent and editor who would make decisions about their readiness for publication and their best future. She told herself that she should think of it only as a matter of economics, of adding to the modest pension on which she had started to draw. Although he could never pay her back for all the years of financial provision he could start to make amends even at this late hour. If the poems were to be published as she expected them to be, then it was probable that they would attract interest, at worst a morbid curiosity. So she tried to concentrate on that knowledge as she carried them over to her seat at the fire.

The opening couple of poems were about his childhood and dedications to his parents. The first one was a homage to his father, a conceit based on the instruments his father used in the drawing office. The slide rule, the set square, the pencil, all became symbols of a way of living 'set sharply square and true', 'the measured moments' on which a life was built. The poem to his mother placed her in the family home sewing by the light of the fire. Then with a rather forced sleight of hand he transformed her into Penelope, a symbol of faithfulness, whose every stitch sealed and shaped her love for her family. She thought it a curiously and uncharacteristically sentimental piece too heavily laden with laboured images of love. Perhaps it was distorted by her own memory of her mother-in-law as someone unfailingly stiff whose approval of her son's choice of wife had been enduringly half-hearted. But she knew already that in relation to the past and the biographical, writing was rarely about how things were, or even how they were remembered, so much as how they needed to be. Then despite her earlier resolve she poured herself another glass of wine.

She had never been much of a drinker in her early life but

in recent years had increased her intake. Sometimes after reading a magazine article warning of the dangers, or feeling the clamouring guilt of working in the health profession and so supposed to know better, she had returned to her abstemious former life but it never lasted more than about a month. Setting the glass on the hearth she told herself it was a comfort, a way of blurring into softer focus things that looked too sharp-edged when seen in their full clarity. She liked the idea that the poem wasn't very good and hoped she might reach the same verdict on those she hadn't read. Because of its proposed prominent position she knew the poem about his mother wasn't considered a filler or piece of 'confetti'. But perhaps she hadn't read it thoughtfully or fairly enough. There was a pleasure in thinking that this final collection might represent a waning and that despite the inevitably respectful reviews it would receive, there would at least be an unspoken suggestion that his best work was perhaps behind him.

But as she turned the pages and slowly read the long poem entitled 'Sea Dreams' she knew there was no falling away of his talents and the knowledge was coloured by both bitterness and the sense of pride she had always felt in his achievement, that in part was made possible by what she did, despite his failure publicly to recognise it. The poem was divided into five sections and chronologically followed his connection to the sea through the various stages of his life. So it began in childhood describing a small boy searching the 'shaded teem of rock pools' where 'braided tresses of seaweed stirred at the brush of his hand' and the sea itself was 'a vast frazzle of timeless light', then ended in his old age with the outgoing tide transformed into 'the final unfathomable wave of mystery'. As she reread and reread, anxious now to miss nothing, part of her insisted as always that she should separate the work from the man but to do that would render the words that she held in her hand beautiful and unflawed and something in her baulked at that.

Feeling breathless and confined again she went to the door of the cottage and opening it looked out at the night. The cool currents off the sea broke against her and in an instant washed the fire's heat from her face. All the lights in the clubhouse were out and there was nothing to be heard except the soft murmur of the tide taking its slow leave of the shore. Once when they had gone out in Gibson's boat on a late-night fishing trip they had sailed under the Mussenden Temple that perched precariously on the lip of the cliff and which one day would surely hurtle on to the rocks below. A folly built supposedly as a result of an infatuation. She thought how often the words 'love' and 'folly' might be inscribed together. They had caught nothing much and her younger sisters soon became frightened by the rising swell. Now the sea was made real only by its sound – that soft rasp and shuck that were the restless prisoners of endless motion. Had her love for Don always been a mere folly? Even now after all the bitterness and recrimination that coursed through her she couldn't bring herself to say so. Once there had been love and passion, words created only for her, whispered in the need of the darkness. And there were her children. Even Rory taken from her had existed and nothing could prise that memory away from her.

She closed the door quietly as if there was someone or something she didn't want to disturb. Part of her simply wanted to pack the poems carefully away in one of the boxes but her curiosity proved stronger and going back to her seat she lifted them and her glass of wine. When she'd had her one affair she had thought initially that for the first time she was experiencing a relationship that was rooted in an equal need so that for a while it felt like an empowerment but before long he had shown himself to be hopelessly weak. And in the moments – once in his car and once in a budget hotel with cigarette burns in the carpet – she had never felt that even the possibility existed of encountering whatever it was of the spirit that was always promised by the giving of the flesh. So as she held the poems she told herself that she could be strong, not intimidated by the voice speaking from the page, but it would have been easier if that voice had been strident or bombastic so that it was her angry resistance that was evoked. She knew already that the voice she was hearing was delicate and at times gentle and that made it harder to fight.

But when she turned the page nothing prepared her to see a handwritten poem that was dedicated to Rory. She felt her anger rising that once again he should write about their son and no doubt parade emotions that she had seen no sign of. She wouldn't read it but even as she told herself this she knew that it was impossible not to.

It began by describing how his offerings of 'sacrificial food, incense, oil-filled bowls' had never been enough to entreat his son's face 'towards the light' and thus like Aeneas he was compelled to journey to the Underworld, 'but as a father searching his stolen child'. Before this journey could be undertaken, however, a sacrifice must first be made from the sacred tree, so the poem offered up his memory of Rory

high in the cherry tree
In spring's first burst, balanced light as air
Dressed in that flounce and shock of white.

But it is his father's shouted warning that his son will fall which 'lays a curse upon his hidden head'.

A description followed of the journey 'through wasted years' until he found his son

in the most distant fields
Where the spirits have their own stars and sun
Sacred ribbons of white about your head.

The white ribbons were linked to the snow-capped mountains that 'cradled' their 'foundling child'. But it was the final two stanzas that affected her most:

I reach out three times to fold you in my embrace
Three times you leave me grasping only air,
Then remember that to return is greater labour, so
Is it love or weariness that makes me take your place
And sends you climbing safely to the light?

And the poem's final lines acknowledging that

there is a price that must be paid
So bind me now to the best of punishments
Stretched and hung out empty, drying in the wind
In slow atonement for the greatest of my sins.

The poem had no final line. At an angle to it was 'A father's words of love I never said' but it had a line through it and other attempts had been scored out heavily as if to prevent them being read. She held her head up for breath then stared at the fire. She wanted to be sure and she couldn't be sure. Was it his voice, or was it his voice in a poem, and what were the chances of these ever being the same thing? If the words were true then it was the first and only time she had heard remorse from him. If the words were false he deserved every punishment that came his way and there was nothing that she could conceive which would ever make atonement possible. Hung out empty, drying in the wind – she tried to think of his final years but could find no trace of such dramatic suffering. As self-contained as always, cocooned in his work, still enjoying the occasional pleasures of the flesh – how could these be reconciled with self-realisation and the crippling press of regret. Did he have two lives, one in the poetry where things were felt, or even felt in the imagination, while the daily pattern of his living survived untouched? Or was it that they had slipped into such remoteness that she no longer had any understanding of what really went on in his head? Some of the lines had double question marks opposite them and a few had scribbled words written in pencil that she couldn't read. She read the poem again and again and still she didn't know what it was it made her feel. In one moment it was as if she held a great weight in her hand, in another it seemed as if the words were so light that she wasn't sure if they were still there or whether they had drifted away beyond her reach, beyond her comprehension.

The white blossom always the harbinger of spring, the tree's bronzed stretched arms suddenly heavily laden with an avalanche of snow. Rory climbing in the blossom. Momentarily hidden from view. Then his smiling face suddenly bobbing like a buoy out of the white-flecked sea. She remembered it. He had told him to get down, that he'd fall and break his neck, and was annoyed when the girls had encouraged their brother to go higher still until he shouted again and eventually Rory had slithered out of the branches and down the trunk, white blossom speckling his hair. A white garland of blossom. But not a garland of blossom, instead a wreath.

They had stored his body in a back room of the local school. A makeshift coffin resting on a table under an ancient map of the world. One of the teachers had given her almond blossom – pale pink and white – and she had placed it on the coffin lid. A makeshift coffin under a tattered map of the world.

She set the poems down and walked back to the uncurtained window but again found just a black pool that showed nothing but her blurred reflection and more than anything she didn't want herself. She let her hand touch the glass as if to brush herself away but its coldness insisted on her presence and then she knew that she had two other children and they would come in the morning for this last thing they had to do. And she would be there for them when they got off the train and she'd be pleased to see them even though she knew that Anna, at least, would have to show her irritation at having to make this journey. But it would be a small price to pay for their company and she would have given anything to have them both there that very night.

She poured herself another glass of wine but made it smaller than the previous ones as a kind of apology for breaking her promise. The fire was fading and she shovelled on what was left of the coal and hoped she hadn't left it too late to save. She even thought of driving all the way home and then coming back again first thing in the morning and so avoid the necessity of spending the night in the cottage but she knew she had drunk too much to make that a possibility. So instead, slowly and as if generated by a great effort of will, she lifted the pages of poems again and started to read. Poems about the seasons and astronomy, about the beach in winter, about politics and the war on terror. She read them all but not as carefully as she had done at the start and it felt now as if there were too many words and she was grateful that none of them seemed to sail close to her. She couldn't concentrate and knew she had drunk too much. She knew she should go to bed and try to sleep it off so that she could greet her daughters brightly in the morning but there weren't many pages left and she didn't want to have to return to them before packing them off to his agent so forced herself to finish the final few. Part of her wanted to leave these last poems until the morning but she told herself that like taking some bitter-tasting medicine it would be easier if she consumed them in one deep gulp.

The collection ended with a sequence of six sonnets called *Legacy* and she didn't need to read very far to know that they were love poems. That awareness prevented her intention of one quick gulp and she read them slowly and carefully, understanding almost from the start that they were love poems to someone who wasn't her. There was nothing by name or physical detail that confirmed this to the world but there was enough in terms of references to place and experiences, enough in their emotional resonances, to ensure she realised that he was writing about a love shared with another. She supposed that love was Roseanne and she was angry that he should write these poems where his lover's 'unbroken constancy of love sustains and endures' and not care that she should know the words belonged to someone else. So this was to be his legacy to the world, his legacy to her. She could have crumpled them in her hand as her anger stirred and flared but something prevented this. What was it? A stupid final loyalty – if not to him but to the work? An insistent knowledge that the words belonged to more than her or even him, that she was their trusted custodian and it was her final obligation to see them pass into the hands of others? So she tried to tell herself it wasn't about the love he felt for someone else, that it wasn't about the love he didn't feel for her – it was about the words, only about the words, and these had an existence and a need to exist that journeyed beyond whatever now kindled her spirit into anger.

She dropped the poems to the floor and stared at the fire that had managed to kick-start itself into a new faltering lease of life. She would take them home with her, photocopy them then send them to his London agent. And then she would never read or look at them again. She'd have them gone from her, dispersed to the world like leaves blown off a tree and if they withered into silence and indifference then so much the better. What she had to do was owed not to him but to something greater and she'd see it through despite everything. She knew too that she would sell the cottage, sell it in part to spite him because he had loved it so much and it was where he had written these last poems but also because it no longer held the memories of her childhood summer or her own children's. The place had been subsumed by more potent memories so let some other family take it on and make something new of it, something that was uncomplicated and which made them happy and stronger.

The urn was still on the hearth but after reading the poems it felt as if he had escaped its confines and blown by some invisible wind the ash of his being was finely riddling and sifting through her no matter how hard she tried to turn herself away. She attempted to convince herself that when with her daughters they released him to the elements she would finally experience her own release but as she climbed the stairs the thought brought no sense of conviction. She wouldn't sleep in the room he used when he stayed in the cottage but rather the front room with its two single beds. That would also bring her closer to the sea and she told herself that its steady ebb and flow might lull her into an easier and quicker sleep, wash away the unwanted whispers of her husband's words.

The room was cold and going to the landing cupboard she found an electric heater and when she turned on both bars the dust-coated elements left a burning smell. She turned back the duvet in the hope it would absorb some of the warmth from the fire and while she waited for the room to heat a little she went to the window and looked out to where the sea was a dark glaze watched over tentatively by moonlight and stars. It stretched uncertainly as her own life and she remembered the final poems and wondered if her need for love was truly over and if so what else did life offer to sustain and endure? Already Anna had suggested she should sell up in the city and move into a modern apartment where there'd be no garden to look after and so much less to take care of. She had said she'd think about it but now as she started to undress she wanted to ask her daughter what she should do all day in this new, pristine apartment. She wanted the garden for as long as she could manage it, wanted the slow turn and unfolding of the seasons.

She stood close to the heater while she removed her clothes and as the heat mottled her skin thought of the cherry-blossom tree in its spring flowering. Of her son disappeared inside the white foam of blossom. She had cried when years later men had come to cut it down as its raised and wandering roots ridged up through the lawn and started to spread under the driveway. She had to agree with his insistence that it had to be done but part of her was glad that her son never saw it. An hour's work to take away what had been there a lifetime, its trunk cut into logs and its branches fed into a machine that spewed out recyclable wood chippings and then finally a machine that sucked up every remaining leaf and twig as if it was forensically important to remove all traces of the tree's existence. It was the first thing Rory had climbed. There wasn't even a stump left because they had ground it down to nothing so all that remained when the lorry pulled away was a slight sump in the ground that was to be filled and regrassed.

The map above Rory's coffin looked as if it had been there for ever, a relic of some colonial power that had left behind their vision of the world after they had taken their leave. None of the people who laid him there could have known how many of the countries he had ventured to or how many of the world's high places he had walked and climbed. She who all her life stayed close to the familiar and had no adventures beyond the journey as a young woman into the unknown world of her husband's desire somehow had a son who loved to follow far-off and mysterious freedoms. She wanted to be as brave as him so that she could still be his mother but as she stood half-naked in front of the fire she trembled a little.

What she wanted to put on now was the white blossom of

the tree that would hide the finite flaws of her flesh and give her some momentary perfection. What she wanted was beyond the world's gaze to climb higher than she'd ever allowed herself to do. She touched her hair and felt it thinning into a coarseness of grey. Rory had pink-tipped petals in his hair when he had been released out of the white-gloved, cupped hands of the tree, standing smiling as if a page-boy at a wedding who had passed under a snow flurry of confetti. How could the mountains hold their whitened caps even in the heat of summer? How could she see them so clearly across the city's dusty roofs where the lines of washing hung motionless in the slow wavering of the day's final hours of heat?

That dusk when the taxi had brought them to the edge of the square what sights had greeted her, their strangeness raging against every unprepared sense. The crowds, the music, the dancers, the animals, the hawkers and the fire-splashed sprawling food stalls. The smells of cooking and perfumes to which she could give no name. The scents of a continent that was unfolding itself before her. Like some landscape of the imagination, some terrible painting by Hieronymus Bosch – it had almost consumed her and only the knowledge that she had come to take her child home had given her the courage to get out of the car. Following an old man who had loaded their luggage in a wooden handcart and was leading them through a warren of passageways from where it was possible they would never emerge. In one of his poems he had described it as a journey to the Underworld and perhaps he was composing it even then as veiled women like shadows averted their gaze while children playing in echoing alleyways paused to look at them curiously.

She knelt naked at the fire and bowed her head, was glad when the familiar sound of the sea reasserted itself in her consciousness. She remembered the two small white fish. Two small white fish and five barley loaves – a miracle to feed the five thousand. She wanted to enter this land of miracles where the dead were raised and storms at sea stilled with the power of words. Her son only sleeping in the boat while the fury raged all about. Finally wakened he tells them not to be afraid and stretches out his arm the way he always does when he's offering shelter. Let the calm come, let it come so that she could still everything that now rose up inside her. Let the calm come so that she could find respite in sleep. Let her awaken and walk free from what cavernous, echoing sepulchre seemed now to entomb her. Then after hugging her naked self she put on her clothes and went back downstairs.

In the morning the sky was bright and when she opened the front door of the cottage the sea seemed skittish, even playful, as thin trills of wave raced each other to the shore and a dog splashed into it after a stick thrown by its owner. There were other people on the beach – a young woman jogging in fluorescent yellow and black lycra, another dog walker and an elderly couple striding purposefully towards the stone pier. The day felt awake and busy and she knew she had much to do before the girls were collected from the train so she began by changing the bed she had slept in and changing the double bed in the back room. She would have to sleep in it to let her daughters have the two singles. She didn't want to sleep in the bed where Don had doubtless conducted his affair but there was no way to avoid it and that reluctance was partially compensated by the fact that she liked the idea of the girls sleeping in the same room they had used as children, liked the idea of them being sisters again and not wrapped up in their separate lives. She wasn't sure but she got the impression they didn't see that much of each other in London. Perhaps if nothing else this last ritual for their father might draw them closer.

At her breakfast she forced herself to eat as much as possible and drank two cups of instant coffee in an attempt to banish the residue of the wine, afterwards hiding the bottle in a cupboard. She opened a couple of windows slightly but turned up the central heating and gave the place a final tidy carried along on her own rising tide of excitement. In the brightness of a new day and with the expectation of their arrival the cottage didn't seem so echoingly empty or ghostridden and the only thing on which she stumbled was what to do with the urn. It still sat on the hearth where she had left it but she neither wanted to confront her daughters with it nor leave it where it might suggest a disrespect, so after some confusion she lifted it and placed it beside his books and papers on the table, trying to make its setting as natural looking as possible. Its black surface was struck by sunlight and she could see the white whorled print of her fingers so taking a teacloth from the kitchen she carefully polished them away. She lit a modest fire more designed to give the room visual warmth than for any practical purpose and brushed the hearth clean of its spill of dust and ash.

It was important to her to present herself as well as possible so she spent more time than usual in choosing her clothes and doing her make-up. But the lipstick she applied seemed too bright and taking a tissue she wiped it off again and settled for a simple brush of lip salve. She hadn't slept well and the dark circles under her eyes looked deeply engrained but after she had finished camouflaging the night's disturbance of broken dreams and time's steady reclaiming she consoled herself that she passed muster and her appearance, however flawed, was better than greeting her daughters as the merry widow. She cleared up the kitchen and was checking the fridge looked respectable when through the window above the sink she saw a gull swooping on the white slivers of fish. Going to the back door she rushed out flapping the tea towel in the air and shooing it away until it lumbered skywards screeching its complaint, then removing what was left of the fish wrapped them tightly in tinfoil and dropped them in the bin. The ring of her mobile phone made her start. It was Francesca telling her that they were about twenty minutes away. Her daughter sounded light, expectant, and that pleased her. As she held the phone to her ear she could smell the fish on her hands and when she had finished she washed them slowly and carefully, then used a hand cream before making some real coffee and placing the croissants she had bought the day before on a plate in the middle of the kitchen table.

There was nothing more to do and after a final check in the mirror and giving herself a modest approval she took one last look round the room before she headed for the car. It was true the station was only five minutes away and easily walkable but they would have overnight luggage at least and might welcome the chance to finish the final part of their journey in comfort. So she parked close by the station exit, saying good morning to those who recognised her and once receiving sympathy from a woman whose name she didn't know but who was familiar to her from her visits to the local Costcutter. As she waited for the train to arrive it suddenly felt like a scene from *The Railway Children* except it was her two daughters who would step on to the platform and not some falsely incarcerated husband. He had his own confinement now even if in the morning they were to release whatever of his spirit still existed. At least then it would finally be over and they could all return to their private places and make what they might of their lives. She wondered if her daughters would now be more forthcoming with their invitations to stay although in their defence she conceded that both inhabited tiny flats for which they paid exorbitant rents. Perhaps the sale of the cottage might be used to help them find the deposits that would allow them to clamber on to the bottom of the housing ladder.

It was Francesca she saw first, hurrying towards her in the slightly childlike manner that still characterised some of her movements, her case bouncing along the uneven concrete. Perhaps her wealthy London clientele found it endearing or perhaps she was able to suppress it in her business dealings. But for the moment at least she looked like a young girl on the first day of her holiday and the affection with which she hugged her seemed sincere and heartfelt.

'Francesca, thanks for coming. It's good of you to come all this way.'

'It's OK, it's OK. Are you all right?'

'I'm doing fine but where's Anna?'

'She's coming. She was filing some copy on her laptop. Here she is now.'

Anna's embrace was hampered by her laptop case but her daughter's kiss on her cheek felt affectionate. As always she wore some indefinable London style that marked her as a temporary visitor rather than a resident. It wasn't that her clothes were particularly modish or sophisticated but rather that she seemed at a slight distance from everything, was constantly evaluating it and perhaps secretly unfavourably.

'I just had to email some stuff,' she said as she sought to strike a working balance between her overnight bag and her laptop case. 'How are you?'

'I'm fine,' she said, thinking that her daughter didn't trust her to know what 'copy' was. 'Good flight?'

'A little bumpy in places,' Anna said as they walked towards the car with the wheels of Francesca's case squeaking in time to their steps.

When their bags were loaded and they had taken their seats silence settled for a moment and she searched for something to say before she started the engine.

'Thanks for coming,' she said, suddenly embarrassed by the fact that she had requested their presence. 'It's what he wanted. I know it's inconvenient after being here so recently for the funeral.'

'And expensive,' Anna said as she struggled beside her with the seat belt.

'Perhaps you'll let me help with that,' she said. 'The money, I mean.'

'It's OK, Mum, Anna and I wouldn't let you do it on your own. And I'm looking forward to staying in the cottage again – it's been so long.'

'You always hated the cottage,' Anna said, glancing over her shoulder at her sister. 'You used to complain about all the things you were missing at home.'

'Only when I was an older teenager and a bit bored. It was good when we were younger children.'

'What do you plan to do with it?' Anna asked.

'It's probably a bit early to make big decisions,' Francesca offered.

'I haven't finally decided but I'll probably sell it.'

'You should wait until the market picks up again,' Anna advised. 'The fact that it's sea front should mean it's worth a good price. Don't be giving it away.'

'We can talk about it later when everything else is out of the way.'

In the cottage she poured the coffee while they deposited their things in the front room. The sound of their feet above her head made her think of all the summers when they had scampered around the place and if their tread was slower and heavier now it still was able to remind herself that these were her children. So it pleased her when they sat at the kitchen table with her and cupped their coffee and helped themselves to the croissants and allowed her time and space to observe them. Francesca seemed restored since the days of the funeral and although she knew it was only in her imagination she liked to think that already something of the sea and the light had coloured her blue eyes brighter and that her customary pallor was less severe. Anna had a new reddish tint through her hair and the recent cut was a little short and functional for her tastes. It would have been pleasurable to believe that her daughters loved to come home but she knew it wasn't true and so she must content herself with what the short time offered. She was surprised when she belatedly remembered that Francesca no longer took milk in her coffee, was interested by Anna's new rings and bracelet, interested above all in the timbre and cadences of their voices, alert to the different inflections of their accents that while not renouncing their origins entirely had learned to accommodate their new home. She thought it incredibly strange but beautiful to have these two young women as her daughters and at intervals almost felt the need to convince herself that they were really hers despite their self-contained differences of personality and appearance and the remoteness of their lives. There were times as they chatted about inconsequential things and sipped their coffee when she felt a surge of emotion and wanted to reach across the table and pull them into her embrace but she knew it would be an embarrassment to them all and confined herself to recording carefully every aspect of them as if their departure might erase the memory.

'So, Mum, talk us through the Don's wishes for his ashes,' Anna said. 'I didn't quite take it all in on the phone. All sounds a bit weird.'

Anna always referred to her father by his first name, frequently adding the definite article to make him sound like the head of a Mafia family. She knew it asserted the absence of deference, her independence, but it always jarred a little. She would rather have put off the detailed explanation of her husband's wishes, sensed that it would spoil the ease that had settled so quickly between them, but knew Anna would persist until everything was fully revealed. So there was little prospect of postponing it until later and she poured them more coffee as a distraction while she considered the best way to go about it before deciding that it was best simply to state the facts and let them make of it what they would.

'In his will, a will I didn't even know existed, your father expressed his wish to have his ashes spread here in the sea.

He wanted you both to be present.' She paused as she raised the cup to her lips. 'He wants it done at the end of the stone pier, wants his ashes to go into the sea early in the morning. And there's one other request – he wants us to do it to the music of "Lark Ascending".'

There was silence for a second and then Anna made a noise that sounded like a snigger. ' "Lark Ascending" – that's a bit of a cliché. You'd have thought he would've recognised a cliché when he thought of that.'

'It was the most popular request on *Desert Island Discs* or something like that,' Francesca added and she was unsure whether her daughter was justifying it or confirming its status of cliché.

' "Lark Ascending"?' Anna continued as she rolled her eyes. 'Did the Don really see himself as a lark, do you think?'

She said nothing because it made her uncomfortable when they were critical of their father in front of her, told herself that she had never revealed her own feelings to them. So why had it been so important to do that? To protect them, she supposed. But had it really protected them by pretending things were different to the way they were and wasn't the truth that she had done it because she was embarrassed for her children to know of their parents' failure?

'So even though he's had his funeral and his tributes – the whole shooting match in fact – he still wants one more epilogue,' Anna said and there was enough irritation in her voice to suggest that she might just take herself back to London on the next plane.

She nodded but said nothing and hoped she wouldn't have to take her daughter's blame for what she clearly considered was an unreasonable imposition. Francesca took her cup in both hands and shuffled a little in the face of her sister's aggression before she said quietly, 'We couldn't let Mum do it on her own so we'll do it for her and when it's done it's done.'

Anna looked at her as if she had just noticed her presence at the table. 'I don't know about you, Francesca, but I'm in the middle of an investigation – an important piece of work that I need to complete on time – so I couldn't really afford to be here right now.'

'I've work on too,' her sister said. 'But it's just two days and we'll be back.'

'It's not just the time. It annoys me that he's thinking of no one but himself. Still pulling the strings even after he's gone and we're all supposed to dance.'

She let the silence settle and when she couldn't bear it any more heard herself say, 'You're right. But when it's done it's done and we can get on with our lives.' They were both looking at her and under the scrutiny of their gaze she told herself that she owed them something, so she said in a voice that she knew sounded tremulous, 'It's the last time any of us will have to dance at his command.'

They stared at her in silence for a few seconds and when Francesca laid a consoling hand on her shoulder she gripped the edge of the table in an effort to stop herself crying. Her daughter's touch was welcome but it made her think of Rory.

'It's all right, Mum,' Anna said, 'we'll do it just as he wants. I'm sorry if I upset you.'

'I'm not upset,' she said, forcing a little lightness into her voice. 'I'm just glad to see you and glad you're here in the cottage even though it might be for the last time.'

'Do you need help packing up his stuff?' Francesca asked as she lifted her arm away.

'It's mostly done, thanks, but when we're going back I'll take these boxes of books – if there's anything you want please just say. I'm getting rid of most of them.'

'Do you remember when he used to read to us from the Narnia books?' Francesca asked.

'And he thought he was Aslan,' Anna added before she

drained the last of her coffee then looked at them and grinned. 'Now he thinks he's a lark,' and encouraged by their smiles, 'more like a bloody cuckoo.'

'Do you remember that interview he did with the paper when he claimed he went swimming every day in the sea?' Francesca asked. Her sister and mother both laughed. 'Swimming? I've never seen him swim in his life.'

'That's because he couldn't swim,' she told them.

'He couldn't?' they echoed.

'Not a single stroke. Never did more in the sea than paddle.'

'So I wonder why he wants his ashes in the sea?' Francesca asked.

She knew that she could say she thought it was about his attempted escape from death, about releasing himself to the sea's endless motion, about giving himself back to light and air rather than the shadows of the Underworld. But she knew if she tried her words would fall hopelessly short and she wouldn't be able to make them understand it as she did, so it was just another part of those things she would never be able to reveal. Instead she said, 'I suppose he just likes the poetry of it.'

'I still think it's all a bit of a cliché,' Anna said after a few moments. 'I thought at least he'd come up with something more original. I'd love a glass of wine, Mum – is there any in the kitchen?'

She produced a bottle of white and poured them both a drink but declined her daughters' invitation to join them by saying it was possible she might have to drive later.

'I'm not sure how original his work is,' Anna added. 'Perhaps that's why he never made it into the big time.'

'He wasn't hugely successful,' Francesca said. 'But he was respected.'

'Yes respected but not really thought of as top of the tree, not in the same league as the others. What do you think, Mum?'

'I think Don was a very fine poet who did some very good work.'

'You don't have to say that any more, so tell us true,' Anna insisted, pointing at her with the wine glass.

'I'm telling you the truth,' she said. 'I think your father has written some very good poems that will endure and that he has a place in the canon of Irish poetry.'

'There must have been times when you'd like to have fired him out of a cannon,' Francesca said, smiling when she saw that she'd made them both laugh.

She wanted a glass of the wine but the day stretched long in front of them and she knew that it was probable that she'd have to drive so she poured herself more coffee. It was good to sit at the table with her children and be included in their conversation, even though it felt like a growing conspiracy against their father.

'Anna, I remember how you really enjoyed winding him up.'

'He was good value for it,' Anna replied. 'He was such a snob. Do you remember he went to school parents' night and asked my English teacher Miss Andrews who was just five minutes out of college what her policy on grammar was and had she ever considered reading Virgil with the class? When he asked her who her favourite writer was she got all flustered and couldn't think of one. It was awful and the next day she told me to tell him that her favourite writer was . . . someone I can't remember and when I told him after school he just made this kind of snorting noise.'

They sat for a few seconds as if lost in their respective memories until she asked them what they would like to do during the rest of the day. But neither had any clear ideas. Anna said she had a few phone calls to make and needed to go online for a while but after that she was free. Francesca stood up and started to clear the table, persisting even when she told her to leave everything, but she was glad when she took the temptation of the bottle of wine away. She remembered her daughter's touch on her shoulder and went to help her.

'Do you fancy a walk on the beach?' Francesca asked as she placed things back in the fridge.

'Need to put your coat on. Even though it's bright it might be cool enough.'

'Blow some of the London cobwebs away.'

Before she got her own coat she put some more coal on the fire and gave the hearth another brush. Francesca's light coat looked as if it would be more at home in a Kensington café rather than the beach but when she offered one of her own, her daughter said she would be fine. They left Anna still at the kitchen table but starting up her laptop and she held her arm in the air in a farewell wave without turning to look at them.

When they had cleared the dunes and were on the beach Francesca linked her arm and she was aware of the light press of her shoulder and the perfume that she always wore. For the first few steps in the soft sand at the base of the dunes they were out of sync before they found a balanced rhythm. The sea was calm, just the way she hoped it would be in the morning, with neat little serrations of waves cutting gently at the shore.

'Very different from London, Francesca.'

'Very different and hardly a soul in sight. Makes a change from crowded streets. I'm glad I can walk to work and don't have to use the Underground. It's a bit of a nightmare in rush hour.'

'And when you were home for the funeral you said business is going all right.'

'Going OK but London overheads are dear so I'm not close to making my fortune just yet. The Royal Wedding was a bit of a godsend for hats.'

'Did you get much business?'

'A fair amount. No one famous, unfortunately, just wives of civil servants and judges mostly. And, I nearly forgot, the wife of some politician I've never heard of.'

They walked close to the sea where at intervals small birds skimmed its surface. Once an eddy of water came shimmying in further than they had anticipated and they had to scurry away, Francesca letting out a pretend scream followed by genuine laughter. Of her three children she thought of Francesca as possibly the happiest, the least prone to unexpected changes of direction, the one who appeared the most settled and content with wherever she found herself. There was little drama about her, no apparent depths of intensity or unfulfilled longings that were evident on the surface at least.

'I suppose I'll be all right so long as people keep on deciding to get married and their mothers want a nice hat to wear on the day.'

'And no sign of you designing a dress for yourself?'

'Afraid not but if I ever do I'll make sure you have the very best of hats.'

'And it's definitely over between you and Matthew?'

'Seems so. But we're still friends and I see him every so often.'

'I liked him – he seemed a gentle soul,' she said as they got closer to the stone pier.

'He was, he is, but we just lost whatever you're supposed to have and drifted apart. Wasn't meant to be. And don't be saying plenty more fish in the sea because I can't see them,' she said, melodramatically shading her eyes with her hand and scanning the horizon.

'I wasn't going to say that,' she said, as she patted the back of her daughter's hand. 'But there'll be somebody.'

They briefly unlocked arms to step on to the stone pier. There seemed to be a swathe of light dusting the shore across the inlet.

'The light often seems to be on that beach when you're on this one,' she said, hoping her daughter would link her arm again. 'Why is that?'

'It's like life, I suppose. Sometimes I think if there isn't anybody, that'll be all right. Might even be simpler.'

She offered Francesca her arm but she was still staring across the water, this time shielding her eyes for real.

'Will we walk to the end, inspect the site for tomorrow?' she asked as Francesca dropped her hand from her eyes.

'Would your life have been simpler without Dad?'

'Simpler? Yes I'd say so,' she said, half-turning to look towards the end of the pier then heading towards it.

'Simpler,' Francesca said, starting to follow. 'And better?'

She didn't reply and instead turned up her collar.

'I'm sorry, that wasn't fair,' her daughter said as she linked her arm again.

So arm in arm they walked on and she patted Francesca's hand to show that it was all right before she asked her how she thought Anna was.

'She's fine, I think. A bit preoccupied with this story about human trafficking that she's working on.'

'And you don't see her that much in London?'

'Now and again we meet up for lunch or a coffee but I don't suppose that often.'

'I imagine life's just too hectic.'

'That's it. We've both got our careers and she often has to work strange hours. But I know she's there if I need her.'

'That's good, Francesca. It's always good to know that there's someone there in an emergency. And is her love life any better than yours?'

'I think she sees someone who works on the paper but I'm not sure. You'll have to ask her, I'm afraid.'

'I don't like to pry even though a mother always wants to know everything about her children. Anna's quite a private person, so I don't want to make her think I'm snooping.'

They paused to look back across the beach they had just traversed. Beyond it there was the bold outline of the apartment block and from its grounds the sound of a lawnmower. Beyond that again, the church with its spire and the village houses. The light had quickened and Francesca tilted her face upwards and she imagined she was absorbing it, storing it to take back with her against the coming winter in London.

'We'll have the sun in our face when we walk back,' she told her daughter.

They walked on until they reached the end of the pier. The sea was stirring itself out of its earlier stupor and there were more strident waves running briskly towards the shore and on the other side the swell was bobbing some birds that had taken rest. Standing at the pier's end where there was no wall or rail they looked out to sea where a cargo ship drifted across the horizon.

'Would my life have been better?' she said. 'I don't know the answer to that, Francesca. Perhaps in some ways but it's also true that I wouldn't have had you and Anna. Wouldn't have had Rory. And that's something I'll always be grateful for.'

'Do you think of Rory often?'

'Every day, Francesca. Every day.'

She felt her daughter put her arms protectively around her and hug her tightly. Then almost as quickly she let her go again as if embarrassed. A thick swell of water shucked up against the wall and a fine shiver of spray landed near their feet.

'When I was a girl we used to fish for crabs here and I was always a little frightened that a wave would come and snatch me. Sometimes when it's very stormy it's not safe to stand here. Do you think about Rory, Francesca?'

'Yes, sometimes. I miss the way he would come and stay a night or so at the beginning or the end of one of his trips. I used to tease him that he thought I was a hotel that never charged for a bed. I still have some of his things – a few books, some postcards and drawings, a couple of maps, even a bit of climbing equipment.'

'What climbing equipment?'

'Just a few bits and pieces – I think they're called carabiners. Things for hooking yourself on.'

'You wouldn't throw any of it out, would you?' she asked, trying too late to edge the concern out of her voice.

'No, Mum, I wouldn't do that.'

'If they take up too much space you can send them to me.'

'Would you like to have them?'

She nodded then turned her face away in case she might cry but she fixed her eyes on the distant cargo ship and forbade herself. There was only the restless sound of the sea. Why had she ever allowed her son to be buried in his father's black suit? Why had she allowed him to be clothed in the vestments of death and buried under the earth when all his life he had sought to be in the light of distant mysteries? But it was her daughter who needed her now as she heard her say, 'Why was Dad always so disappointed in me?'

'If there's disappointment, Francesca,' she said, taking both her daughter's hands as if they were about to share the first steps in some dance to silent music, 'then it should be yours because if he didn't realise that he had the most lovely of daughters who's kind to everyone who crosses her path and who is talented and creative and who's worked so hard to make a successful business, then he didn't deserve to be your father.'

'Sometimes we talk about him as if he's still here and it matters what he thinks,' she said, sniffing and breathing deeply as if suddenly there wasn't enough air. 'But he was disappointed, wasn't he? He was always disappointed.'

'There was something in Don that grew bitter over the years. Maybe he felt his talents were overlooked, maybe he didn't feel as if he'd completely fulfilled them – I don't know.

It wasn't anything that was your fault and you shouldn't think that even for a moment.'

She pulled Francesca into her embrace and as she nestled her head on her shoulder she felt the shock of hearing her crying. 'Francesca, Francesca,' she whispered. 'It's all right, it's all right.' She rocked her a little as if she were a child again and as if the motion might free the pain. 'Soon we won't have to worry about what he thought, and there was no one who disappointed him more than I did.' She gently prised her daughter free from her but only so that she could see her face. 'Francesca, we don't need to care any more. And tomorrow morning it's all over for good so please don't punish yourself. Please don't.'

Francesca nodded but wouldn't look at her and she felt suddenly angry, angry with him but also with herself for letting him do this to her child. Then taking her hand she moved them both closer to the edge. 'Look, Francesca, this is where it ends.' A light wisp of spray dark-spotted their coats and they stepped back again. 'In the morning we'll do as he wanted and put his ashes in the sea and pray it doesn't throw them back at us.'

Francesca pretended to laugh before she said, 'I'm sorry. I didn't mean to give you this. I don't know why I'm saying these things – it's really stupid. Let's go back before the sun goes in again.'

They walked back along the pier separated by their silence but uncertain about what should be said and whether too much had already been spoken. On the beach now there was a jogger, a couple of dog walkers and a mother and father shepherding a toddler away from the water. Francesca lifted her face again to the light and breathed deeply as if inhaling all the freshness of the morning. Her eyes closed for a second.

'You wouldn't mind if I sold the cottage, sure you wouldn't?'

'No, you must do whatever you think is best for you now. It'll probably take all your time keeping up one place without the cottage as well. But the market's not good now, so Anna's right, perhaps you should wait a while and see if it picks up. And you're all right for money, aren't you?'

'Yes, there's enough to get by on if I don't go crazy.'

'Maybe, Mum, you deserve to go a little crazy – live a little.'

'Francesca, even if I wanted to go crazy I wouldn't know how.'

They nodded as the dog walkers passed them and watched as the dogs were sent scampering after balls that were thrown by a plastic stick. The jogger was a young woman who ran along the water's edge and puffed out a red-cheeked 'morning' to them when they crossed. Out at sea the cargo ship had disappeared as if it had simply fallen over the edge of the horizon.

'You could go on a cruise – lots of single people take them.'

'There is somewhere I'd like to go,' she said, hesitating for a second. They were almost stepping in the footsteps they had made earlier. 'I'd like to go back to Morocco and visit the village, make a small donation to the school – they were kind to me.'

'Are you sure, Mum?'

'I'm sure, Francesca. I'm going to go before the end of the year.'

'Would you like me to come with you?'

'That's good of you but I want to go on my own.'

They followed their prints back across the beach talking about inconsequential things but she was conscious of everything that had passed between them and had surprised herself by saying that she would go before the year's end. It was as if the decision had been finally and impulsively made during their walk and the words spoken before she had time to allow doubts to consolidate. And she'll take a brand-new map with the world's countries marked as they really are and just maybe they'll give her theirs in exchange. She'll give them money to buy new books and things they need for the school and she'll take a guide and walk in the mountains. The decision filled her with new determination and all that seemed to stand between her and its fulfilment was the required ritual in the morning.

When they returned to the cottage Francesca said she wasn't used to so much fresh air and was going to lie down for half an hour. Anna was still sitting at the table at her laptop and talking to someone on her phone and it sounded as if she was speaking to a child, trying to reassure them about something, making promises. She went into the kitchen and made some new coffee and when it was ready took one up to Francesca who had got under the duvet.

'It must be the travelling,' Francesca said, 'and all that fresh air out there.'

She set the cup at the side of the bed and briefly stroked her daughter's head before telling her she deserved a rest and to stay there as long as she wanted. As she walked back down the stairs she told herself that it was like having a child again who was feeling unwell and there was a pleasure in being there to look after her. She took Anna a cup, Anna who never seemed to need any nursing and always appeared to be imbued with an inner strength. The phone conversation had ended but her mobile rested on the table close to her hand and as she drank the coffee she lifted it from time to time and turned it in her hand like a worry stone before setting it down again. Her daughter's restlessness made her uneasy but she didn't know what to say so instead she sipped her coffee and waited silently for whatever conversation, if any, might begin.

'I suppose I should get a walk on the beach and blow some of the London air out of my lungs.'

'You'll have your chance tomorrow morning. I hope it's a day like this and not stormy.'

'Is Francesca all right?'

'I think she's just a bit worn out. She'll be all right when she gets a rest and we get this over with.'

'Why is he making us do this?' she asked, lifting her phone, almost as if she was going to ring him and demand an explanation.

'Because he was selfish and always insistent on what he believed was his entitlement, I suppose.'

'Selfish in life and selfish in death,' Anna said as she set the phone down again. 'I don't know how you stuck it all those years.'

'It wasn't always like that.'

'So what was it like?'

She looked at her daughter who was scrutinising her intently in a way that made her uncomfortable and which made her feel as if she was about to be interviewed professionally rather than personally. She felt too that if she were to be weighed in her child's judgement then she would be found wanting. It wasn't judgement she wanted now so she said, 'I suppose like most marriages it had its ups and downs.'

'So there were ups?'

'Yes and as I said to Francesca my marriage gave me three children I'm very proud of. That's something I'm grateful for.'

There were a few seconds of silence while Anna appeared to be pondering her mother's words and momentarily unsure of what her next question should be so she took advantage of the hesitation to ask about the story she was working on.

'I'm doing a series of articles on human trafficking – it's the most important thing I've been given to do so far. It's an ongoing piece of work and I'm investigating how illegal immigrants are farmed out to various industries where they work for minimal wages, often in appalling conditions, and then get most of the pittance they've been paid taken off them for the privilege of being allowed to live in some doss house.'

'It's a terrible thing. But how do you go about finding out about it?'

'It's not straightforward because everything's controlled by fear so it's not easy getting someone to talk to you. I've had to do a little undercover work a few times and I have a contact in the Met who's allowed me to follow some of their investigations first-hand. The sex trade is the worst – what happens to some young women who think they're coming to decent jobs and better lives.'

'God help them. But it sounds dangerous, Anna – you're careful, aren't you?'

'I'm careful, Mum. It's not a world where you can afford to take big risks. There's too many dangerous people who have too much to lose by being exposed. But there's experienced people in the paper advising me and I have to get their approval for everything I do. So I'm not about to disappear at any moment or anything.'

She was frightened for her child but knew that if she were to show it or make too much of a fuss then she would be told nothing more.

'Was that someone you were talking to on the phone who's helping you?' she asked.

'Yes, it's a young Chinese girl who's labouring for a gang-master on farms. Back-breaking work for less than the minimum wage and sleeping in a Second World War Nissen hut. She's educated, paid the equivalent of two years' salary to come and this is the life she's found. I've got to know her as much as that's possible. Given her some money and a phone.'

'I didn't hear what she was saying but I guess from the way you were speaking to her that she was frightened.'

'Yes she's frightened but frightened even more of what might happen to her in the future.'

'Anna, you'll take care of her, make sure no harm comes to her, won't you?'

'Of course, Mum.'

'And take care of yourself as well.'

Anna stretched her hand across the table and patted her arm but it was like the half-hearted reassurance that might be given to a child by a weary parent and she took no comfort in it. She was glad when her daughter closed the laptop and slipped her phone in her pocket as if to signal that this world of potential danger had been set aside. However it was difficult after what she had heard to know how to make further conversation without it sounding like inconsequential and even insensitive small talk so she got up from the table and busied herself about the kitchen. She heard Anna go into the front room and then her voice asking, 'Was the Don working on anything?'

She turned from the sink and watched her daughter perusing his writing desk.

'I suppose he was always working on something but there was just bits and pieces. I'll send whatever there was to his agent.'

There was something forensic about Anna, in the way she touched things, the way she lifted objects and looked at them. She wondered if that was a good thing in relation to love and thought that it might be in that it would prevent her ever being taken in by the false but also that she might never be able to see beyond the flaws, the fine cracks that veined most people's souls.

'If you see anything you want please take it.'

'You didn't find a diary or a journal, did you?' Anna asked as she examined a fountain pen.

'No, as far as I know Don didn't keep a diary and if he did I'm not sure I'd want to read it. I suppose the poems were his diary.'

She watched Anna sit at his desk and place her arms on the wood at right angles to her body as if weighting herself while she saw what her father saw when he looked through the window.

'Did he ever read any of my pieces?' she asked.

'I don't know for sure but my guess is that he did. Even though he liked to pretend indifference or that he was too preoccupied I think he was always curious about things so I think that he probably read them all.'

'He never said once.'

'I'm sorry about that, Anna, I'm truly sorry.'

'It's not for you to be sorry.'

'It feels like I should be.'

Her daughter said nothing but lifted the pen up to the light before asking, 'Can I keep this?'

'Of course but is there nothing else you'd like?'

'No, just this pen.'

The light streaming through the window illuminated the side of her daughter's face and glinted the thin streaks of red into life. She saw for the first time that she seemed older, older and a little tired. She wanted to go to her but in the passing seconds where she weighed up whether her daughter would want it or not the opportunity slipped away.

'Let's go out for lunch,' Anna said, suddenly standing up. 'Let's all go out together. Why don't we go round to the Ramore? Is it still there?'

'It's still there but I've lots of stuff in if you just want to stay here.'

'No let's all go out and have a change of scene. Whenever Francesca comes down,' she said as she slipped the pen into the pocket of her trousers. 'I'll go and check on sis.'

'Don't waken her if she's sleeping. I think she's a bit drained.' Anna smiled at her and she knew she'd told her something that wasn't necessary. Wanting to redeem herself she asked, 'What's the girl's name – the Chinese girl?'

'Jiao.'

'What age is she?'

'Twenty-six.'

'I know it's a stupid thing to say but if there's ever anything I can do to help her, with money or anything, I'd like to.'

'It's not a stupid thing to say – it's a nice thing – but I'm hoping the paper might be able to pull some strings when we publish,' she said as she paused at the bottom of the stairs.

Her hand held the banister and her new rings caught the light. The sun coming in through the porch window nestled against the side of her face and revealed the first fine lines beginning to linger at the corners of her eyes.

'Strangers were good to Rory when he was in a different country,' she said, her voice shaking a little. 'So if there's ever any way we can help this young woman we should.'

For a second she thought that Anna was going to come to her but instead she simply nodded and then went upstairs, her steps muffled by the carpet.

She went back to the kitchen and pottered aimlessly about trying to calm herself through being busy. It would be best to go out and escape the confines of the cottage. And if neither of her daughters did nostalgia then it might still be nice to retrace some of the places they had frequented as a young family. She heard both their voices but couldn't make out what they were saying. In the riad where they had stayed there were two young women who did all the work, cooking and serving the meals. Working from early in the morning. When she woke their voices talking quietly in the small kitchen close to her room was the first thing she heard. Unobtrusive, moving like whispers through the courtyard and with whatever was their own lives entirely hidden from public view. She wanted to ask if they too had children but knew they didn't wish to have conversation beyond what was the polite necessity. When on that morning the younger of the two brought her a breakfast unasked to the roof terrace where she sat looking at the distant mountains she wondered if she knew she had a dead son. She thought of asking her name but hesitated because when so much of her was hidden

259

it seemed like an intrusion. She had made herself eat what little she could of the breakfast but without taking her eyes away from the mountains.

When Francesca eventually appeared she seemed restored to her former self and Anna was close by her side as if in custody of her younger sister.

'So, Mum, are we going to do a tour of the north coast's exciting attractions?'

'Can we get ice-cream in Morelli's?' Francesca asked as she pinned up some wisps of her hair.

'Yes and you can go on the dodgems in Barry's if you want and eat candyfloss,' Anna said.

'I would think the dodgems are out, girls – from memory it's closed now for the season. But if you're serious we can go to Morelli's,' she said. 'When you were children you used to think it such a treat except you used to drive your father mad because you took so long to make up your minds about what flavour you were going to have. But let's get lunch first. It'll be good to get out and you can see how things have changed, if they have of course.'

So she drove them round the coast to Portrush and they had lunch in the Ramore and both daughters laughed at how big the servings were.

'People obviously don't think they get value for money unless it's reflected in the quantity,' Anna said but neither of them seemed to have any trouble finishing their portions. And then when they had gone up to the dessert counter and laughed again at the baroque sculptures of cream and cake, they eventually opted to share something, giggling like school-girls at their indulgence and declaring they'd have to do a month's diet to atone for the excess. It pleased her to see their heads bent close and to hear their laughter and for a moment she was almost grateful that they had been summoned to this final ritual. There had been no real time during the funeral period for her to talk to them at length and all her focus and energy were taken up by the arrangements for the service and receiving the constant stream of visitors who came to pay their respects. So even for this short time it felt as if her children had returned to her and she was their mother again, driving them, supplying them with information about things and even despite their objection paying the bill.

'There's no way I could even look at an ice-cream now,' Francesca said.

'Nor me,' Anna echoed, 'although I would quite like to see if it's how I remember it. It was a place I always liked – you felt you were an adult if you were able to go with your friends and no parent.'

'I think you'd find it changed – everything's modernised and plushed-up,' she said. 'And the last time I was there with your father he thought the price for a coffee and a scone was outrageous.'

'Tell me, Francesca,' Anna said as she wiped her lips with a napkin, 'when a very overweight young Henrietta arrives in your shop for a wedding dress does your heart sink?'

'Not at all. It's a challenge. Covering up what needs covered up, drawing the eye to what's best. A customer is a customer and anyway who's perfect, Anna?'

'I see lots of perfect specimens everywhere I look in London.'

'Think of the price they pay for it,' Francesca said, sipping her black coffee. 'It can't be worth it, can it? But do you remember what the Don used to call what I do?'

She knew the words that were about to be spoken by her daughter and so heard them simultaneously in two different voices as Francesca said, '"Coating debutantes in icing sugar" – that's what he called it. Don't laugh, Anna – I could have strangled him.'

'You'd have had to join the queue.'

She didn't want them to talk about their father, didn't want anything to spoil the pleasure she found in their company, so she went and paid the bill, then ushered them into the car. It was her conviction that he had been the one who had driven their children away so she had to believe that if they finally accepted his absence then her daughters might return, if not to the place where they were born but to her life.

After they had driven to Portstewart she parked the car and they took the cliff path round to the beach. Down below, the sea pushed in roughly against the rocks. There wasn't room for them to walk three abreast so Anna went in front setting a brisk pace while she stayed with Francesca. Her daughters expressed their surprise at how many apartments and new houses they passed and when eventually they reached the steps down to the beach they stopped and looked across the water to the village they had left earlier in the day.

'Would you believe the sun seems to be shining over there but not here any more. I told you it was what life was like,' Francesca said.

A rising breeze trembled a fine mist of sand along the stretch of beach.

'So how do we do the "Lark Ascending" bit in the morning?' Anna asked.

'I've an old cassette player with me and a copy of it on tape.'

'So then he doesn't expect a violinist and a piano player performing at the end of the pier?'

'Thankfully not.'

'I'm glad it's early in the morning so we don't get an audience. It would all be even more embarrassing than it's already going to be,' Anna said.

'And he doesn't expect us to dress in black gowns or something,' Francesca said as she brushed a wind-stirred strand of hair from her eyes. 'I could always knock us up some sackcloth and ashes.'

'I think our normal clothes will do the job just fine,' she said.

'Do you think we should do it in our pyjamas?' Anna said, smiling at her own joke. 'Like the way you now see women going to the supermarket for milk, or driving their children to school.'

'Normal clothes might just be best,' she said, worried for a second that they might conspire the joke into a reality.

'We're only joking, Mum. We'll turn ourselves out appropriately,' Francesca reassured her, patting her arm.

'So, Francesca, fashion expert, what is an appropriate mode of dress for dumping your father's ashes off the end of a stone pier?'

'Well this season I think it's something a little subfusc, perhaps trimmed in ermine and sensible shoes of course – flats, I think – and definitely no heels to prevent the risk of accompanying the ashes.'

As it was getting colder they decided not to walk the beach and instead retraced their steps and at her daughters' insistence they went into Morelli's, but for hot chocolate and coffee rather than ice-cream. Anna inevitably expressed her disappointment at the modernisation then reluctantly conceded it was more comfortable than the place she remembered from her childhood. She was telling them of some really great spot in Brighton she had discovered that retained its fifties décor and furniture, preserved in perfect retro aspic, when her phone rang briefly before going dead and she excused herself and went outside to try to get a signal. She watched her daughter through the glass as she paced up and down then crossed to the sea side of the road. Her frustration was obvious from her body language and the way her arm jerked the phone again and again to her ear as if an excess of energy might shake it into connection. Francesca was saying something but suddenly it seemed important to keep focused on her other child, the one she now believed she knew least about. So she felt a moment's irritation when passers-by briefly blocked her view or a waitress collecting trays lingered too long. She wondered if Anna's instinctive impatience with whatever was faulty or too slow in offering the response she desired now secretly extended to her. And she worried about a Chinese girl whom she had never met and whether her daughter's impetuosity might lead them both into dangerous waters. But she knew there was nothing more that she could say and to try and do so would risk pushing herself even further out of her orbit. She wanted to blame Don but knew that it must also be in part due to herself and her failure to present Anna with any sense of an independent life. Her daughter doubtless thought that she couldn't come to her without coming to her father. She glanced briefly at Francesca who was sipping hot chocolate and watching a toddler at another table while talking about Eugenie's hat but the words slipped away and she stared through the glass wondering if this was always how she would be destined to see her daughter, at a distance and separated by the mistakes she had made in the past.

When she returned to Morocco she wanted to stay in the same riad, hoping that the two young women would still be there and that they might remember her. Was it even possible that they too might be willing to share something of their lives with her? All her marriage she had held on privately to her life, giving only of herself to her children and at the mercy of what they chose to give back. When this thing was done in the morning might she not find some new strength to reach out beyond the confines of herself?

'Did you get a signal?' Francesca asked as Anna sat down with them again. 'Do you want to try my phone?'

'No,' Anna said as she tipped her cup towards her and inspected the remains. 'I'll try again later.'

They sat on, ordered more coffee, whiling time away with conversation and in no hurry to return to the cottage. At intervals she glanced at her watch wondering if their seeming slip into lethargy was a result of boredom. She didn't know what to talk about any more and it felt as if she had used up most of the potential topics already. If they had both married or had children's progress to share then she knew things would have been easier, but what right had she to wish husbands and families on to them when neither displayed any great desire for either? She no longer knew if it was self-ishness on her part to want them married. She was hardly in a position to advocate it and once again wondered if what they had seen of their parents' marriage had been enough to prejudice them against the idea. Anna was talking about some film she had just seen and as she listened to her asser-tive judgements she took comfort in the knowledge that her daughter would never let her life be absorbed and lessened by another.

She thought too of Jiao who had probably journeyed to England over many months, a frightened hungry human cargo transported in the back of lorries or in the holds of ships; Jiao who had come with such high expectations and now found herself little more than a slave, prisoner of the destructive desires and whims of men, and it made her angry. So she shouldn't find fault with Anna if there was something that was hard and strong at her core. It should be welcomed even though at times she thought of it as the same quality that served to exclude her from her daughter's full embrace. And she still wanted that embrace, one that was true and deep and not governed by a filial sense of duty.

She went to the bathroom and when she returned Francesca told her that she and Anna would like to make the tea in the cottage but just as she started to think that it was because they didn't relish the prospect of her offering, Anna said that it was something they would like to do and she knew it was meant as a kindness. So she accepted and told them what she had brought and before they returned Anna bought two bottles of wine and Francesca purchased a few bits and pieces in a small supermarket close to the car park. The wind was strengthening now and as she drove back she resolved to light the fire but when they arrived she suddenly felt overwhelmed with weariness, having to force herself to kneel and light it. It was her job, she told herself, and when it was about to take there was a knock on the front door and as she turned with her hands dusted by ash and coal she saw both her daughters staring at each other and then looking at her.

'You'll have to open it, Francesca, see who it is,' she said, holding both her palms upwards towards them as if offering evidence why she couldn't.

Still kneeling at the hearth she heard the voice of John Gibson and his wife Gillian. It was clear that Francesca wasn't sure who they were and hadn't invited them inside so she called to them to come in.

'It's John and Gillian,' she told her daughters as she stood up and dropped her hands to her side. John was wearing a jacket and a shirt and tie. He had clearly dressed for the visit. 'You remember John, don't you, girls? You've been out in his boat more than once and he's been good enough to look after the grass and generally keeps an eye on the place for us.'

'Of course,' Francesca said, shaking their hands and apologising for not recognising them. 'It's been so long.'

'It has indeed now. Right enough,' he said and then nodded to his wife who stepped forward and handed her a bunch of white, globe-headed chrysanthemums.

'We're sorry for your loss,' she said, handing her the flowers and nodding at both daughters to show they were included in the expression of sympathy.

'They're lovely, Gillian. Thank you.'

'The last of the summer,' John said as he dropped his eyes momentarily to the floor. 'We're not intruding, are we?'

'No, no, have a seat,' she answered as she glanced with surprise at both her supposedly sophisticated daughters who suddenly seemed to stand awkwardly, momentarily deserted by an understanding of how to show simple hospitality. 'Francesca, put the kettle on and, Anna, clear a seat for John and Gillian. You'll have to excuse the mess – we've been sorting out stuff. And I'm just going to wash my hands – I was lighting the fire.'

She carried the flowers into the kitchen and found a vase while telling Francesca what biscuits to put out and which plate to use. As she washed her hands she strained over her daughter's clattering to hear the conversation from the other room and hoped that Anna was making the effort to put them at their ease. So she was pleased that when she went back in Anna was talking naturally to them and they seemed a little more relaxed and with their former nervousness less obvious. For a second she thought John was going to stand up and offer her his seat so she hurried to take her place on the footstool at the side of the hearth.

'There's still a little of the summer lingering on,' he said, looking towards the window's brightness.

'It must be a trick of the memory but the summers all seemed much warmer when we were here as a family,' she said as she stared at the fire and wished she had managed to get it going properly before their arrival.

'That's not yesterday,' he offered and glanced at his wife perhaps as an encouragement to speak.

'And, Lydia, your girls are all grown up now and living in London,' Gillian said. 'Anna was telling us she works on a newspaper. Don must have been very proud of her.'

She was relieved to see Anna smile and nod lightly in apparent affirmation.

'He was a great man, was Don,' John offered. 'All those words in his head and many's the night I'd be out walking the dog and go past the window and he'd be sitting there at his desk writing his poems.' He pointed to the desk as if its physical reality was a necessary confirmation of his memory.

'He had a mighty send-off,' Gillian said. 'All those writers and famous people. We cut out the bits in the paper afterwards.'

Francesca came in with the tea and biscuits on a tray and rising she told her daughter to take her seat while she served. There were no napkins but she supposed it didn't matter and she poured the cups and passed round the plate of biscuits.

'The paper said there was someone from the government there but we didn't see her,' John said as he balanced his cup and saucer on the broad flatness of his thigh.

'We might have seen her but we don't know what she looks like so we wouldn't have known it was her if you see what I mean,' Gillian explained.

She was pleased to see her daughters politely nodding their understanding and pleased too when a few minutes later Francesca offered to top up their cups.

'When I see these two girls all grown up I still think of them as wee'uns playing on the beach with buckets and spades,' John said. 'So how do you like living in London?' he asked.

'I like it fine,' Francesca said, 'but it's always nice to come back home for a visit. We had some good times here in the cottage when we were younger.'

She caught her daughter's eye contact with her sister but their expressions didn't change.

'I mind one summer when you were all mustard keen into catching crabs and I used to tell you that if you caught any more there'd be none left in the sea,' he said, smiling at the memory.

'Francesca makes wedding dresses and hats now in London,' Anna said, gesturing towards her sister. 'Isn't that right, Francesca?'

'Yes that's right,' she said, glancing again at Anna. 'Keeps a roof over my head.'

There was silence for a moment and she looked intently at Anna and hoped she wasn't going to be mischievous.

'Making wedding dresses – that's a nice job,' Gillian said.

'But in no rush to wear one, neither of them,' she said, making the joke then wondered if she should have.

'Sure there's no rush any more. They say women are all getting married later now and better to decide at leisure than repent in haste,' Gillian said, adding, 'isn't that right, girls?'

'That's right,' Anna said. 'But you'd think we'd be able to find Mr Right in a place as big as London.'

'You'd think someone would like a nice Irish girl,' Francesca suggested, playing along with her sister.

'Their loss, their loss,' John said in what she suspected was a genuine offer of consolation. And then after silence had settled again, 'I suppose you've come over to spend some time in the cottage.'

Her two daughters looked at her, giving her the time to say, 'Yes and to help me tidy everything up, sort out Don's things.'

'A right lot of books and papers,' he said, looking around the room and at the packed boxes. Somehow he managed not to see the urn or if he did perhaps mistook it for something else. 'I don't know how one person could read so many books.'

'John's not a great reader. But I like a good book.'

'So what do you read?' Anna asked.

'I'm sure you'd think it was rubbish but it keeps me entertained. I get books out of the mobile library – the girl knows what I like and always keeps me something.'

'And did you ever read any of our father's poetry?'

'A bit beyond us, I'm afraid,' John said as his wife nodded in agreement. 'But it must have been right good stuff if even half of what those other poets said at the funeral was true. And it would never have been in books if it wasn't best quality.'

Before Anna could ask any more questions she quickly turned the conversation back to the weather and the latest news in the village and nodded as she listened to a long, slow litany of births and deaths, weddings and builders gone bankrupt. When the news had been exhausted they sat in silence for a few seconds until John stood up and announced that they wouldn't trouble them any more and as she took his cup and saucer from him he offered as his final requiem, 'The place won't seem the same without him,' then formally shook hands with them all before assuring her that he was happy to go on looking after the grass for as long as she needed.

She thought Anna was going to say something about her intention to sell the cottage but her fear was misplaced and after their visitors had departed both daughters stood smiling at her.

'A good soul,' she said before any of them could speak and then turned her attention to the fire, kneeling down at the hearth.

'I'll do that, Mum,' Francesca offered, placing her hand on her shoulder.

She shivered at her daughter's touch and when Francesca asked, 'Someone walk on your grave?' she nodded then concentrated on getting the fire going. She felt weary again and without turning her head told them that she was feeling a little tired and if they didn't mind she was going to have a lie-down before tea. They could call her when things were ready and after making sure they knew where everything was in the kitchen she excused herself and climbed the stairs to the back room. She pushed the door lightly closed after her and shut the wardrobe door that had been left open. Now it gave back her reflection and she turned her eyes away almost at once because it seemed to offer too sharp a scrutiny and she was no longer sure if any of the things she had done were right. She wondered why she couldn't remember the faces of the young women in the riad – it was as if their full formation in her consciousness had been softened and rendered vague and indistinct. Yet there were so many other things that seemed to press their sharp reality into her memory, some of which she was glad to have, others that she wished could be removed but over which she found herself unable to exercise any control.

Not then married, it was the bed in which she had first secretly slept with Don. Down below she could hear the clang of cooking pots and the laughter of her daughters and the girls' whispered voices in the riad, see again their ghost-like movements when they glided in and out of rooms or appeared suddenly in doorways, framed only by the light behind them. What ghosts now hovered over the bed with its creaking mahogany frame and ancient mattress? She had been young, but not so young that she hadn't known what she was doing or what it meant, and if the rawness of desire had been tenderised by the spill of words then she was grateful for all of it. The sun, the moon and the stars. She couldn't remember exactly but they had probably been present in the moment. Or perhaps it was the sea and maybe even the universe itself where love reached through the dark oceans of space to the very edge of time. So the act of love was leavened with so many words, sifting through her senses like some impossibly warm fall of snow, and if she had taken her pleasure in them then it was as a listener with no words of her own. Even then right at the start no words of her own. Perhaps she wasn't capable of her own. Then his words had come to a sudden and permanent halt. There was the arrival of children of course and the inevitable silencing of passion but whispered words in the darkness where had they gone? Then there was only the inarticulacy of need, the years of taking whatever was required for self. Had she been a fool? She didn't think so because what she had once felt was as real as anything she had ever known and if with the passage of time she had come to feel something entirely different it didn't lessen the truth of that earlier experience.

She felt cold and hugged the duvet tighter. Even when everything else might have gone it was what she missed the most – the simple shared warmth of a bed. Perhaps she would be foolish to shut the door to that possibility, however slim, in the future. She felt confused about everything and above all what still had to be done. Too late now to go back but even that knowledge failed to renew her sense of resolution. So in the morning when the light was bright and young she would go to the end of the pier and slip the ashes in the sea. And she would be watched over by her two daughters who even now were making her a meal – she couldn't remember the last time such a thing had happened. Perhaps as far back as when they were teenagers and it was Mother's Day. What did they think of her? What did they really think in those moments when they were able to set aside what they were expected to think under the bind of filial obligations? As she listened to the low murmur of their voices, unable to distinguish the words, she felt once more that she had failed them but in ways to which she could no longer give a simple name.

The ghosts of their childhood were in the cottage too. Their fall-outs and their laughter. Huddled at the fireside around their father as he read the Narnia books, urging him to read on when he pretended he wanted to stop. It wasn't just a way of postponing bed – she could see it in their widening eyes, flecked with the fire of imagination, that they were desperate to follow the story's steps ever further. And once when Rory, exhausted by the day's activity, had drifted into sleep, his father had carried him in his arms up the stairs and gently slipped him into bed the way he might slip a letter into an envelope. She too had been a child in this place. She tried to remember the life that child had dreamt for herself but nothing would come. Perhaps she never dreamt; perhaps that was the seed of her failure, always just being prepared to accept whatever happened. She thought of the sea dreams of the poetry and slipped a page out of her pocket and read the poem about Rory again. She had read it many times already but it had not lessened her confusion or understanding about what it really meant. She looked across at the pillow where her husband's head had once rested and wanted to ask him if his poem was true, if the words were real and not just images that were momentarily infused with whatever fleeting meaning coloured them. Was the poem a true offering to his dead son or just another tribute to some divinity he hoped would benignly bless his words and disperse them like holy seed? Just another way of ensuring the propagation of his own life? If it were true why the need to put it in a book? Why the need to give it to anyone other than his son?

She had first slept with Don in this bed that seemed now to be cavernous and patched with coldness. So it was here in this very place that she had thought love held out to her the possibility of something that could endure in the face of life's transience and here she first came to believe that words were strong enough to bear you up above the reach of whatever it was in time's grip that deadened and rendered all else meaningless. But what were words now without love? She tried to tell herself that words alone had no special claim over life, that it was the heart that spoke truest always, but even in the same moment her conviction faltered because she knew that throughout her life she had believed words were holy things that should be reverenced. Always she had bowed her head to them and so it felt strange even then to fold the page again and replace it in her pocket as if it was entirely at the mercy of her control.

She would sleep now and when she woke share whatever her daughters had made for her. She found it difficult at first and wondered if a glass of wine would have helped but then her body somehow generated enough heat to smother the coldness nipping at her and freezing so many of her memories into what seemed like an icy permanence. She looked at the wardrobe with its shut door, its frosted mirror with the mottled glass. Had any of her children ever tried to hide themselves in it or intoxicated by the stories thought it might be the portal to some magical world? She thought again of Jiao stumbling out of the back of a lorry, momentarily blinded by the light and then opening her eyes to what she thought would be a better place. Rory far from his home, mysteriously taking a narrow night path under the stars; his fallen body looking as if it was only sleeping. Everything drifted hazily through her and then a sea was ebbing slowly out and gradually she released her weariness to it and let herself slip into the solace of sleep.

When she woke she was confused for a second about where she was or how long she had slept. The bedroom window was a dull square of grey and then she was conscious of the smell of cooking and everything came tumbling back. The door was bevelled by a thin strip of yellow light. She knew she had to get up but it felt as if even the greatest act of will couldn't lift her head from the bed so she closed her eyes again and tried to ease herself slowly into waking. She was frightened she had slept too long, that she had spoilt her daughters' meal. And then there were footsteps on the stairs, light as a child's, a knock on the door and Francesca's voice asking if she was OK and telling her that the meal would be ready in about twenty minutes. She didn't want her daughter to come in and see her so sleep-muddled and was glad when at her reply the footsteps went away.

She smoothed some of the creases out of her clothes and in the bathroom splashed her face. In the mirror it looked blotched and she tried to conceal and restore it with make-up and a brush of her hair. When she was satisfied that she had made the best of herself she sprayed a little perfume on her wrists and then, after lightly touching the mirror with the tip of one finger as if in her own private leave-taking, she closed the door and holding on to the handrail went carefully down the stairs.

It was not what she expected to find. They had cleared Don's desk and moved it into the middle of the room, covered it with a cloth that she had forgotten was in the back of a drawer and formally set the makeshift table with the best plates and glasses that could be found in the kitchen cupboards. Only the blazing fire and candles on the table that were pressed into saucers or jam jars now lighted the room. In the middle of the setting were the white chrysanthemums arranged in a blue glass vase that she recognised as a wedding present from a lifetime ago. Suddenly she remembered the urn and looked around the room desperate to see it.

'The urn?'

'Over there on the bookcase,' Anna said. 'Don't panic – we haven't got rid of it.'

It nestled inconspicuously on one of the shelves she had cleared of books. She nodded and looked again at the table. They were using four chairs out of the kitchen.

'It's beautiful,' she said. 'What made you do it?'

'Just as a small thank you and I suppose as a farewell to the Don,' Anna said as she opened a bottle of wine. 'A kind of last supper.'

'Is that why there are four chairs?'

'No, we're not setting a place for the Don – it just looked unbalanced with three,' Francesca said.

'Can it be for Rory?' she asked before she could stop herself and then observing the glance that passed between her daughters knew she shouldn't have said it.

'It can be for Rory,' Francesca said and she was grateful for the kindness. 'Sit here, Mum, where you can see the fire.'

Her daughters looking after her like this made her feel old and then she realised that sometime in the future they would return once more together to take care of everything that had to be done. She knew that she would make it straightforward for them, have all her affairs settled and easily accessible.

There would be no list of requirements except a desire for as simple and speedy a conclusion as possible. She looked at their faces and even in the softened light saw their sharp excitement, their childlike desire to play at making everything perfect, and for the first time she felt both the pleasure and the inexpressible sadness of having children.

'There's nothing matches,' Francesca said. 'Everything's a bit hotchpotch.'

'It's beautiful,' she said.

'You could have done with a trip to IKEA, got some cheap sets of things,' Anna said as she poured wine into her glass.

'I quite like it this way,' Francesca said, slightly altering the placement of some cutlery and then holding out her glass for her sister to fill. 'What shall we drink to?'

There was a moment's hesitation and she saw Anna look at the extra chair. She didn't want to embarrass them any further and so she raised her glass and said simply, 'To us.' They leaned across the table and lightly clinked her glass and she saw it kissed by the light as she held it briefly in the air.

'Your father once asked me what I saw in the fire and I didn't know what he meant and I said something stupid like "flames".'

'I hope he didn't do that terrible snorting noise he did when I told him my English teacher's favourite book,' Anna said.

'I don't remember but he said something about me being a literalist and I think he was probably suggesting that I had no imagination.'

'You certainly did have an imagination because you were able to see something in him,' Francesca offered in a way that made her defence seem sincere but somehow childish.

'Although he didn't meet my parents' approval he was seen as a great catch by my friends and sometimes even by complete strangers who would sidle up and tell me how lucky I was.'

'I can imagine strangers would think he was quite the

catch,' Anna said. 'Might have changed their opinion if they had to live with him.'

She looked at the snowy-white globes of petals that were tinged pink at their tips. She didn't want them to talk of Don any more.

'So what culinary treats have you in store for me?'

'Well now, that's for us to know and you to find out,' Francesca said. 'But I wouldn't get too excited about it in case we disappoint.'

'I blame you, Mum, for our very mediocre cooking skills,' Anna said. 'You always did everything in the kitchen. You should have trained us up.'

'You always seemed so busy with school stuff and your social life. And I don't recall either of you showing much enthusiasm or inclination to learn.'

'First term at college was a real shock,' Francesca said. 'The realisation that you had to feed yourself. It was really sink or swim.'

'You phoned me up once to ask how you made gravy,' she said, smiling at the memory.

'A couple of Oxo cubes and boiling water, Fran. Even I knew that.'

'Proper gravy, Anna, like you get with Sunday roast. Not that in student digs we ever had Sunday roast.'

'At least you both didn't have these terrible fees and ending up with all that debt.'

'It must be awful,' Francesca said. 'To be starting out on some career with all that hanging over you.'

'If they're lucky enough to find a job at all,' Anna said as she sat down at the table. 'And the paper's full of young people working for nothing. Calling it an internship doesn't hide the fact that it's just a form of legal slave labour.'

Francesca went into the kitchen and returned with the starter. 'A kind of retro prawn cocktail. Very fashionable,' she said, smiling at her own joke.

'Let's face it, Francesca – it's just a prawn cocktail. Like something out of *Abigail's Party*. And anyway why do you always have to see everything in terms of fashion?'

Francesca pulled a face at her sister and joined them at the table. Something in the fire sparked and they all turned their heads to look.

'I did the starter and Anna's doing the main. And the dessert is contributed by Costcutter's freezer.'

'It's very nice,' she said, holding up her fork as a kind of testimony. 'It's always nice to have something made for you, don't you think?'

They both nodded. Anna poured her more of the white wine. The vein of red in her hair seemed at first to have been absorbed by the subdued lighting but from time to time when she turned her head it glinted again. The corners of the room were folded in shadows and all the light seemed pulled into the centre about the table. One of the four candles they had found was scented and although she knew it was only in her imagination it reminded her of the almond blossom she had been given in the village. They never spoke of him unless she found some way to engineer it. Perhaps they would have if they had known how much it pleased her to hear his name on their lips. Their young brother who should have been at the table with them, teasing them as he liked to do and talking of where he'd been or where he was just about to go. Talking as if going to some far-off destination was nothing more than a stroll to a local park and never once in the lightness of his voice or in the quickening spark of his eyes was there even the most fleeting premonition or awareness of death's possibility. She drank more of the wine, stared at the candle flame, the hollowing, trembling scoop where the wick had burned. She heard the words,

> I find you as always in the most distant fields
> Where the spirits have their own stars and sun.

She wanted above all things to bring him home. To have him safely home from those distant fields to be with her and his sisters. Not to be in the earth in his father's suit.

'Are you all right, Mum?' Francesca asked.

'Yes, I was just thinking of . . . thinking of tomorrow.'

Her daughters looked at each other and Francesca nodded a forceful encouragement to her sister.

'Look, Mum, Francesca and I have been talking and we think that maybe tomorrow might be a big strain on you and that we should just do it on your behalf. What do you think? We'll get up early in the morning and do it and then it's over. We'll do it properly, "Lark Ascending" and all. What do you say?'

She glanced to where the urn sat. It was almost absorbed into the shadows with only one little pinhead of light on its dark surface ensuring its presence remained a reality. She couldn't let them. Couldn't let them for reasons that she could never hope to explain but she sipped her wine as if she were considering the suggestion, before saying, 'That's very good of you, girls, very kind, but I need to do it. It wouldn't be right.'

'It's not as if he'll come back to complain,' Anna insisted, holding her arms wide in a way that suggested her indifference to her father's wishes.

'I feel I have to do it, Anna. Do this one last thing. And I know I can get through it fine with both of you there to support me. That's why I'm so grateful that you were willing to come.'

She could tell Anna was going to try and persuade her and so was glad when Francesca stood up and at the same time as she reached for the bowls told them both that the matter was settled and they'd do it together in the morning, ending with the words 'all three of us'. Anna nodded but she could see the traces of exasperation in her face and that she was thinking of saying something more when Francesca reminded her from the kitchen doorway that her course was almost ready and she needed to see to it. She strained to hear what they were saying to each other in the kitchen but their words were lost amidst the sounds of serving and the opening and closing of drawers and cupboard doors. She wondered if they needed any help but thought it best not to offer and so she sat in the candlelight and stared at the fire that consumed a little by its earlier vigour had collapsed in on itself but which still offered a bright brace of heat.

Her daughters reappeared and Anna served her glazed salmon on a bed of rice and vegetables. There was a bowl of salad and a dish of olives, sliced ciabatta bread and another bottle of wine appeared.

'We couldn't find napkins,' Francesca said, handing her a square of white paper, 'so we're making do with kitchen roll.'

'It's all beautiful,' she said as she took in everything on the table. 'You've gone to so much trouble.'

She saw how her praise pleased them and then was sad to think how often they had gone without it, how often they had to find some other approbation for themselves. How even now in adulthood it still mattered. What did he want of his children? She presumed it was that they should achieve something he would consider worthy of himself, but she understood him well enough to know that even if they had been able to do that his pride would eventually have been consumed by jealousy. She told Anna that the salmon was lovely and asked her if she cooked much at home.

'Mostly just at weekends. It's sometimes easier during the week to stick something in the microwave. Cooking takes so much time when all you want to do is flop down and stare at the television. Sometimes, though, I make something at the weekend and freeze part of it to use later.'

They chatted about food, about restaurants, both of them comparing notes on places in London that did good-quality take-away for lunchtimes. They asked her why she didn't try to get tickets for the Chelsea Flower Show in May and come and stay with one of them. The idea appealed to her – it was something she had always wanted to visit. She felt the future opening up with them in a way that previously didn't seem possible. She didn't say anything but perhaps when she made her trip to the village in the mountains before the end of the year she might stay with one of them for a night before coming home. She didn't want to impose herself – it would have to come from them and she would be grateful for whatever they found themselves able to give. And she knew that a great deal of time had passed and the patterns of their lives had become established without her deep involvement. She wasn't entitled to expect that suddenly to change.

Anna put more coal on the fire and opened the second bottle of wine. They each had a slice of the supermarket chocolate cake and Francesca made coffee, apologising for the fact that it was only instant. After she had served them she moved her chair sideways to the hearth saying she had forgotten how nice a real fire was.

'When you stayed here as children you used to squabble about who would get the closest seat and, Francesca, you used to sit so close you'd get your legs all measled.'

'I remember how Don made us all gather driftwood and pile it up behind the kitchen and then some nights he'd make these great bonfires with sparks flying everywhere – you can still see where the carpet was burnt,' Anna said, pointing at the marks with the toe of her shoe.

They sat on, in part it seemed to her because there wasn't really anywhere else to go and in part because of the warmth of the fire, but also because she wanted to believe that it was the three of them together. From time to time one of her daughters would say something about their father and then her own eyes would turn to the urn as if to confirm its reality but even having done so it didn't always prevent his image, his voice, some memory drifting out of the thickening folds of shadows that appeared to be slowly enveloping the room. She looked at the empty chair beside her and saw him in the court-yard of the riad down below her seated at the small round table with the mosaic tiles, writing in his Moleskine notebook, pausing only to sip from the mint tea one of the young women had brought him. Writing out his grief, writing out his loss, writing her out and everything inside her that threatened in those moments to render her asunder. She thought too of the new love poems he had written – his final legacy – blind to the irony of his praise for 'the unbroken constancy of love'.

Her daughters chattered, the second bottle of wine and the pleasure of having carried off the meal loosening their tongues as if to make up for the long periods when there had been silence between them. She listened to the timbre of their voices, recording and preserving every inflection; the places where their accents diverged from what she had known when they were growing up. She wondered how many other things their lives now possessed that ran counter to the identities she had attributed to them in the past. She wasn't sure but she thought Anna might smoke. She had smelled the slightest trace of it in their embrace at the station, perhaps on her clothes but more likely on her hair as they brushed cheeks. She wondered if Francesca wanted a child – she had seen the way she had looked at the toddler in Morelli's, her eyes flick-ing again and again in the child's direction.

They had slipped into a kind of competition now, an adult echoing of a teenage habit, with Francesca telling her sister that although she made wedding dresses and hats she too encountered life in all its forms and when her sister emitted some sound that was clearly an expression of doubt, Francesca insisted, 'It's true, Anna. It's not all ribbons and bows – I get all kinds of trauma.'

'Like someone doesn't like their dress or some stitching unravels,' Anna said.

'No, like the woman who came for a dress last month who's terminally ill and has less than a year to live. Like the women who come to do their final fitting or even to collect their dress and then cry their eyes out and you don't know what to say to them.'

'So why are they crying?' Anna asked.

'Sometimes because they're frightened. Once because she knew she was making the worst mistake of her life.'

'So why was she going to go through with it?'

'Because it's complicated and sometimes there are other reasons and other pressures than are obvious. Things aren't always as simple as they seem.'

'I don't know why anyone would want to be with a man they didn't love,' Anna argued but then stopped abruptly. Francesca said nothing in reply but glanced quickly at her. The silence lingered too long.

'When I married your father I loved him. I believe he loved me equally,' she said.

'You don't have to talk about it, Mum,' Francesca said.

'No, it's all right. I think there are things you're both owed and perhaps the truth is one of them.'

She saw her daughters looking at each other. The light from the replenished fire rouged their cheeks and burnished the glasses they held. But she didn't know what it was she should say to them and so she too sipped from her glass and stared at the fire.

'Is it true that Don had other women?' Anna asked.

'Anna! You've no right!' Francesca's voice was raised and the effect was so unfamiliar that they both were taken by surprise.

'It's all right, Francesca,' she said, 'you've both a right to know whatever it is you want. So yes Don had other women but how did you hear?'

'We would all hear gossip from time to time, mostly about him and that woman Roseanne. Was it true?'

'Yes, it was true. I'm sorry if you were embarrassed or upset by hearing about it.'

'She was at the funeral, wasn't she?' Francesca asked.

'Yes, she was there and I think she was probably entitled to be as much as anyone else.'

'Why do you say that?'

'Because, Francesca, I think she was the person who still loved him.'

'And were there others?' Anna asked.

'Yes, there were always others.'

'Why did you stay with him?' Francesca asked without looking at her.

She had to think about what it was she should say and faced with her mother's momentary silence Francesca told her she didn't have to reply. But she knew that the words were for herself as well as for them so she sipped the wine again before she said, 'I don't know that I have any answer to that which will make sense or be easily understood and I'm not sure that I really understand either. So I suppose I stayed with him because I loved him for what now seems like a long time and when that love had finally faded on both our parts there were three children and I was frightened of admitting failure to them, even when they were grown up. Probably, if I'm honest, frightened too of being on my own. There was also a time when I wasn't a particularly strong person and I suppose I let your father's will override my own.' She looked at them to see if their faces reflected any of the meaning she was trying to grasp. 'And there's another reason which might be difficult for you to understand but it's to do with the poetry, to do with your father's words, and for a very long time, all our marriage I suppose, I felt that something was always owed to it. That the words were something precious so even when his failings were in the front of my head I still respected the written words and his struggle to find them.'

284

She paused and looked at them again but they sat silently and their expressions gave no clue as to whether they had understood or not.

'And do you regret that now?' Anna asked.

'It's not easy to say that because there's so many good bits mixed up with all the rest. Like Francesca said, things aren't always so simple.'

'Maybe nothing ever comes as just one thing,' Francesca ventured. 'Maybe things are always mixed up.'

Anna poured them more wine but said nothing. She wanted her to speak but didn't know whether what she had said had weakened her further in her daughter's estimation. Francesca broke the silence by saying she would clear the table but Anna told her to leave it, her voice edged with insistence, and she sat down again. They began to talk about their childhood, safe, shared memories of holidays in the cottage, and Francesca even succeeded in making her sister blush when she reminded her of the time she had gone on a date with the greenkeeper's son. As a payback Anna asked why she didn't stop being such a style snob and get in on some of the Big Fat Gypsy wedding action.

'Cash in hand – they carry a big fat wad of it in their pockets. You could charge them by the yard and the trains stretch into infinity.'

'Not a bad idea. I read somewhere that the giant wedding cakes are mostly polystyrene.'

Her daughters laughed and she laughed with them even though she only had a vague idea of what they were talking about. More wine was poured for her despite her halfhearted protests and telling them that she needed a clear head in the morning. She sensed there was a feeling that this experience might not be repeated so no one wanted to be the one who brought it to an end. More coal was put on the fire and even though the candles burned ever lower there was no desire to switch on lights. It felt as it had done when their father had read to them except then she had watched and listened from the edge. Now she had them to herself even though she had no story with which to enthral them, no range of voices or dramatic characterisations. She only had what was left of herself and she didn't know if that could ever be enough. But as she spoke about things that had happened on those holidays when they were very young they looked at her with interest and she was surprised by how many things they had forgotten or claimed to have no memory of. Sometimes when their faces registered a struggle to recall something it felt as if she too was recounting a fiction and the events in which she made them characters merely products of her maternal imagination. But just when she ran out of memories and glanced towards the urn to find that it too had disappeared into the shadows she heard, 'Perhaps he wasn't such a bad father.'

The words didn't come from Francesca but Anna. They both looked intently at her as she continued, 'Of course he had his faults. We all know that. But if we're fair you'd have to say that there are worse fathers in the world – men who beat or abuse their children, men who don't provide anything.' She paused as if to gauge whether her own words carried the necessary conviction. 'I'm not saying he wasn't pretty awful on occasion and I'm ready to believe that he was an awful husband – well some of the time at least – but maybe now we should try to dwell on the better sides.'

'Where does this come from all of a sudden?' Francesca asked with what sounded like genuine confusion. 'You're singing a very different tune. What brought this on?'

'I'm just saying. That's all.' But as if because she had failed to convince her sister, or failed perhaps to convince herself, she added, 'I'm reporting on human trafficking and I've come across cases where fathers have sold their own daughters.'

'You were always his favourite, Anna. Because you were smarter than the rest of us.'

She looked at Francesca and at Anna. There was a trace of resentment in Francesca's voice even though she had tried to disguise it with a lightness of tone.

'Being his favourite didn't really get me very much – if I was his favourite.'

'Come on, Anna, you know you were.'

'I never felt it.'

'Well Rory and me did.'

She needed to say something but didn't know what it was. She could neither say something good about him nor criticise without losing one or the other. She didn't want him to do this even now to her children, wanted to embrace them both, but knew that to say the wrong thing, or do the wrong thing, might send them spinning away. So instead she simply stood up and started to clear the table. In the candlelight the flowers looked like slowly melting snow.

'Leave it, Mum, we'll do it,' Francesca said, but it was as if the earlier spell had been broken and she carried on until they started to help. In the kitchen the electric light seemed harsh and intrusive and no one looked at the other's face as they moved back and forwards, carefully avoiding each of their burdened pathways. After it was done her daughters moved the desk back to its former place at the window and replaced the chair with its battered green-velvet cushion, as if in the morning he would be coming to sit at it once more. Under the overhead light she saw the colour on the tips of the petals was brown not pink – they were already beginning to wither. She filled the sink with hot water and started to wash up. Anna excused herself, saying she had a phone call to make but would be back to help, and eventually after making her a coffee she managed to persuade Francesca to sit back down by the fire.

She saw Anna standing across the road looking out to sea, the red tip of a cigarette scoring the darkness while in her other hand flared the light of her mobile phone. She hoped the Chinese girl was safe and that soon she might know what it was to be free. She felt the warm water in the sink comforting her hands, held them there for a few moments even after the last dish was done then went in to see Francesca.

'We should all go to bed soon,' she told her gently. 'It's been a long day.'

Her daughter sat with both hands cupping the mug in front of her face, her bare feet resting on the edge of the hearth.

'Careful or you'll measle your legs again. That wouldn't go down too well in Kensington.'

Francesca attempted a smile but almost at once started to cry for the second time that day.

'Anna thinks she's the only one who sees what life's like. But she's not, she's not.'

She put her hand on her daughter's shoulder and tried to soothe her, saying, 'I know, I know.' Anna came in, giving a shiver as she closed the door behind her, then seeing her sister crying said in a voice that registered genuine concern, 'What's wrong, Francesca?'

'That young woman who had cancer, when she came for the last fitting she'd lost her hair. And she never got to wear the dress,' she said, her speech breaking in little sobbing breaths.

'She died before she could get married?'

'No, she did get married. In the hospice. But she was too ill to wear the dress. Afterwards her husband told me they laid it across the bottom of the bed so at least she could see it.'

She was crying now and taking the mug from her hands they cradled and hugged her, stroking her hair and holding her as best they could until she told them she was all right, and when she apologised for crying they hugged her again. Anna got her a tissue from the kitchen and then pulling two chairs up they sat beside her and no one spoke for a long time but simply stared at the hollowed-out caverns of the fire.

'What do you see in the fire, Mum?' Francesca asked eventually as she slipped the tissue under a cuff but the attempts she had made to restore her voice only drew attention to her efforts.

'I see three tired girls. Perhaps it's time we went to bed because we've to be up early in the morning. I think we need to be on the beach for about seven to be sure of avoiding an audience.'

'What's the forecast?' Anna asked.

'Generally bright, I think. Perhaps rain later in the afternoon was what the radio said.'

'We'll be long gone by then,' Anna said, resting her hand on Francesca's knee.

'I'm OK now. I'm OK. Sorry for embarrassing everyone.'

They reassured her again and then Anna told them how mild and still it was outside. 'Hardly a breeze blowing,' she said and all three of them glanced towards the window.

'Perhaps before we go to bed a little night air might clear our heads,' she told her daughters and they followed her to the door, Anna still holding her glass of wine.

The night was immensely still and even the soft moan of the retreating sea seemed to lull everywhere into such a calm that it almost felt as if they were intruding when they walked across the road and stood on the edge of the beach. She looked for the green light but couldn't see it. What inescapable folly existed in the world! What unspeakable follies of the human heart! The sky was folded tightly in a starless gauze over a sea that looked broken and spent. The stone pier where they would walk in the morning was a distant shadow and she wasn't even sure if what she saw was real or merely constructed from her memory. When the children were young they often played hide and seek in the dunes, the searcher having to count inside the cottage while the others hid where they wouldn't be found. If such a place existed now she would go to it, listen while her pursuer's cries sought her in vain. She was frightened of what the morning might bring, of walking to the end of the pier where as a child she was scared that a wave would snatch her. Her daughters who stood on either side of her linked arms with her and she tried to tell herself that there was strength in the chain but it was Rory she thought of and how in the brightness of the morning she must try to bring him back into the light in the only way she knew.

When she woke she wanted her window to show the sea but instead all it revealed was the back square of grass, the mist-silvered field and the grey ash pile at the foot of the separating hedge. She showered and dressed quickly but took longer than usual over her make-up, trying to repair the strains of the night before and a dream-riddled sleep. She had allowed plenty of time but heard no hint of her daughters stirring. What she did hear, however, was the sound of the wind rousing itself into life and when she looked out again saw it shivering the top leaves of the hedge. She went out to the landing, standing still to listen for signs of life from her daughters' bedroom, but there was nothing and only the knowledge that they had both said they were used to getting up early in London, and that they were setting their alarms, prevented her from thinking of them once more as sleepy-headed teenagers who needed to be wakened by an urgent knock on their door.

Going downstairs the first thing she looked for was the urn as if it might have been secreted away during the night. But it still squatted on the same empty shelf. She didn't want to have to touch it but knew there could be no other way. Then as she filled the kettle she heard one of her daughter's phone alarm ringing and while she waited for the water to boil she opened the front door and took stock of the morning. It was clear and bright and the wind although wakening a little was not gusting in any great strength. She couldn't tell whether the tide was going in or out. She returned to the kitchen but despite her intention couldn't make herself eat anything and instead drank coffee while sitting at the kitchen table as up above her unfolded the first sounds of activity.

On this morning with the snow-capped mountains in the distance, a young woman whose face she couldn't remember had brought her breakfast and she had tried to eat what she could. The journey to the village followed narrow corkscrewing roads that wound precariously around the mountains, and if again and again they edged closer to the vast drop, what did it matter when she was already falling, finally snatched by that wave that others called grief? She comforted herself with the knowledge of how in a short time she would walk to the end of the stone pier that reached itself into the sea and tell her son that she hadn't drowned but had finally come to bring him home.

Anna appeared, bleary-eyed but dressed more formally than the clothes she had travelled in, and kissed her lightly on the side of her head as she said good morning.

'If you like, I'll do the music,' she offered. 'I'll practise before we go to do it for real.'

Francesca too was soberly dressed. In her hand she held what looked like a white wreath.

'I made it with the chrysanthemums and a wire coat hanger. What do you think?'

'It's very nice, Francesca,' she told her but worried whether her daughter would be able to do this thing without getting upset again.

'I thought we would drop it into the sea with the ashes.'

They wanted nothing more for breakfast than the toast and tea she made for them and when they enquired whether she was having something she said she'd already eaten. Anna went into the front room to try the tape.

'Will you be all right, Francesca? It'll all be over very quickly and then you'll be on your way home.'

'I'll be fine if you are. But it doesn't seem fair that we have to go through what feels like a second funeral.'

'I know but when we do this it's over for ever. And you'll be back home making your beautiful dresses.'

As Francesca nodded they heard Anna swearing loudly and going to see the cause they found her looking with dismay at the cassette player.

'It's eaten the tape. I only pressed play and it's eaten the tape,' she said, trying carefully to eject it, but already they could see that the tape was spooling around the heads. Despite her efforts delicately to tease it out it was clear that it was caught tightly.

'Oh, Anna,' Francesca said, pressing her hands together in front of her face as if she was about to pray for a miracle.

'It wasn't my fault. I don't know what's more ancient – the tape or the player. If we can get it out maybe we can rewind it.'

Anna carried it over to the light of the window and setting it down on the table started to ease it out again but when she met resistance her impatient tug resulted only in the tape emerging with a broken tail. She looked at them, slowly shook her head in disbelief, then said, 'Sorry, Don.'

'It wasn't your fault, it wasn't anyone's fault,' she told her daughters.

'You'd think a journalist would be good with this sort of machine,' Anna said as she held up the cassette with its broken spool of tape.

'It wasn't your fault, Anna,' Francesca said.

'We'll do it without the music,' Anna said. 'No one gets everything they want in life and perhaps death's no different.'

'Don will be rolling his eyes and making that snorting noise,' Francesca said. 'It's not as if we can sing it.'

'We've saved him from a cliché,' Anna said, throwing the tape on the table. 'He should be grateful. Let's do this thing, Mum.'

She nodded and each of them put on their coats. Even if she had wanted there was no way back, so going to the bookcase she carefully lifted the urn and when Francesca offered to carry it she told her it was better if it stayed with her. There was a moment's delay as Francesca went back upstairs to get her scarf and as they waited just inside the open front door Anna whispered, 'Sorry,' but she told her that it didn't matter, that everything would be all right.

The morning air was sharp but already a strengthening sun was beginning its work. Over the headland of Donegal clouds buckling with their own weight smudged the ridge of higher ground – it would be where the rain would come from later in the day – but above them the sky was patched with blue and the light, glassy and sharp-edged, already mirrored the sea into reflected life. They took the path through the dunes and she gripped the urn tightly despite its coldness, her greatest fear of dropping it a companion to her every step.

They walked in single file along the narrow path and when it broke on to the beach and they slithered down a slight slope into the soft sand she could see that it was completely empty. The stone pier stretching into the sea had never seemed so far away. She couldn't tell whether the tide was still going out or coming in. The lower half of the beach shimmered and was dressed in a transfer of mottled sky. They headed closer to the sea glad to be out of the softer sand. Four seabirds stood motionless on spindle legs as if anchored, their white breasts glinting in the light. A solitary bird bobbed further out, its orange beak bright against the blackness of the water. As they walked none of them spoke, little lisping spurts of white christening each of their steps.

On this part of the beach the waves rose lightly but as her eyes carried towards the pier where the stronger currents often encouraged surfers, she could see already that they were stirred into a stronger motion. The three of them walked steadily on, her daughters slightly behind her and everything pressed against her with its own intensity, and she wondered if it was the presence of death that so heightened the awareness of life. Now her eyes picked out the cappuccino-coloured foam that splurged at intervals on the wet sand, the spiral coils of sandworms, and when she looked up at the sky saw the fragility of its faltering shifts of blue.

She paused to ask them if they were all right and when they told her they were she nodded and headed on again. The beach stretched out before them, sea-washed and striated in wavy patterns as if hundreds of snakes had wriggled over its pliant surface. Some birds skittered into directionless, haphazard flight before wheeling away in tight formation. She wanted her children beside her but it felt as if something held them back and so they followed a step behind like a procession. Perhaps the urn cowed them. If that was true then soon they would be released. Soon they would all be released.

She could see the stone pier clearly now, its protective ramparts of rocks sea-splashed but stoutly resisting the waves' angry insistence when their slick black underbellies ripped in a furious flurry of foam. Further out the unfurling, curving runnels broke white, each one back-combed with spray. She wanted her daughters to take the comfort of each other but couldn't think of what she should say to encourage it so with her breathing a little heavy simply offered, 'We're almost there now.' There was no response and so still gripping the urn in front of her in both hands like a chalice she led them on to where they had to step up from the sand.

After its softness the pier felt solid under her feet despite its pitted, uneven surface and regardless of the fact that some of the bigger pockmarks held the trapped splash of the sea. They passed the rusted relic of a warning light. She tried not to look to either side of the pier but kept her eyes steadfastly on its end where from this distance it appeared to stretch into the very heart of the ocean. When she glanced questioningly to her daughters they nodded to say they were all right and then they were almost there, almost at the very end. Stopping just short of where it met the sea, she set the urn down on the ground, carefully seeking out a spot where it secured a balance. She hugged each of them tightly before saying, 'Anna, Francesca, this is something I'd like to do by myself. Will you let me?' They looked at each other and then, in turn nodded and Francesca hugged her again, the white flowers pressed between their embrace. She thanked them, then lifting the urn took the final few steps towards the edge and knelt down at it, the cold points of the stone pressing against her knees. Glancing back towards the beach she saw it burnished with light and into that momentary bright grasp of life stepped all those who were now part of her – her two children, Jiao, the two young women in the riad, the man who stood fishing at this very place, John and Gillian, the bride whose wedding dress was a shroud. All of these and more and then she took the lid off the urn and placed it on the ground beside her.

He tries once more to embrace his son but it's too late and so three times he's left grasping only air, weightless as the wind, as light as the flight of sleep. And his journey has already begun because she's sent him spinning to the Underworld, spilled on the pyre of ash, stretched and hung out empty, drying in the wind. So it is only his words she now gives back to the world, emptying their ash to the freedom of the air and the shifting motion of the whelming sea. They puff up like smoke, threatening for a second to engulf her, but then slowly fall, before drifting away and seeping into the slick of the swell. Nothing can snatch her now. And then as she lifts herself up her children come and stand beside her, rest their hands on her shoulders, and Francesca drops the white flowers into the water. The tide is going out, the final unfathomable wave of mystery – in that at least he was right. She smiles at them both and hopes as they stare at the sea that they too can see her son shaking off his father's dark vestments of death, his eyes full again of the future's light. She stretches out her hand, not in what they must think is a farewell, but in a greeting to her lost child who's coming home from the earth's distant places and is even now forming about her, reclaimed at last, she silently tells them, not by the drifting ash of words splayed out on the water below, but by the constancy of her love.

Author's Note

In creating a fictional portrayal of Catherine Blake I am indebted to many books but principally to Alexander Gilchrist's *The Life of William Blake*, *The Letters of William Blake*, edited by Geoffrey Keynes, and Peter Ackroyd's *Blake*, for furnishing all the known facts about Catherine's life.

The part of the novel dealing with Nadezhda Mandelstam was inspired by her own accounts of her life, *Hope Against Hope* and *Hope Abandoned*. In some parts of my novel I have stayed deliberately close to her remarkable story, in others I have imagined. In both cases my aim was to honour her life of witness. *Hope Against Hope* remains one of the twentieth century's greatest records of the struggle of the individual against totalitarianism, and an enduring testimony to the capacity of literature and language to survive the silence some sought to impose on them.

Ireland is an island overflowing with poets but all the characters who appear in the final part of the novel are entirely products of the imagination and not intended to resemble anyone either living or dead.

I would like to thank Sinéad Morrissey for her thoughtful advice and also Colin Watson for creating the illustrations.

Finally I acknowledge the generous support of the Arts Council of Northern Ireland and the National Lottery for a Major Individual Artist Award.

ALSO AVAILABLE BY DAVID PARK
THE LIGHT OF AMSTERDAM

Shortlisted for the Irish Novel of the Year

It is December in Belfast, Christmas is approaching and three sets of people are about to make their way to Amsterdam. Alan, a university art teacher, goes on a pilgrimage to the city of his youth with troubled teenage son Jack; middle-aged couple Marion and Richard take a break from running their garden centre to celebrate Marion's birthday; and Karen, a single mother struggling to make ends meet, joins her daughter's hen party. As these people brush against each other in the squares, museums and parks of Amsterdam, their lives are transfigured as they encounter the complexities of love in a city that challenges what has gone before.

'Marvellously compelling . . . Park takes that most difficult of subjects – recent history – and with graceful integrity explores the difficulties involved in coming to terms with the legacies of the past . . . Beautifully described in Park's crystalline prose'
DAILY MAIL

'Subtle, understated, not without a hint of menace and always courageous . . . An important book'
Eileen Battersby, **IRISH TIMES**

'A stealthily affecting novel, this could well give more famous names a run for their Booker money'
GQ MAGAZINE

ORDER BY PHONE: +44 (0)1256 302 699; BY EMAIL: DIRECT@MACMILLAN.CO.UK

DELIVERY IS USUALLY 3–5 WORKING DAYS. FREE POSTAGE AND PACKAGING FOR ORDERS OVER £20.

ONLINE: WWW.BLOOMSBURY.COM/BOOKSHOP

PRICES AND AVAILABILITY SUBJECT TO CHANGE WITHOUT NOTICE.

WWW.BLOOMSBURY.COM/DAVIDPARK

BLOOMSBURY